the happy room

Also by Catherine Palmer
in Large Print:

A Whisper of Danger
A Touch of Betrayal
A Victorian Christmas Tea
Prairie Rose
Prairie Fire
Prairie Storm

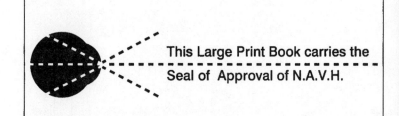

This Large Print Book carries the
Seal of Approval of N.A.V.H.

the happy room

catherine palmer

Thorndike Press • Waterville, Maine

Published in 2003 by arrangement with Tyndale House Publishers, Inc.

Thorndike Press Large Print Christian Fiction Series.

The tree indicium is a trademark of Thorndike Press.

The text of this Large Print edition is unabridged. Other aspects of the book may vary from the original edition.

Set in 16 pt. Plantin by Elena Picard.

Printed in the United States on permanent paper.

Library of Congress Cataloging-in-Publication Data

Palmer, Catherine, 1956–
    The happy room / Catherine Palmer.
      p. cm.
    ISBN 0-7862-4849-1 (lg. print : hc : alk. paper)
    1. Children of missionaries — Fiction. 2. Brothers and sisters — Fiction. 3. Anorexia nervosa — Fiction.
4. Large type books. I. Title.
PS3566.A495 H3 2003
813′.54—dc21   2002032448

*This book is for all those who
seek the road through the forest.*

author's note

No fiction author writes in a vacuum. Our experiences, the people we have known, and the things we have learned all interweave to form the fabric of our stories. These threads are drawn from real life and they contain truth, but when we place them on the loom and begin to fashion our tale, they become fiction.

The fabric in which you are about to wrap yourself is such a work. The characters are not people I have known, nor are the events factual recountings of my experiences. Yet in the weaving, a verisimilitude emerges. It is the essence of this reality that I pray may enfold you in its truth, its pain and joy, and — ultimately — its healing.

chapter one

Julia Chappell dreaded the phone call she'd been waiting for all morning. Lately, she'd had about all the turmoil she could take. Her older daughter — newly graduated from high school — lived on the edge of hysteria at the prospect of leaving her boyfriend when she headed for college. The other daughter, at sixteen, acted like she'd been chosen eternal queen of the universe. And Julia's husband, a youth minister for almost twenty years, suddenly wasn't sure he could relate to teens anymore. He was thinking about becoming a pastor. In a small town. In Wyoming. All that, on top of a surprise pregnancy, was almost more than Julia could handle. And now her doctor had ordered an ultrasound because something didn't seem right.

Julia set her cell phone on a tree stump, knelt, and dug her fingers deep into the soft dirt of her freshly spaded garden. Moisture seeped through the knees of her sweatpants as she carved a small hole in the soil. To Julia, gardens meant flowers. And flowers meant life. Let the neighbors plant their tomatoes and cucumbers. Julia would have hot pink begonias, primrose yellow marigolds, purple petunias, bright red geraniums. No matter what turmoil life tried to hand her, Julia could always find serenity in her garden.

Slipping the root ball of an orange-pink lantana into the hole she had dug, Julia let her thoughts drift back to her childhood, a magical time when lantana blossoms made perfect wedding bouquets for her dolls. She and her little sister, Debbie, had each placed their Barbies — stiff-legged, half naked, and barefoot — along the edge of a tissue-box altar. And there they had vowed to love, cherish, and obey their barefoot Kens until death did them part.

Julia's own daughters had grown past the age when they played with Barbies. Down in the basement lay boxes of tiny shoes and wedding gowns — not to mention four versions of Ken, a camper with a swimming pool, and a pink-and-blue plastic mansion. Julia sighed as she set a second lantana into the ground and covered its roots with dirt. What on earth was she going to do?

Leaning back on her heels, she studied the rows of flowers she had planted this spring. The possibility that something might be wrong with the tiny life she carried had brought back, full force, all of her mixed emotions about being pregnant at all. She couldn't be pregnant, she'd thought when the possibility first presented itself. That was all there was to it. The grocery-store test with the little blue line just had to be wrong. Mike had been "snipped," as he endearingly put it, and besides, she was too old to have another baby.

"Been there, done that," as her younger daughter liked to say. Julia and Mike had married in college, and she had given birth to Jessica barely a year later. Heather followed in eighteen months, and Julia had dropped out of school to spend her time chasing toddlers. She had loved motherhood. Loved everything about it — her pregnancies and even the births of her babies. Tiny feet and reaching fingers delighted her. Years of baking cookies and sewing frilly little dresses and smooching sticky cheeks were heaven on earth.

But she did not want to be pregnant

now. Not at thirty-seven, when she had almost raised her daughters. Not when Mike was wallowing hip-deep in a midlife crisis. Not when . . . Julia pushed back a wisp of hair with the heel of her hand. Could she really admit to herself why she didn't want to have a baby? And if something was wrong with the child . . . it would just compound her guilt over not receiving the unexpected gift with the proper gratitude and anticipation.

Of course the doctor had been optimistic. His theory was that she was expecting twins. Twins. Right. Julia was so ambivalent about the idea of even one baby that she had yet to break down and buy any maternity clothes. Her big T-shirts and baggiest sweatpants were getting tight, she had to admit, but she wasn't able to make that emotional leap yet. How could she possibly cope with the idea of having twins?

She wiped her hands on the thighs of her sweatpants and stared at the cell phone. God already knew the innermost desires of her heart. So, why did she feel uncomfortable praying about this? Maybe because it seemed wrong not to want the precious new life that was growing inside her. Maybe because what she *did* want felt selfish and sinful.

Her whole life — from the time she was seven years old and sailing to Africa on a ship with her missionary parents — Julia had tried to do what was right and good. Even though she despaired at being sent away from home, she had attended boarding school without a complaint. As a teen, she had gone to the small Christian college her parents chose for her. And she had married a minister, of course.

Standing, Julia picked up her basket of garden tools. She loved Mike, and theirs was a strong marriage. But wasn't she ever going to get to do something just for *herself*?

"Okay," she said, dropping the basket and laying her hand on her stomach. "God, I know I haven't been too happy about this pregnancy. I don't want to be pregnant because I . . . okay, it's because I want to go back to college and get my nursing degree. There, I've said it. I don't want Mike to move us to Wyoming. And I don't want Jessica and Heather to be so . . . so difficult! And most of all, Lord, I just really —"

The phone's warbled tone cut off her words. She stared at it. Good news or bad? And what exactly would good news sound like at this point?

She picked up the phone. "Hello?" she said, and she could hear the quaver in her voice.

"Julia? You sound so far away! Is something wrong?"

"Mom — oh, it's you." She let out a breath. "No, I'm just . . . I'm out in the garden. I've been planting lantana."

"Lantana! But that's a weed, honey. We used to have such trouble with lantana. Snakes love to hide in there, you know."

"Mom, lantana's an annual flower here in Santa Fe. It doesn't survive the winter. No problem with snakes."

"Well, but it can be such a pest. It was all our garden boy could do to keep that bush cut back. The cobras were just thick in there." Julia's mother paused. "You do whatever you want, honey. I'm sure your garden will look very nice, even with lantana."

Julia smiled. Her parents had retired to Missouri from the mission field two years ago, but sometimes it felt to Julia as though they were still living on another continent. Often, they seemed to be viewing the world from the window of their small corrugated tin house under a thorn tree in the African bush.

"You don't usually call during the day,

12

Mom," Julia said. "Is Dad all right?"

"Oh, he's fine. Busy as ever. But listen, this is about your sister."

"Debbie? What's wrong?"

"It's nothing serious. Well, we don't think it is. Anyway, the doctor felt she needed to be put in the hospital — just to keep an eye on her."

"Why?"

"It's her weight. Personally, I've always thought Deborah was just the right size, so cute, and such a good athlete. But, anyway, yesterday after church she fainted, so they took her to the hospital. The doctor put a tube down into her stomach —"

"A tube? Mom, what's going on?"

"He says she needs extra nourishment right now, until she can get back on her feet."

"Did the doctor give you a diagnosis?"

"He called it . . . *anorectica*. Something like that. But you know, Deborah's always been thin. All right, I'll admit she was a little pudgy when she was a toddler, and she had that kind of fattish stage in high school. Then she lost her weight so nicely, and she's really done well keeping it off. You know how most people's weight just seesaws up and down? But Deborah's always been trim and fit."

"Anorexia? Mom, that's a serious disease. People die from it." Julia sat down on the stump and cradled her stomach.

"Well, they don't really *die*, do they?"

"Yes, they do. Sometimes. I read about it in a magazine, or maybe I saw a TV program on it. Anyway, girls who have it think they're too fat, so they starve themselves. Even when they start looking like those kids in Africa during the famine years, they think they're too fat. Mom, how much does Debbie weigh?"

"Do you think I would ask her that? Really, Julia." She hesitated. "Your father and I drove over to Bolivar to see her —"

"She's not in Springfield?"

"I'm sure the hospital in Bolivar is perfectly capable of handling something like this, Julia. I wish you would calm down. There's no need to get so agitated, honey."

Letting out a breath, Julia shook her head. Mike liked to joke that her mom held the original patent on denial. No matter how bad things got, Olive Mossman put a smile on her face and blankly refused to admit there was a problem.

"Mom, is Dad there?" Julia asked. "Can I talk to him for a minute?"

"Your father is in his study preparing for the Vacation Bible School speaking en-

14

gagement we have next week in Joplin. I really hate to disturb him. We have to make two presentations every single day, you know. This is a very large church, and they've done an amazing outreach program into the community, Julia. They're expecting nearly a thousand children. Can you imagine that?"

"Wow."

"Mike scheduled your church's Vacation Bible School for August, didn't he? I wonder how many he's planning for. Maybe we could talk to the youth minister in Joplin and ask him what he did to increase their attendance so dramatically. What do you think? Would Mike be offended if we passed along some suggestions?"

"That would be fine, Mom." Julia could just see Mike's reaction. *The Meddling Mossmans are back in action,* he would say. "Listen, would you mind getting Dad for me? I'd really like to hear his opinion about Debbie's condition."

"He did ask me to make this call, Julia. And it is high rates. But if you insist."

Julia could hear Olive calling her husband, and in a moment, Don Mossman's gentle voice came on the line.

"Hello, Julia. Your mother says you

wanted to talk to me about Deborah." He cleared his throat. "Well, I have to tell you that your sister is looking very frail. I think she's not feeling well at all. Her weight is a concern, and the doctor decided that a feeding tube had to be put in. It's hard to see her that way, hooked up to the tubes, you know. There's an IV in her arm, I think. Yes, I'm sure there is. But she was smiling at us. She looked very pretty, even though her hair has gotten kind of thin. Maybe she's just taking after her ol' dad. You know I'm awfully thin on top!"

A joke. Julia gave the appropriate chuckle. "What are they saying about Debbie getting better?"

"They're going to run some tests. I think when you have this weight problem there's a danger of bone density loss. The doctor told us the condition sometimes leads to osteoporosis, which we know about because your mother has a touch of it. And it seems Deborah's hormones are a little out of whack."

"What do you mean?"

"Well . . ." He was probably cleaning his glasses. When he was uncomfortable, he took them off, blew on the lenses, adjusted the earpieces, and put them back on. "Well . . . it's her . . . female . . . cycle. The monthly cycle. It stopped some time ago, and of course, she couldn't be pregnant."

Julia rubbed her hand across her own swelling stomach. No, of course not. Olive and Don Mossman would never believe their unmarried daughter could get pregnant. Even though Deborah had a long-time boyfriend and was thirty-four years old.

"So, the doctor wants to test her blood and take some X rays." Don rushed ahead now that the awkward part was over. "She's going to have to be in the hospital for a while, and they're planning to do several types of therapies. They've assured us if the situation worsens, they'll transfer her immediately to a hospital in Springfield."

"How could the situation worsen, Dad?"

"Well, you know Deborah doesn't have a lot of strength, and her immune system is down. There's a possibility of infection. They've got to get her to start eating again. For some reason, she just won't eat regular food. It's hard to understand, honey, but the doctor says your sister is quite sick. Mentally as well as physically."

The picture was becoming clear, and it wasn't good. How could this have happened without Julia's knowing anything about it? She and Debbie talked on the phone a couple of times a month, and they e-mailed each other regularly. But, of course, Debbie wouldn't have thought she had a problem, so why would she mention it?

The baby of the family, Debbie had always been adored. Her long blonde curls and the dimples in her cheeks had stunned villagers in the remote part of Kenya where the Mossmans had lived and worked as missionaries for many years. Small children loved to touch her golden hair or stare in starstruck fixation at her blue eyes. Debbie had sailed through her teenage years without a blemish to mar her velvety skin. As an adult, she studied fashion design and became a buyer for a small chain of ladies' clothing stores in southwest Missouri. While Julia lived in her blue jeans and tennis shoes, Debbie wore the latest styles and loved to walk the edge of high fashion. Thin was in, and the thinner the better.

"Dad, when you say Debbie is mentally sick, what do you mean? Is she depressed?"

"I'm not sure what you'd call it. Let's just say she isn't talking much. Maybe she doesn't feel up to it. But the doctor told us that with this anorectica thing, there's a sort of distortion in the patient's mind."

"*Anorexia*, Dad."

"Oh. Are you sure? Your mother wrote it down in her schedule planner, and we thought the doctor called it *anorectica*. An-or-ec-ti-ca." He said it several times, as if learning a new word in one of the African languages he had studied.

"*Anorexia*," Julia corrected again. "Dad, do you think I should fly out there to see Debbie? Is she that bad?"

"Well, I'm sure she would love to see you. She mentioned Peter, too." He was blowing on his glasses again. "In fact, your mother and I were wondering if you could call Peter and let him know about this. We're trying to get ready for this speaking engagement next week, and your mother has a large dinner scheduled tomorrow night for her Sunday school class. We're having about twenty people —"

"Twenty-five!" a voice sang out in the distance. "Three widows. And you're really running up the phone bill, Don. Why don't we let Julia call us back this evening when rates are down?"

"Your mother says —"

"It's fine," Julia cut in. "I'll call Peter. We'll decide what to do about Debbie."

"That's wonderful, honey. You know Peter just doesn't seem to —"

"Don! The phone bill!" Olive Mossman's voice was louder now, obliterating any chance that her husband might mention the strife that plagued their relationship with their son.

Julia shook her head. "Thanks for the call, Dad. I love you."

"Be sweet, honey!" Olive had taken the phone. *"Kwaheri — tutaonana!"*

Julia rolled her eyes at the Swahili farewell as she spotted Heather sashaying out of the house, her shorts slung low on her slender hips and her little tank top just this side of indecent.

"Here comes Heather, Mom. I'd better go." As her mother gave a final good-bye and the line went dead, Julia pressed the button to turn off the phone.

"Mom, have you been on the phone for, like, hours or something?" Heather's long brown hair was tied up in a messy ponytail. "People can't get through to you, so they keep calling our line. And I'm waiting to hear from Ashley!"

Using more effort than she liked to acknowledge, Julia stood up from the stump. "Who phoned?"

"Dad, of course. He got a call from some mom whose son is acting really weird, so he's going over there to talk to them. I bet it's that Darren Whitlock — he's so bizarre. He's got those freaky little eyes."

"Heather."

"Well, his eyes give me the creeps. Yuck." She shivered. "And some nurse called. She said their office was closing for the day, so she wanted me to give you the message that you don't need to worry. They have good news for you, and they need to schedule an appointment with you, so, you're supposed to call them in the morning. I don't know why Ashley hasn't called. We really need to go to the mall this afternoon, because that sale at The Gap is —"

"Wait a minute." Julia held up her hand. "What did the nurse tell you?"

"It's 'good news.' The doctor was right, whatever that means."

"The doctor was right?" Julia sucked down a breath. "Are you sure that's what she said? The doctor was right?"

"Wow, Mom, chill out. You're acting like I'm some kind of idiot who can't take a phone message. It was good news, okay?"

"Oh no." Julia laid a hand on her stomach and sat back down on the stump. "Call your dad. Get your dad on the phone. Here!"

Heather took the phone. "Mom, I told you. He's at some lady's house from the church. Dad never tells us who's having trouble, you know that. What is with you? Gosh."

"Don't say that! Don't use that kind of slang, Heather, and I mean it! It sounds like you're taking God's name in vain —"

"Mom, what is your problem?" Heather took a step toward her mother. "Are you all right? What kind of a test was it? Is something wrong with . . . you know, the baby?"

"I need to talk to your dad. Call Mrs. Moore at the church and find out where he went. Get her to page him."

"Do you have like . . . cancer . . . or something?"

Julia hung her head. They would all know soon enough. But she needed time. Time to think it all through, time alone with Mike, time to figure out how she was going to cope.

"It's not cancer, Heather."

"Well, what is it? Mom, you're freaking me out!"

"I'm . . . I'm going to have twins." Julia lifted her head and met her daughter's deep blue eyes. "I'm going to have two babies."

"No way. You're so old. I can't even deal with the fact that you're pregnant, Mom!"

"Thanks." Julia studied her younger

daughter and watched the reality settle in. Heather took another step closer and hunkered down beside her mother on the stump.

"Twins." Heather's voice grew soft. "Wow. I've got to call Ashley —"

"No you don't!" Julia grabbed the phone from Heather's hand. "Don't tell anybody until I've talked to your dad. There are a lot of things we need to talk over — such as, I just found out your Aunt Debbie is sick."

"What's wrong? *She's* not pregnant, is she? Grandma Mossman will have a heart attack!"

"She has anorexia."

"I thought only teenagers got that. Like Jenny Lieberman in Jessica's class who had to go away to some rehab center because she was so skinny she almost died. She weighed like eighty pounds or something. How much does Aunt Debbie weigh? She's not going to die or anything, is she?"

"I hope not. I may need to fly to Missouri to see her."

"You can't go flying off, Mom! You're pregnant! With *twins!*" She got to her feet. "Look, here comes Jessica. Can I tell her? I really want to tell her. She's going to have a cow."

Julia studied her older daughter as she pulled the compact car to a stop in front of the house and climbed out. Carrying her Wal-Mart uniform vest, her hair up in a pretty bun, her shoulders straight and high, she looked so mature. A young woman.

Heather hadn't waited for her mom's response. Like a colt, she was galloping across the lawn, all arms and legs. She grabbed Jessica's hands and started jumping up and down. In a moment, Jessica's jaw dropped, and she turned to stare at her mother.

"It's true! It's true!" Heather skipped beside her sister as the two of them hurried toward the flower garden. "Hey, Mom, I told her. She's in total shock!"

Jessica reached out to her mother and folded her in a warm hug. "Mom, congratulations!"

"Thanks." Julia tried to smile. "Surprise!"

"No kidding. Does Dad know?"

"Not yet. Maybe I ought to take him out to dinner."

"Maybe you ought to wait until he's lying down," Heather said. "He's going to faint. He was shocked enough at the idea of *one* baby."

"Mom, are you feeling okay?" Jessica asked.

"I'm fine. It's just something we'll all need to get used to."

"Wow." She studied her mother for a moment. Then she turned to Heather. "Has Danny called yet? We're supposed to go to the mall."

"The mall! Ashley and I are going there. Would you take us? We want to go to that sale at The Gap."

The girls, lost in a heated exchange, started for the house. "You can't ride with Danny and me. We hardly ever get to see each other. Get Ashley to drive!"

"I can't get ahold of Ashley. It's like her pager is off or something. But I have to go to that sale. It's not fair that you get the car all the time, Jess. If you had a halfway decent boyfriend, he'd have a car that wasn't always in the shop. . . ."

Julia watched them go and tried to imagine — again — starting all over. In eighteen years, she would be fifty-five. Fifty-five, and the mother of two teenagers? Her urge to scream was quickly replaced by the image of two tiny pink newborns with little pug noses and skin like eiderdown. *Cute.* Yes, the babies would be cute. And funny and precious and adorable. A surge of joy spilled through her chest, and she hugged herself.

Twins! As Jessica and Heather had said — *wow*. And maybe at least one of them would be a boy. Double wowsers. What on earth was Mike going to say?

She had just begun to punch in the numbers for Mike's secretary at the church when she remembered her promise to call her brother. Peter . . . with his long hair and angry blue eyes and messed-up life. Peter . . . who hadn't finished college and at thirty-six still didn't know what he wanted to be when he grew up. Peter . . . whom she loved and agonized over and prayed for . . . but barely spoke with anymore. When had they grown apart? As kids they had been so close.

"Hi, Peter," she would say. "Debbie's dying of anorexia, and I'm having twins. Welcome to reality."

Julia turned the phone around in her hand, trying to decide whom to call first. Then she switched it off, set it on the stump, and went back to her lantanas. The crises could wait for another hour. Things were growing. Flowers and babies and teenagers. And things were wilting. Sisters and brothers and husbands. It was time to tend the garden.

chapter two

Peter Mossman pushed open the door to his small apartment, dropped a sack of groceries into a chair, and focused on the blank canvas staring at him from across the room. Nothing. Empty. He kicked the door shut behind him. Yesterday evening, he'd spent three hours staring at that canvas. Waiting for something to come. Trying to find a vision. But all he felt was anger and confusion.

It was Maria's fault, he thought as he stripped off his uniform shirt. If she hadn't walked out on him . . . if she hadn't taken their son . . . if she hadn't filed for divorce . . .

He threw his shirt on the chair, grabbed the plastic grocery bag, and stalked into the kitchen area of his efficiency rental. Opening the freezer door, he tossed in three TV dinners and a carton of ice cream. He stared at the canvas again, re-

27

sentful of the unblinking white eye that focused on him like a condemning judge.

"What?" he snarled at it. "What?"

He kicked off his shoes near the chrome-and-glass dining table and checked his answering machine. Nothing. Of course, she wasn't going to call. She hadn't called since the day she'd left the message about the divorce papers. Well, fine. He didn't want to talk to her anyway.

Maria had no idea how to carry on a conversation. "Stop yelling at me!" she would complain. "You're always so mean, Peter. Don't shout. Why do we have to fight all the time?"

She thought any discussion that held the slightest note of conflict was a fight. Her parents had never argued, she insisted. Well, neither had his — Mr. and Mrs. Perfect Missionary Mossman.

But Peter wasn't that stupid. He knew his parents' marriage hadn't been flawless. His mother had resented spending all those years out in the boonies with no friends and no dinner parties and no little Sunday school classes to teach. And Dad hadn't always been too thrilled with Mom either, burying his nose in a Bible commentary when his wife went off on one of her tangents.

"The children are growing up wild, Don," she would say in her sweetsy voice — honey laced with poison. "You really ought to take Peter out to the churches with you. He spends all his time in the kraal. You're not listening to me, are you, Don? Have you seen the way Peter carries that spear around, just like one of the natives? How are we supposed to teach him to grow up to be a responsible young man when he's always off with his Maasai friends? And what about the girls? Well, it's a good thing the kids are all away at boarding school most of the time. These days I can hardly pull a meal together to feed my family. Do you realize I haven't had any flour in three months? And safari ants have invaded the storage room again — a whole stream of them. Don, are you listening to me?"

Peter shook his head. Maria thought she had it rough because he didn't bring in enough money. She didn't have a clue what rough was. "Why do you have to work as a mailman?" she would complain. "Why don't you apply for a maintenance job over at the law enforcement training center? Why don't you try to get on with one of the refineries? Why don't you work out in the oil fields? You could make a lot more money, Peter, if you'd just try harder."

But the truth was, Peter liked working for the postal service. His delivery route through the small town of Artesia, New Mexico, took him through the Hispanic section where Maria had grown up — where the exotic aromas of roasting chilies and freshly grilled tortillas greeted him each morning, where people spoke in a different language and children ran around half naked. It felt slightly foreign there, slightly like home. Like Africa.

Besides, as a mail carrier, Peter didn't have to work odd hours or carry a pager. He could come home and paint. That was where his passion lay. His painting really should be taking off now that Maria was gone. She was always rearranging his oils and dusting his canvases before they were dry. And Angelo, crawling around under the legs of the easel or crying to be held, kept him distracted.

Ever since Maria took their son — their "Angel" — and headed back to her mama's house several weeks earlier, the apartment had been quiet. Serene. Uncluttered. So, why couldn't Peter paint?

He felt like ramming his fist right through the canvas. All he'd ever wanted was a loving woman, maybe a couple of kids, and a chance to grow as an artist. Why couldn't Maria understand how much his art meant to him? It was his only way of going back, of touching the past, of salving the hidden hurt of his thousand losses. When he painted, he connected with his inner self. Painting healed him.

Why couldn't Maria see that? She wanted things he couldn't give her. Curtains and tablecloths and rugs and a new bedspread. She wanted pots and pans. She complained about buying Angelo's clothes at garage sales and having to stretch leftovers into more than one meal. She wanted spending money and a new house and pretty clothes. Peter's dreams of showing his work in a Santa Fe gallery, of making a living as an artist, of being able to paint full-time meant nothing to Maria. Those kinds of things weren't real to her. Working in the oil fields was real.

With a sigh, Peter walked back into the kitchen and chose a Salisbury steak dinner from the selection in the freezer. He peeled back the corner of the packet and slung it into the microwave. The beeps of the electronic timer sounded too loud in the deserted apartment.

Maria had always been a great cook. She made enchiladas and tamales and refried beans to die for. Peter had always told his wife how much he loved her cooking. In fact, he'd made sure to admire and compliment her up one side and down the other. And his flattery was genuine. With her black hair and big brown eyes, Maria radiated youthful beauty. Not only was she lovely, but she kept the apartment clean, she took good care of Angelo, and her kindness extended throughout the whole neighborhood. Maria had been exactly what Peter wanted in a wife. So what had gone wrong?

The beeping confused him at first — he thought it was the microwave, when actually it was the phone. His heart contracted. Maybe Maria was finally calling. Every time he had phoned her since she'd left, her mother had answered and told him that Maria didn't want to speak to him — now or ever. What would he say to her now? How could he let her know how much she meant to him even though she'd hurt him so badly?

He picked up the phone.

"Hey, little brother!" It was Julia. His sister never called unless something was wrong.

"Hey," he said. "How's everything up in Santa Fe?"

"Pretty good. The girls are out of school. Did you get Jessica's graduation invitation?"

"Uh . . . yeah." He rubbed the back of his neck, feeling guilty because he hadn't sent his niece a gift.

"I mailed you one of her prom pictures," Julia said. "What did you think? She's really grown up, isn't she?"

"She's pretty. I didn't like the looks of the guy with her. Too skinny."

"Oh, that's Danny. The tux didn't do much for him, but he's really a very nice young man." She paused, clearly waiting for him to ask more questions about her wonderful, all-American family. "Heather's driving now. It seems like she's always out at the mall."

Again she hesitated. Peter tried to think of something to say. He knew Julia had called for a reason, and he wished she would dispense with the polite chitchat. All through their childhood, he and his older sister had been buddies. Together they had braved boarding school and explored the bush country and fought off malaria. "Peas in a pod," their mother used to say about her three children with their wavy golden hair and deeply tanned skin. What had happened to turn his sister into a stranger?

Time, he supposed. Time and distance.

"So, how's Maria?" Julia asked. "Is Angelo walking yet?"

Peter hadn't yet told his family about the trouble with Maria. Why should he? It wasn't like they cared. Now he searched his memory for an answer to Julia's question. "He's pulling up. Trying to stand on his own." He reflected on the son he hadn't seen for several weeks. Maybe Angelo *was* walking by now. What a thought.

"Well, listen, Pete. I wanted to call and let you know something. It's about Debbie."

A jolt of concern shot through him. "What's wrong? Did something happen to her?"

As a boy, he'd always felt it was his duty to protect his sisters. Julia had been fairly resilient, but skinny, blonde, little Debbie with her scuffed-up knees and tear-filled blue eyes was Peter's baby girl. Though she was only a couple of years younger than he was, she had been fragile, delicate, too pretty and gentle for the harsh world of their upbringing. He adored her, and though their paths hadn't crossed in years, his "big brother" defenses were instantly on the alert.

"Did that creep of a boyfriend do something to Debbie?" he asked. "I'll kill him."

"No, it's not that. She's sick, Peter. They've got her at the hospital in Bolivar. It sounds pretty serious."

"What happened to her?"

"She has anorexia. Can you believe it? I had no idea anything was wrong with her. The doctors put in a feeding tube, and they're worried about her ability to fight infection. She might have osteoporosis, too. I guess anorexia involves a whole realm of other problems. Mom and Dad have been to see her, but it's hard to get an accurate reading of the situation from them." She hesitated. "Pete, I think you and I need to talk this over. Make some decisions. I was wondering if you could drive up to Santa Fe for the weekend. You can bring Maria and Angelo, if you want. There's nobody in the guest room right now."

Pete glanced around at his microwave dinner and his blank canvas and his empty apartment. There was nothing to keep him in Artesia. But he didn't like the idea of visiting Julia either. She'd want to know all about his problems with Maria. And he'd have to look at the perfect little family she'd created for herself. A preacher for a husband, two beautiful, smart daughters, church three times a week, and a house in the suburbs. And what did he have to show off in return? A broken marriage, an efficiency apartment, a high school education, and a job that was taking him nowhere.

"I can't come," he said. "I'm busy this weekend."

"But, Pete, this is about Debbie."

He thought of his baby sister, the way she had always clung to his hand, her fingers tight and warm. "Do Mom and Dad think she's . . . I mean, is her life in danger or something?"

"I'm not sure. That's why I want to talk to you. We might need to fly to Missouri and spend some time with her."

Missouri. No way. That would mean an extended period with the elder Mossmans, too. Seeing his parents was the last thing Peter wanted to do. He had embarrassed them, failed to live up to their expectations, slid away from his Christian roots. It would be the same as ever with them — all huggy-kissy for a few minutes, and then the barbed comments would begin. Criticisms. Complaints. Mournful recitations of his failures. The news about his impending divorce would knock them flat. They'd probably fall to their knees in prayer right on the spot.

"And there's something else I want to talk over with you," Julia said. "I . . . I know we haven't been too close lately, but I still feel like you're the only one around here who might understand what I'm dealing with."

"What's going on, Jules? Are you all right?"

"Yeah," she said, and he recognized the thin thread of her voice on the other end of the line. "I'm okay . . . I guess."

"You don't sound okay."

"I'm pregnant."

He took a breath. "Wow."

"With twins."

Peter felt his mouth drop open. "Wow," he said again.

She gave a weak chuckle. "That seems to be the consensus. I just told Mike. I think he's in shock. We've only known I was pregnant for a couple of months, even though I'm about six months along. Things were so busy around here, and I kept hoping it might be early menopause or something else. Anyway, I just couldn't believe it might be true, so I didn't check it out."

"Julia, you've had two babies. You should know the signs." It looked like his big sister was following the good old

Mossman tradition of being able to turn a blind eye on reality.

"Yeah, I guess. Anyway, we were just starting to get used to the idea of my being pregnant at all when we found out it's twins. Pete, listen, Mike's not going to be in any condition to talk seriously about this for a few days. The girls are each in their own little universe, of course. I could really use someone to lean on right now. I need my brother."

He closed his eyes, feeling a warmth spread through his chest. How long had it been since someone had wanted him, needed him? "I'll leave in half an hour," he said. "I should be there by midnight."

"What about Maria? Angelo might do better if you left tomorrow morning."

"Maria's been staying with her mom for a few weeks."

"Oh, Pete."

He studied the empty kitchen counter. "See you soon, Jules."

"Okay," she whispered. "I love you."

"I love you, too." He set down the phone and opened the microwave. With a flick of his wrist, he sent the Salisbury steak tray sailing into the trash like a Frisbee. He would stop at McDonald's on his way out of town. No point in wasting time.

"How about a cup of chai?" Julia asked. At the Swahili word for tea, Peter grinned. *Chai* might mean some gourmet blend of spiced tea to most Americans. To the Mossmans, it would always be a strong, amber-colored drink heavily laced with milk and sugar. *Chai* was African tea, preferably with a few dark leaves floating at the bottom and a side order of *mandazis* — fried donuts coated in sugar.

"I haven't had any chai in years," he said.

"I drink it every day. Decaf, of course." Julia pushed up out of her chair, probably as eager as he was to have something to distract them from the awkwardness they felt at seeing each other again after so long. Julia had explained that, as usual on a Tuesday morning, Mike had gone over to the church to take care of his office paperwork after being off on Monday, and both girls were sleeping late. Peter felt somehow odd to be alone with his sister, as though she had become a stranger.

"Come on into the kitchen," Julia beckoned him. "I'll show you my stash."

"You have the real stuff?"

"The genuine article." She padded barefoot across the vinyl floor that looked impeccably clean and opened a cupboard filled with several varieties of teas. She selected a colorful tin and extracted from it a plastic bag sealed against moisture. "Remember my friend Emily Porter from boarding school? She married Jacob Myers, who was a year older. Anyway, they went back to Kenya as missionaries, and she sends me a packet of chai a couple times a year. She and Jacob have four kids; can you believe that? They work up near the Northern Frontier District with the Samburu tribe, but Emily home-schools. Don't you think it's interesting that she won't send her kids to boarding school?"

Peter studied his sister as she fluttered around the kitchen filling a kettle, selecting a teapot, measuring out tea leaves. It looked pretty obvious to him that she was expecting twins. Only six months along, her belly protruded round and smooth beneath her T-shirt, a pink glow brightened her cheeks, and she had taken on that wide-hipped waddle he remembered from Maria's last months. His wife's pregnancy had amazed and bewildered him. He wondered how Julia was feeling now.

"I think it shows that things are different when it's your own children," she said, answering her own question. Long ago, Peter had learned that his big sister could carry on a conversation all by herself. "I mean, we all had a good time at boarding school, but the thought of sending your own kids there is —"

"Wait a minute. We all had a good time at boarding school? Is that what you just said, Jules?"

"Oh, Pete, you have to admit it was fun. All our friends were there, and —"

"And we had that great food — my favorite was the cauliflower flavored with caterpillars — and those loving, caring teachers, and the comfortable iron beds with their two-inch-thick mattresses, and don't forget our regular bouts of dysentery and malaria."

Julia leaned back against the counter, looking at him through narrowed eyes. "If that's how you want to remember Kenya Christian Academy, fine," she said. "But I choose to look back on the friendships I made and the things I learned. We got a very good education —"

"And you're a housewife, and I'm a mail carrier. A lot of good that education did us, huh?" He glanced at the teakettle as it began to whistle. He didn't want to hurt her, but the facts were clear. "We should have been home-schooled."

"Oh, I'm sure you would have *loved* Mom as your teacher. We could have experienced an in-home demonstration of World War II. Come on, Pete, KCA wasn't so bad. You had fun there."

"Breaking rules, yeah. I spent most of my spare time off campus in the forest. We poached small game all the time; did you know that? Sneaking out after midnight, walking the railroad tracks, drinking chai down in the African village . . . Did I ever tell you about that shopkeeper who would trade us beer for T-shirts?"

Julia's mouth dropped open. "Beer? You were drinking beer at boarding school, Peter?"

"Tusker lager, East Africa's finest brew."

"No wonder Mom used to complain that you had lost so many of your clothes in the school laundry. You'd traded all your T-shirts for beer."

He laughed. "I was such a mystery to our dear mother."

Peter wondered how his older sister had turned out to be such a great mom, with the role model they'd had. On the phone, Julia had sounded kind of nervous about the prospect of the new babies, but he couldn't figure out why. She was a perfect mom. "Debbie never complained about

KCA," Julia said as she carried the teapot back into the living room. "She liked boarding school."

Oh, brother. How out of touch had Julia been during those years? Peter wondered. "Debbie hated boarding school," he told her.

"Why would you say that, Pete? Debbie had so many friends. She was homecoming queen her senior year, remember?"

"Did you ever read her poetry?" That had been Peter's first clue that their beautiful little sister was unhappy.

"Oh, I think that was just a phase. It's a teenage thing to be melodramatic."

"Debbie was suicidal, Julia."

She sat down and stared at her brother. "Suicidal?"

"She didn't want to go on living. It was clear in her writings. She used to fold up her poems and hand them to me when we passed each other in the cafeteria. I always felt like she was crying out, begging me to save her. But there wasn't anything I could do." Outwardly, his younger sister had always seemed so bright, the center of the most popular clique. Had Julia been blind to their sister's pain all those years? Debbie had been three years behind Julia in school, so maybe the two girls hadn't seen much of each other. Class schedules, different dormitories, and strict curfews kept the siblings apart most of the time.

Julia stared at her cup as she stirred sugar cubes into her tea. "I never knew anything was wrong with Debbie," she confessed. "I wonder if it's the same now."

"What do you mean?"

"Maybe this anorexia problem is her way of sending out a cry for help. I feel like she needs us, Peter."

"What good can we do? I don't have any money to help her pay bills, and it's not like we can force-feed her. Besides, you know what'll happen if I go to Missouri." The spark of Peter's concern for his younger sister was extinguished as he thought of their parents. "Mom and Dad will jump all over me. Especially when they find out about Maria."

"What happened between the two of you, Pete?"

He shrugged, unwilling to go into details. "I don't really know. She wants me to work in the oil fields."

"Are you still painting?"

He thought of the blank canvas in his apartment. "Trying. An art career is probably just a pipe dream. Maybe I ought to do what Maria wants. But —" he bit back a curse — "Julia, I've spent my whole life trying to do what other people wanted. I've never managed to make anyone happy, and I just don't see why I should even try anymore!"

Julia sipped her tea, taken aback at Peter's vehemence. She had almost forgotten how easily her brother was roused to anger. He had always been disobedient and rebellious. But this time, she had to admit to a certain empathy with him. Wasn't that exactly what she'd been arguing about her pregnancy? All her life, she'd tried to do what other people wanted. She had been the good girl, so obedient. Now she wanted to finish her college education and establish a nursing career. Peter's description of how he felt sounded uncomfortably familiar — confined, hemmed in, forced to spend his days in a prison that others had created. No, that was too harsh. Julia loved her family and her role as a youth minister's wife. She just wanted . . . what did she want?

Pouring her brother a second cup of tea, she felt an overwhelming sadness. What had happened to Peter in the years since they had left Africa? She remembered him as a tawny young lion, thick golden hair drifting in the breeze as he crept through the brush with his spear, tracking an antelope or bringing back a small gazelle for their dinner. He had been all grace and beauty, a handsome warrior with a smile that set girls' hearts afire and eyes the color of the African sky. Now his body seemed tense, his eyes cold and gray, his smile empty.

They were heading for forty — all three of the Mossman siblings. Yet, none of them seemed to have found a comfortable skin to fit into. Each had tried one thing or another, stumbling through life, guessing at what "normal" life was supposed to look like. Why were they still struggling to figure out who they were? Why didn't they fit? And whose fault was it, anyway?

"It's our parents," Peter said, as if he had read her mind. "The thought of seeing them again just knocks the wind out of my sails. I'd like to be with Debbie. I'm really worried about her. But you know what would happen, Jules."

"Well, I'd hope we could all get along — for Debbie's sake. But the thing is, I really don't think I can go right now. Mike is dealing with some stuff related to his ministry. Jessica is a mess over leaving her boyfriend when she starts college. And Heather —"

"What about me?" Still wearing her

nightshirt, the teenager sauntered into the room and eyed her mother accusingly. Then she flipped her long hair over her shoulder and gave a wide grin. "Hey, Uncle Pete! Did you get in last night? I didn't hear a thing."

Reaching out her arms, she gave him a hug.

"You're looking good, Heather," he said, holding her at arm's length. "I bet all the boys are after you."

"Boys." She rolled her eyes. "I have better things to do with my time, thank you very much. Hey, what are you guys drinking? Is that chai? Mom guzzles the stuff. Did she tell you she's pregnant, Uncle Pete? Isn't that the weirdest thing you ever heard?"

Heather's bare feet slapped against the floor tiles as she headed into the kitchen. Peter settled back into his chair. With a mixture of amusement and pride, Julia watched her daughter over the counter that divided the two rooms.

"Why don't you fly out to check on Debbie?" he said, drawing her attention. "You're good with that kind of thing, Jules. And Mom and Dad would enjoy seeing you."

"I don't want to go without you, Peter. I

think this is a family thing."

"Family? Julia, when was the last time the Mossmans were a family? Come to think of it, were we ever a family? I mean, during our whole childhood, Mom and Dad were doing their God thing, and the three of us were off at boarding school. Even on holidays, it was clear we played second fiddle to pastors' meetings, Bible commentaries, sermon preparation —"

Peter was such a mystery, Julia reflected as she poured herself a second cup of tea. Sometimes she wondered if she even knew her brother at all. They had grown up in the same world, yet their memories were so different. And now look at him. Who was he? What had he become?

And what about Peter's unhappiness? Was he just choosing to focus on the bleak memories, or had he really been so miserable?

"This is so cool," Heather said, carrying a bowl of cereal back into the living room. "The two of you sitting here drinking chai. It's like that picture down in the basement. You know, Mom? You and Uncle Pete and Aunt Debbie are on this blanket under a tree, and you're drinking tea."

Julia searched her memory. "I don't remember a picture like that. Are you sure?"

"Duh, Mom. It's on that shelf by the old encyclopedia set." She plunked her cereal bowl on the coffee table and straightened, heaving a sigh of exaggerated tolerance. "Okay, I'll get it for you. Gosh."

"Heather!" Julia felt her blood pressure rise. "I told you not to use that slang. It's inappropriate."

"Sor-ry! Chill out, Mom."

As Heather vanished down the basement stairs, Julia set her teacup on the low table. "We *were* a family, Peter," she said. "We still are. We're a very good family. Our parents might have made a few mistakes, but who doesn't? They were committed to their mission work, and we have to respect that. God called them to Africa to evangelize the Maasai, and they were faithful in their ministry. We had lots of great experiences, we learned several languages, and we made good friends. I don't think we got shortchanged at all, and I can't see why you —"

"It's not me. It's them. They don't like who I am."

"Who *are* you, Peter?" Julia felt tears spring to her eyes as she spotted Heather returning with a small framed photograph. "What happened to all of us?"

"Right here!" Heather crowed. "Look,

here's you and Uncle Peter. And there's Aunt Debbie crawling around in diapers. You're drinking chai, am I right?"

Julia took the picture and studied the three children gathered on a cloth under a thorn tree. Now she remembered the photograph. Sure enough, they were drinking chai and munching on *mandazis*. In the background, the corner of their corrugated tin house was just visible, and there was the storage room that the safari ants were always invading.

"Who's that lady in the back? Over in the shadows?" Heather asked, plopping down beside her mother on the couch. "Was she one of the natives? She's kind of creepy looking."

"That's our *ko-ko-o!* Look, Peter!"

He took the picture and peered down at the black-and-white figures. "It is. It's her!"

"Who is she?"

"Her name was Vanoui, but we called her our *ko-ko-o*, our African grandmother," Julia said, gazing down at the kindly face. "She was a good friend to our whole family, but she especially loved us kids. Ko-ko-o always made our tea in the afternoons."

"She used to tell us stories, too." Something in Peter's voice made Julia wonder if he felt the same welling of emotion that she felt. "Remember, Julia? She told us all the legends."

"And songs."

"And prayers, too."

"Prayers?" Heather asked. "Was she a Christian?"

"In the later years," Julia said. "But she still prayed all the old Maasai prayers. Remember what she used to say to us, Pete? After teatime, she would make us hold hands, and then she'd tell us to take care of each other. We had to make a vow every day."

Her brother looked up at her. "Love each other. That's what Ko-ko-o made us promise."

"Love each other. Take care of each other. . . . Peter, we have to go to Debbie."

"Dad's gonna go ballistic," Heather warned. "But don't worry, he'll get over it. Besides, me and Jessica can take care of everything around here."

Julia fought the panic building inside her. Mike would argue against a trip — especially in light of the news about the twins. And the thought of Heather and Jessica trying to run the household sent chills down her spine.

"You ought to go, Mom," Heather said, taking the picture and running her finger over the dusty glass. "Jessica drives me crazy most of the time, but if I got sick, I'd want her around. She's my sister."

Peter took Julia's hand. "A long time ago, I made a promise."

She nodded. "Love each other. Take care of each other." She let out a breath. "Okay, I'll go call Mike and let him know what's happening. Then we can call Deb and tell her we're coming."

chapter three

As Peter drove the rental car into the small town of Bolivar, Missouri, he shook his head at how little the place had changed. After leaving Kenya, each of the three Mossman children had begun college at the Christian university here. But Julia had met and married Mike almost right away. Peter survived only a year at the school before heading off to work at a church camp in the New Mexico mountains. After that summer, he drifted south, ending up in Artesia. When Julia and Mike went out to visit him, they decided to make the state their home. Only Debbie had stayed in college, graduating with a degree in home economics and then going to work for a chain of ladies' boutiques. Though she had risen to the position of buyer, she still lived in Bolivar in a little white clapboard house near the campus.

"This is like a time warp," Peter said as he and Julia crossed the college campus. "Look, there's the old dorm where I lived. And there's the basketball gym and the soccer field. Nothing's changed."

"I was just thinking how different it all seems," his sister said. "They've added a football stadium and a cafeteria and even a new administration building. What a lovely campus. You know what? I always liked Bolivar. It's quaint."

"I think the word you're looking for is *rinky-dink*."

"Oh, Pete, it's a nice little American town. It has a courthouse on the square and cafés and doughnut shops. It's cute. And the people are so kind."

Peter turned onto Oakland Street toward Citizens Memorial Hospital. Had his sister always been such a Pollyanna? He glanced over at her, marveling at the way her newly purchased mother-to-be wardrobe had transformed her. No more oversized T-shirts and baggy sweats. Julia was a bona fide pregnant woman, and she looked it.

That Tuesday after she and Peter had made their decision to travel to Missouri, Julia's daughters took her shopping for maternity clothes. Peter had phoned and left a message for Maria, who had still refused to speak to him. Then he called the Artesia post office and explained about his sister's situation. He had so much vacation time built up that the postmaster had given him two full weeks off. And then he and Julia had booked their plane tickets.

"What are we going to say to Debbie?" Julia asked as they approached the hospital. "Do you think there's anything we can do to help her?"

"I haven't even gotten that far yet. I'm just hoping I can keep things calm with Mom and Dad. That's my goal: peace on the home front." Ha. As if he could be in the same room with his parents for more than five minutes without an argument erupting. But, hey, it was worth a try.

"Good. It'll be upsetting to Debbie if there's tension," Julia was saying. "But I think we can do something to help her. We ought to see if we can take her out of the hospital now and then. You know, drive her around Dunnegan Park and watch the swans. Or maybe just take a ride through the countryside. Being around flowers and trees is so healing, don't you think?"

"I wish we could take her back to Africa. She'd get well there."

"Yeah," Julia said softly. Images of the country she had loved so dearly floated through her mind. As always, she felt her-self instantly transported there with the sun-warmed wind playing across the plains, the melodic cry of the African dove — *ku ku kuru ku ku* — the scent of euca-lyptus trees and tall golden elephant grass spicing the air. Miles and miles of golden grass — grass as far as you could see — and thorn trees dotted here and there across the savanna. Sometimes huge rock formations, red and pink and gray, rose out of the grass like ancient castles. Julia used to try to imagine what it would be like to climb to the very top of one. She was sure that if she ever got there, she would be able to see all the way to Mount Kilimanjaro.

What she loved most was seeing wild animals grazing by the roadside — Thomson's gazelle, impala, wildebeest, eland, topi. It wasn't unusual to see a few elephants, too. Giraffes were the prettiest. She smiled as she remembered the way they would walk in a line, with their long, graceful legs like ballerinas dancing in slow motion. Sometimes a warthog would dash across the road, tail straight up in the air, with several little babies racing behind in a row, their tails straight up, too.

"Here's the hospital." Peter's voice was tense. "I wish we'd brought a present or something. Maybe a box of chocolates."

Julia forced herself back to the present. "She won't eat chocolate. You know Deb." Even as she said the words, Julia recalled her sister's growing aversion to food. Through the years, Debbie had slowly cut one thing after another from her diet. She had grown thinner and thinner — and been heaped with praise by the whole family for how lovely she looked.

"Let's see if we can get her some flowers," Peter said as he pulled the car into a parking space. "There'll be a gift shop inside."

"I wonder what she looks like. The thought of that feeding tube is just awful. What if she's really sick, Peter? I mean dangerously ill?" Julia was feeling more and more nervous.

"Then we'll make sure she gets well. If we have to, we'll kidnap her and force-feed her. We'll take her back to New Mexico and you can ladle chai down her throat."

"This is not funny, Pete."

"I'm serious. I mean, how hard can it be to make someone eat?"

"Evidently pretty hard, or she wouldn't be in this shape."

They got out of the car and began walking toward the hospital. Instinctively,

57

Julia reached for her brother's hand. His fingers were large and warm, and she thought of all the times she had relied on Peter's strength.

My brother killed a lion, she used to boast to her friends at boarding school. But at college in America, her pride in his accomplishment only drew looks of shock and scorn. Weren't lions an endangered species? How could your brother have done such a thing? The poor lion!

Julia realized there was no point in explaining about the need to protect the Maasai cattle and their kraal from predators. And the notion of proving one's manhood by spearing a lion was totally foreign to her college classmates. But Peter was strong and brave and clever and, to Julia, that was everything a brother ought to be.

He led her toward the gift shop, where they purchased a large bouquet of bright spring flowers. Julia hoped her sister would be cheered by the colorful assortment. As they carried it down a hall toward the room they had been directed to, she could feel her heart beginning to quake. She had experienced harsh reality helping out in bush clinics during her school vacations, tending to patients with tuberculosis, leprosy, trachoma, and terribly infected thorn wounds. But this was Debbie. Her Debbie.

"I'm scared," she whispered as they reached the door to her sister's room. "Peter, you talk first. Give me a chance to get adjusted."

"It'll be okay." He squeezed her hand. "It's just Debbie."

He pushed open the door, and they stepped into the cool, darkened room with its single bed against the far wall. Appearing empty of all signs of human habitation, the place smelled vaguely of antiseptic. As she focused on the bed, Julia smothered a gasp. Debbie lay there pale and unmoving, her blonde hair reduced to thin, brittle wisps that fell limp on the pillow. Both her arms extended across the sheet, bone-thin and eerily white, like those on a glow-in-the-dark Halloween skeleton. She had clasped her hands together as though she had been praying before she fell asleep. An IV line ran from one wrist, while the feeding tube that had been threaded through her left nostril was secured to her face with white adhesive tape.

Peter breathed hard as he drew his older sister toward the bed. This was worse than he'd imagined. A lot worse. Debbie looked like a corpse, lying there so stiff and bloodless. A surge of anger ran through his veins. How had this happened? How had anyone who lived or worked around her failed to see what was happening to Debbie? Why hadn't his parents done something to help?

"Where are Mom and Dad?" he whispered to Julia. "I thought they'd be here waiting for us."

"I don't know, Pete. I didn't get a chance to talk to them. I just told someone on the nursing staff we'd be coming in this morning."

Struggling to contain his rage, Peter stared down at his sister. Debbie's eyes fluttered and slid open. Big blue eyes, still beautiful, studied the two figures hovering by the bed.

"Hey, you guys." Debbie's lips cracked into a pained smile. "Mom told me you were coming. You didn't need to do that."

"Oh, Debbie!" With a stifled sob, Julia rushed forward and took her sister's hands. "Why didn't you tell us you were so sick? We would have come sooner."

"I'm okay," Debbie said. "I just fainted after church, that's all. I think everyone's overreacting to this."

"Overreacting?" Peter frowned. "Debs, you look like a refugee from Somalia."

"Peter!" Julia grabbed the bouquet from his hands. "Look, Debbie, we brought you some flowers. Aren't they pretty? They might need some water, though. I'll check. Is it okay if I put them on the shelf? Hey, how come it's so dark in here? Wouldn't you like a little sunlight? It's a beautiful day outside, Debbie. Let me open the curtains for you."

"No, really." Deborah tried to lift a hand. "I'm all right."

She blinked as Julia whisked open the curtains and set the flowers on a shelf near the window. Peter pulled a chair to the side of the bed and sat down, watching his older sister go into her motherly flurry. How many times had he seen her do this very thing? Drawing back curtains, making beds, whipping up grilled cheese sandwiches, arranging toys on the shelves. Even at boarding school, she had straightened Peter's collar, and tucked in his shirt, and made sure to sneak him any extra food she was able to hoard.

"Ignore her," he told Deborah. "She's just doing her thing."

"She looks good. Different, sort of."

"She's pregnant."

"Peter, I was going to tell her," Julia scolded. "I'm pregnant, Debbie. It was a total surprise. I've only known a couple of months. I was already four months along when we found out."

"Four months? Julia!"

"I know. It was dumb of me not to check it out sooner, but things had been so hectic at home. And the really wild thing is, I just found out it's *twins*. Can you believe it? We're still in shock. And you should have heard the girls' reactions!"

Peter sat back as Julia went into a lengthy monologue on the trials and joys of mothering two teenagers. Then she segued neatly into the saga of Mike's emotional turmoil as he tried to decide whether to be a youth minister or a pastor. Like it was some kind of an earth-shattering choice. She talked about the possibility of their moving to Wyoming, and she mentioned several new things she had done to decorate their house in Santa Fe, and finally she ended with a brief explanation of Xeriscape gardening, as though Debbie might have been considering a move to a drier landscape.

"I put in a few roses this spring," Debbie offered. "Along the south side of my house."

"Roses grow very well in Santa Fe. Have you ever heard of Olympiad? It's a big red rose with great disease resistance —"

"Speaking of diseases," Peter cut in, eager to change the subject, "what does the doctor say about this deal of yours, Debbie? This anorexia. Is he thinking you'll be in the hospital awhile, or what?"

"He's not sure. I guess I got pretty weak somehow." She looked out the window. "I don't really understand the problem. I've always kept my weight under control, and you know how focused I am about exercising. I run three miles every morning, I do my treadmill and weights at night, and I drink gallons of water. I really do take very good care of myself."

"But, Debbie, you're obviously not eating enough," Julia pointed out. "If the doctor felt he needed to put in a feeding tube —"

"That's just because I got a little dehydrated. I've had some problems with my stomach lately. So, I started trying a few different kinds of laxatives. I think that might have started the whole thing."

"What's wrong with your stomach?" Julia asked.

"There's no food in it," Peter said, before Debbie could answer.

"No," Debbie said defensively. "For your information, I eat plenty for my frame and height. My stomach just gets tied up in knots sometimes. It starts feeling so bloated that I can't stand it. I've worried there might be something else going on. Like cancer."

"Maybe you're working too hard," Julia suggested. Peter could tell their older sister was unwilling to entertain the thought that Debbie could have cancer. "Maybe you need to take a vacation."

"I'm fine. I really am."

"You don't look fine," Peter said. "You look skinny. Bony."

"Peter, could you please make an effort to be more polite?" Julia asked. "You're not being helpful here. You're being offensive."

"You sound like Mom. Speaking of whom, where are the elder Mossmans, anyway, Debs? I figured they'd be camping out here day and night."

"They haven't been around too much except in the beginning. I think this is upsetting to them. Anyway, they had a Vacation Bible School to help with this week, so they've gone to Joplin."

"Joplin?" Peter felt a familiar red rage boil up inside him. "You're lying here with a feeding tube, and they're doing Vacation Bible School in *Joplin?* Are you *kidding* me?"

"I told them it was okay. I'm just resting here. I don't need anyone to be here."

"But, Debbie," Julia said, "you really do seem very sick. Did Mom and Dad understand what your situation is?"

"They talked to the doctor. He'll call them if I get worse."

"Worse?" Peter exploded. "How can you get *worse?* If you get worse, you'll be *dead,* and then what good can they do?"

"Pete!" Julia cried.

"It's true, Jules! Look at her. She's half dead already. How could they have the gall to go off and do their missionary thing when their daughter is in this condition?"

"She's not dying, Peter. She's getting better."

"Better than what? Where's her long wavy hair? Would you tell me that? Look at it now. It's like her head's been cooked in a microwave."

"Stop it, Peter." Julia could feel tears of dismay threatening. She could hardly believe her brother would get so angry so quickly.

"Why?" he challenged. "She's obviously living in some kind of fantasy world. Mom and Dad, too. How can they not see how sick she is? They probably do, and they just don't care. Got that Vacation Bible

School on the old calendar. Gotta do God's will. Gotta run here and there following the call to missions. Never mind that your daughter's in the hospital dying."

"Peter, please don't."

"Don't what? Don't be real? Don't be honest?" He stood, clearly exasperated. "This is so typical of them. First of all they do their big denial scene — *Oh, she's not so bad.* And then they skip off to get the celebrity treatment in some church."

Julia felt sick with panic. The things Peter was saying in front of Debbie! She swallowed the lump in her throat. "You have to try to understand, Pete. I'm sure the VBS is something they scheduled a long time ago —"

"Of course they did. So when is a schedule more important than a family? I'll tell you when — always. In the Mossman family, *always.* I come here prepared to do my best to make peace with them, and they go and do this."

"I'm sure they wouldn't have gone to Joplin if they'd felt like it was an emergency."

"Don't kid yourself, Jules. They'd have gone. They were always gone. Did they come up to school when I got an amoeba that put me in the infirmary for two weeks?

Did they come to the States when I was in that car wreck? Did they come to my wedding?"

"Well, Peter —"

"Did they come to yours? How about the birth of your kids? Were they there for that? Have they ever been doting grandparents to your daughters, Julia?"

"Peter, please." She couldn't stop the tears now. "Our parents have always done the best they could. They act the way they feel is right under the circumstances. Please stop being so angry. It doesn't do any good."

"That's true, and you know why? Because they never listen to us. And even if they did, they'd go ahead and do what they thought God was telling them to do —"

"God does call people into his service, Peter —"

"I don't want any part of a God like that!"

"Oh, Peter!"

Julia groped in her purse for a tissue. This was turning out horribly, just as she had feared. Peter couldn't keep his feelings under control, and Debbie was in terrible shape, and Julia wished she hadn't come. Things were probably a mess at home with the girls trying to take care of the house and Mike so confused about his future. Besides, what good was she doing here? The whole thing had provoked another one of Peter's outbursts, and the minute their parents walked into the room, the situation would explode. And what good would that do Debbie?

"Peter, I want you to calm down," she said. "Just take a deep breath and —"

"Don't talk to me like I'm some kind of child, Julia! I'm the only one in this family who can see reality."

"You know what?" Debbie said, her voice hovering in a detached whisper over the bed. "This reminds me of the time Mom and Dad put us in the Happy Room."

"The Happy Room?" Peter asked.

It had been years since Julia had thought about the Happy Room.

"Don't you remember?" Debbie said. "You yelled all the time in there, Peter. You were so mad. Julia cried her eyes out. And I just sat there watching you both, scared to death and wondering what was going to happen to us."

"I don't remember that," Peter said.

"Oh yes," Debbie said. "We were on that ocean liner on our way to Africa, the time Mom and Dad put us in the Happy Room.

I was only four, and the boat seemed so big and scary . . ."

The boat is big and scary. Mommy holds my hand so I won't fall off the boat. There's water under the boat. Mommy says I will drown if I fall into the water. Peter tells me that drown means die.

I look through the bars on the edge of the boat, and I see lots of people standing on the land. They wave. Everybody on the boat throws something. Daddy says they're throwing streamers. Pink and purple and blue streamers. The streamers land in the water and on the land. Everyone is happy to be saying good-bye.

I'm not happy. I'm sad. I remember our house where I have lived all my life, for four whole years. We won't ever go back to that, or our green plastic swimming pool, or our doggy. Julia told me we're going on the boat to Africa. Peter said natives live there, and they put missionaries in a pot and cook them and eat them. We are missionaries.

I'm afraid to go to Africa. I'm afraid of

falling off the boat into the water. I'm afraid of the streamers. When somebody blows a loud horn, that's when I start to cry. Julia puts her arm around me. She tells me everything is going to be okay, and Africa will be wonderful. I ask her about the pot, so she thinks I need to go to the bathroom, even though I really meant the pot where the natives cook the missionaries. When Julia and I come out of the bathroom, the boat is sailing away from the land, and the Statue of Liberty is passing by, waving her big arm at us, good-bye, good-bye.

After that, it seems like things might be okay after all. We go down some long steps into the bottom of the boat, and we find a nice room with a bed for each of us. We're all together, Daddy and Mommy, Peter and Julia, and me.

We go to a big room full of tables. We eat supper. Then we go back to our new bedroom. We get into our beds. I can't go to sleep, because I am afraid the boat will sink. Peter says sometimes boats do that. He says if the boat sinks, we'll put on our life jackets and swim to shore. But I can't swim, no matter how hard I try. I am too little.

Pretty soon, I get out of my bed, and I climb into bed with my brother. Peter knows how to swim. He puts his arm around me and says I better not wet the bed, or he'll kill me. Peter says things like that, but I'm not afraid of him.

The next morning is when the terrible thing happens. After breakfast, Mommy and Daddy take us to a door. "This is the Happy Room," Mommy says. The door opens. A lady looks down at us. All of a sudden we are inside the Happy Room with the door shutting behind us. Right away, Peter decides he doesn't want to be there. He turns around and runs to the door, but it is locked. We feel just like Hansel and Gretel in the wicked witch's house. Julia starts to cry. Then I cry, too. If Julia cries, I usually cry. Julia is the biggest, and she knows if things are going to be good or bad. The Happy Room is bad.

"I want my mommy!" Julia says, wailing through her tears to the wicked witch. "I want her to come back. Where is she? Where did she go? I don't want to be here!"

Peter picks up a jack-in-the-box. He throws it across the room. It hits the wall and pops open. A little clown bursts out and bounces up and down. It scares me to death. I cry harder.

"Where are my mommy and daddy?"

Peter shouts. "I don't want to be in this stupid room!"

We're not supposed to say *stupid*. It's a bad word. I am so surprised that Peter said it, I sit down on the floor. That's when I notice there are some blocks and some books and some other children in the room. They stare at Peter and Julia and me, and I stare at them. We don't know what's going to happen to us — not a single one of us. We have been put into the Happy Room with a wicked witch, and she might boil us in a pot and eat us. Maybe she's a native. Maybe this is Africa. Oh, where are we, and what happened to our mommy and daddy?

Forever and ever, we stay in the Happy Room. Julia cries. She cries all the time, without ever stopping, even when sandwiches come and purple juice to drink. Peter yells and throws toys. Sometimes he hits the other children. He is very mad. I watch Peter and Julia, but I also keep my eye on the witch, in case she turns into a monster. This is a very scary place.

Then we get a big surprise. Mommy and Daddy suddenly open the door! They're alive! I can hardly believe they came back for us. We run into their arms. We tell them how much we hate the Happy Room. They take us away, across the boat, down the stairs, to our beds.

"The captain agreed that we could hold worship services on Sunday," Daddy says. "Olive, this may be a great opportunity for us to share the Word."

Olive is the other name of my mommy, and sharing the Word is what missionaries do. Daddy told me it means telling people about Jesus. We're going to do it a lot when we get to Africa. I'm glad, because I love Jesus. I want everybody in the whole world to know about him. Especially natives.

"I could offer to teach a Sunday school class," Mommy says. "And there are quite a few foreigners on board. I met some Italian ladies at lunch today. I wonder if I ought to give a few English lessons. That might be a way for me to reach out to them with the gospel."

I'm not sure what the gospel is. I know you can spread it, and you can share it. I think it might be kind of like peanut butter. I haven't seen it in our suitcases, but Mommy and Daddy packed a lot of things. I might have missed it. I know they didn't pack our doggy.

I fall asleep thinking about her. She was very soft in my arms. She liked to lick my nose. I wonder if there are doggies in Africa. But it doesn't matter. Everything is going to be okay now. We're all together in our room — Mommy and Daddy, Peter and Julia, and me. I feel warm. The boat is rocking. I know I'm safe.

But the next day, something terrible happens! Mommy and Daddy take us back to the Happy Room! The witch is still there, and so are all the other children. I wonder which ones she ate during the night. Julia starts to cry right away. Peter throws blocks at the little round window. This time, I know Mommy and Daddy are gone forever. Where can they be? Why did they leave us here? What will happen to us?

I love the smell of my daddy, his big gentle hands, his brown eyes. I love the way my mommy's lap feels when I sit and listen to stories she reads. I like to play with her pretty necklace and touch her hair. I miss my mommy and daddy so much. I know I will never see them again.

I feel very small, like a little ant crawling across the floor. Somebody could step on me, and they would never know it. My tummy hurts.

But then, after a long, long time, something amazing happens. Our mommy and daddy come back! There they are, standing in the doorway, giving us big hugs and kisses. We skip across the deck. I feel so good! I forget all about the Happy Room. We're all together again. We laugh and talk. We listen to Mommy and Daddy tell each other about who they shared the gospel with that day on the boat. The Word of God is going everywhere on that boat, and it's all because of my mommy and daddy. I love them so much!

But the next day, Peter and Julia and I are back in the Happy Room. We all cry and tell Mommy and Daddy we don't want to go there. They tell us there is work for them to do on the boat, and we can have fun with the other children in the Happy Room. I try to talk about the wicked witch, but Mommy just kneels down and gives me a kiss on my cheek. She tells me she loves me so much. Then the door closes behind her. I am very sure I will never see her again. I have lost my mommy and daddy forever and ever. I have never felt so sad or lonely in my whole life. I just want to drown in the ocean. And then the door opens, and there they are!

This happens *every day*. Every single day. Morning is when you get up and go to the Happy Room. Evening is when you go back to your bed and sleep. There are lots of days. One right after the other. Mommy and Daddy come and go, come and go.

They are getting used to it. Used to leaving us. Used to saying good-bye.

I am not.

I try to think about a different kind of day when I will get up and go somewhere besides the Happy Room. But that never happens. Daddy says there is always work to do on the boat, sharing the Word of the Lord and spreading the gospel.

Julia still cries every morning, but she has started to help the wicked witch pass out sandwiches and purple juice. Sometimes she rocks the babies who live in the Happy Room. One day the witch gives her a doll to keep forever, even when we get to Africa. Julia hugs that doll. She won't let go of it even in her own bed. I ask Peter about Africa. I think the Happy Room is Africa, I tell him. I think the boat and the purple juice and the witch will last forever, and this is Africa. He says no. Peter says one day we will get to Africa, and we will be free forever.

I don't believe him. I am only four years old, but I have learned a little bit.

The Happy Room is how things will be. Forever.

chapter four

"So, Debs says I was angry even on the boat to Africa," Peter said. He and Julia carried their trays to a small table in the hospital cafeteria, where they'd gone to get a bite of supper. "The Happy Room. I barely remember it."

"I remember it. I remember it very clearly." Julia held up her hand as they sat down. "Just a second, Pete. I want to pray before we start talking."

She bowed her head and closed her eyes. Peter glanced around the room and wondered who was watching. Wasn't it just like Julia to be so pious? She had never gotten past the religious indoctrination their parents had stuffed down their throats. In fact, Julia had swallowed it all — hook, line, and sinker. But Peter had long ago seen through the simplistic belief system that controlled his family's lives.

Oh, he believed in God, of course. Anyone who had ever been to Africa and had seen its natural wonders would have to be nuts to doubt that the world had been created by an intelligent being. Peter even suspected God might still be interested in the earth and its inhabitants, and during rough periods he sometimes prayed for divine help. Once in a while during their marriage, he had gone to church with Maria. But there he confronted all over again the outlandish claims of Christianity. Miracles, rising from the dead, the Holy Spirit's indwelling . . . it was hard to imagine that his intelligent, insightful sister still bought into it.

"You bet I remember the Happy Room, Peter," Julia said, lifting her head and pinning her bright blue eyes on him. "I can't believe you've forgotten."

"If Debbie was four, that means I was five or six. And you were seven, Jules. Come on. I have a hard time remembering what I did last week."

"The Happy Room was where I got Baby."

"Well, I remember Baby, of course. Who could forget that doll you hauled around with you until you were . . . what, eighteen?"

78

"I wasn't that old. And I never took her with me to boarding school. Mom wouldn't let me, remember?"

"No, I don't. I can't recall all those little tiny details the way you do. And Debs — wow, it's like she's still living in the Happy Room. Could you believe she remembered something as trivial as me throwing a jack-in-the-box?"

"You were always throwing things, Peter."

"Glad I finally got my spear." He gazed down at his plate. The Maasai spear had been as integral a part of his life as Julia's doll had been of hers. He wondered what had happened to it. Somehow the spear had vanished along with all the other things he had lost . . . his childhood, his home on the African plains, even many of his memories. . . .

"I kind of liked that lady who took care of us in the Happy Room," Julia said. "I never knew Debbie thought of her as a wicked witch."

"Debs probably believed the woman had something to do with the disappearance of our parents."

"I guess so. Somehow I must have understood that Mom and Dad actually started their missionary service on the ship. I don't think the mission board required it. It was just something they wanted to do. I remember they held worship services and taught the Bible to the other passengers — stuff like that. And I wasn't as scared of the Happy Room as Debs, because I was old enough to know our parents would come back for us."

"Ha! They never came back." Didn't Julia realize that Debbie was right? The Happy Room was the place their parents learned to let go of their children so they could throw themselves into doing God's work for him.

His sister stared at him. "What do you mean by that?"

"I mean the Happy Room was the beginning of it all. Don't you see? That's when they started abandoning us so they could go off and do their missionary thing."

"Abandoning us? That's pretty strong, don't you think?"

"That's exactly what it was. First, they left us in the Happy Room. While we were living in Nairobi, they hired that African lady to watch us so they could go to language school. And finally, when we moved out to the bush, they sent us away to boarding school. Even when we were home on vacation, we spent most of our time under the care of Ko-ko-o. Face it, Julia. Our parents abandoned us."

"Then you'd accuse me of abandoning my own daughters right now." She leaned across the table. "Peter, people have to make choices that aren't always easy. I decided Debbie needs me more at this moment than Heather and Jessica do. So, I left them behind and came to Missouri with you. It's a matter of prioritizing. But not being with my girls doesn't mean I've abandoned them. I love them. I would do anything for them. It's just that right now, I need to be somewhere else."

"*Somewhere else* always came first with our parents, Julia. How can you not see that? They were always somewhere else! Language school, sermon preparation, mission meetings, pastors' conferences, English lessons —"

"You've abandoned your son, Pete!" she cut in. "Don't you see that what you've done is much worse? At least we always knew our parents loved each other and they loved us. There was a reason we went to boarding school. What reason are you going to give Angelo for abandoning him?"

"I haven't abandoned my son, Julia. I live in the same town, and I can see him every day if I want to. Besides, it wasn't me who walked out. If you want to accuse someone of abandonment, talk to Maria."

"Oh, Pete, I'm sorry." Julia reached across the table and laid her hand on his arm. "I don't know anything about your situation with Maria. I was just reacting to your accusations against Mom and Dad."

Peter let out a breath. "It's okay. Things have been a little rough on me lately."

"I'm sure they have."

"And now there's this whole problem with Debbie. I realize she's been sick for a while, but I can't help feeling like the issue goes way back to our childhood. A long time ago, the three of us lost track of who we were. You're the most stable, but look at you. All you've done is follow in our parents' footsteps with the whole Christian bit. Conform, conform, conform. It's not like you've made any decisions for yourself."

Julia looked hurt at his words. "I don't think that's true at all, Peter. I'm a Christian because, on my own, I chose to follow Christ."

"Are you sure?"

"Yes, I'm sure. I remember when I decided to give my life to Jesus. I was eight years old, and I haven't wavered since."

"You were a kid. What kind of rational

decisions can a kid make? Even a child as serious and responsible as you were. Are you sure this faith of yours belongs to an adult, Julia? Or are you just toddling along after Mom and Dad, being the perfectly obedient child you always were?" He looked into her eyes, trying to read her response.

Rather than answering, she picked up her soda and took a drink.

"Our parents are the ones who need to answer for what Debbie's going through," he went on. "I think we ought to confront them about why they aren't here. Why did they run off to do their church work, instead of being here when we need them? And while we're at it, we should ask them where they were our whole childhood. I don't have any problem with demanding some answers. I'll stand up to them. I'm not afraid."

Julia set her glass down and leaned back in her chair. "Peter, you've been standing up to our parents your whole life. You've argued with them, fought with them, raged against them, and accused them of everything under the sun. It hasn't ever done any good, so you might as well forget it."

"You're talking about when I was a kid. Of course it didn't do any good. I wasn't worth their attention back then. But I'm my own person now, and I refuse to stand by and watch my sister suffer."

"You really think Debbie's anorexia goes back to the past?"

"Yes, I do."

"But how can you blame our parents, Pete?"

"How can you *not* blame them? You always defend them, Julia. Take a look at reality. Take a look at what happened to us in our childhood. We did not have a normal upbringing."

Julia set her fork down on her empty plate. Peter could tell she really didn't feel like arguing with him.

"Peter, I'll admit our childhood was unusual. Lots of joys, some sorrows. Like most kids, probably. Maybe some of what Debbie's going through does stem from the past, but confronting our parents is not going to make a difference. It never has. It never will. They believed they were doing God's will in Africa, and that covered all the choices they made. You're not going to change their minds on that. And besides, you told me your goal in coming here was peace on the home front. Peter, please. I absolutely dread the idea of your confronting them. Especially with Debbie so sick. Try to let it go."

"I'll never let it go," he said. "They need to see what they did. They used 'God's will' to justify everything they did, no matter how it affected us. They never hesitated to lay that guilt trip on us if we made a peep of protest. Maybe if they can admit the pain they caused her in the past, Debbie will get better."

Julia sighed. "Debbie's going to get better when she decides to eat some food. Let's go back to the room and see if she managed to get down any of her dinner."

As they left the cafeteria, Peter put his arm around his sister. She was right about one thing. Their childhood was not without its high points. They had met interesting people, seen cultures of every imaginable variety, had some amazing adventures. Not for anything in the world would Peter have traded the joy of running through the bush with his Maasai friends. The day he had killed his lion had been the greatest moment of his life.

But something had been wrong during their childhood, too. Something sharp and painful, like a thorn from an African acacia tree — a barb that had buried itself inside his chest and would never come out.

The thorn was abandonment by his parents, he realized. And then one loss after another had driven that thorn deep into the flesh of each of the Mossman children. He knew it was true, even if Julia wouldn't admit it. He wondered if any of them knew what it meant to be loved. Truly loved.

"Hey, Debbie," Julia said gently, as she and Peter walked back into her room. "How was your supper?"

"Fine," Debbie whispered.

A nurse looked up from his work on Debbie's IV and gave them a smile. He was a short man, and though he seemed quite young, he had a thatch of thinning gray hair and an odd little mustache. His brown eyes were filled with compassion, as if he truly cared about his patient.

"Is this your family, Miss Deborah?" he asked.

Debbie's focus wandered across from the bedside tray where her full plate and glass sat apparently undisturbed. "Oh yes, excuse me. You guys, this is Ralph." She lifted a thin-boned hand. "Ralph, meet my brother, Peter Mossman, and my sister, Julia Chappell. They came all the way from New Mexico."

"Olé!" Ralph exclaimed, snapping his fingers like a mariachi dancer.

Julia laughed. "That's *New* Mexico, not

the old country. I live in Santa Fe, and Peter lives down in the southeast corner."

"Cha-cha-cha!" Ralph did a little twirl under the IV line. "I went to Cancun on my honeymoon, but I haven't been back. My wife passed away a few years ago, and I just never had the desire."

Peter tried to hide a smile at the man's cluelessness. At least it was clear he truly cared about his patient's well-being, and that thought warmed Peter's heart.

"But I'll tell you what," Ralph was saying, "I like a taco as much as the next guy. I'm a pretty good cook, too, and I can whip up a mean batch of enchiladas. Where are you folks staying? You over at the motel on the highway?"

"I've offered them my home while I'm in the hospital," Debbie said. "I have two bedrooms."

"Well, that is really nice. Now all we need to do is get you back on your feet, Miss Deborah, so you can enjoy your company." He paused and looked down at her. "You know, you remind me a little of someone I once knew. Blonde hair, blue eyes, and a pretty smile. I didn't have her long enough."

"I'm sorry," Debbie said.

"You get well, okay?"

"I'll try." As he turned to go, she weakly grasped his arm. "Ralph, what's on my charts? I mean, do I have something they're not telling me about? Do I have cancer?"

"You can read your charts yourself if you want to, Miss Deborah. The doctor has run just about every kind of test available. The only thing giving you any trouble is your malnutrition."

"Malnutrition," Julia echoed, sinking into a chair.

Images of tiny children with frizzy orange hair, skinny legs, and swollen bellies flooded into Peter's mind. "Growing up in Kenya, we used to see little kids suffering from malnutrition all the time. So, malnutrition — that's what anorexia is."

"Bottom line, that's it." Ralph picked up the chart. "Miss Deborah, you have starved your body of just about every kind of nutrient it needs to keep functioning. Bad as it may sound to you, fat is a great thing. It keeps your brain working. And calcium holds your bones together. Protein makes your hair grow. All those essential amino acids —"

"I do eat," Debbie said in a soft voice. "But I need to stay fit. I'm in the clothing business, and I have to take care of my appearance."

Ralph put his hand on her shoulder. "You do some thinking about those kids you saw in Africa — the ones your brother talked about. Remember how they looked?"

"But they were starving because of the famine. This is nothing like that. How can you compare my situation to theirs?"

"Doesn't matter how it came to be, Miss Deborah. The fact is, you're malnourished just like those children. If you could see that —"

The bedside phone rang, cutting off his words. Julia picked up the receiver. Peter felt his heart constrict as he realized from her tone of voice that their parents were on the line. He glanced at Debbie to check her reaction. Her eyes were wide, anxious. She reached up and laid her hand on Ralph's.

Peter took a step toward the phone. "Let me talk to them," he demanded. He was going to stand up for Deborah, no matter what Julia thought he should do.

"She's very weak," Julia was saying as she waved him back. "The nurse here says she's malnourished, like those children we used to see out in the bush. The ones with the red hair."

"Give me the phone, Jules." Peter

couldn't believe she would have this polite little conversation — not after he'd shown her so clearly that their parents were at fault in this.

"So, how's Vacation Bible School going?"

Peter shook his head. Debbie's fingers had closed around Ralph's hand. She was scared, just as he had suspected. Instead of giving her comfort, their parents' very presence on the telephone stressed her out.

"Wow, that's a lot of kiddos," Julia was saying. "They must have had a very successful outreach program."

If he could just get the phone away from his sister, Peter would tell his parents exactly what they needed to hear. But even as he planned a vehement speech putting them in their place, he could hear Julia's voice reminding him that his way of handling things had never done any good. Anger and accusation never made any difference to their parents. She was right. But what would make them see that they needed to be here with their daughter? What would motivate them?

"Listen, Mom and Dad, Peter wants to talk to you," Julia said finally. "Yeah, he's right here. Just a second."

She handed over the receiver, her blue

eyes flashing. "Be nice!" she mouthed.

Peter took a deep breath. "Hey, Mom and Dad," he said, forcing his voice to a friendly tone. "How are things in Joplin?"

"Things are fine here, Peter." His father sounded surprised to hear him. "And how are you?"

"Well, I'm very concerned about Debbie."

"We are, too." His mother's voice came on an extension. "She's frail, isn't she?"

"She is. But she seems a lot more cheerful now than she did when we came in this morning. I guess having family around her is helping a lot."

He glanced at Julia, who was eyeing him warily. He gave her a wink.

"You know Debbie's always been such a loving person," he went on, "and I think it means so much to her that we're here."

"Well, I'm sure it does," his mother said.

"It makes a difference to have a warm, supportive family upholding you when you're going through a time of struggle."

"That's exactly right, Peter," his father said. "Your mom and I are very grateful that you could come all the way from New Mexico to be with your sister."

"Well, I just think a family ought to stick together as much as they possibly can.

When one of them is suffering, they all ought to be right there to support her." He looked across at Julia. She was glancing back and forth between him and Debbie. Debbie had an odd smile on her face, but she hadn't let go of Ralph's hand.

"The three of us have been through a lot," he continued. "We made a vow a long time ago to be there for each other."

"And your mother and I would be right there with you if this VBS commitment hadn't been on our calendar for months," his father said. "In fact, I've been wondering if we ought to leave a couple of days early. I'm sure the director would understand the situation with Deborah."

"Oh, I don't know about that, Don." Olive Mossman's voice held a note of warning. "You know they have us scheduled twice a day right up to the end. They set it up that way so we could speak to every group of children."

"I understand," Peter said. "The Lord has a plan for each of us, and we all have to do God's will. For Julia and me, that's being right here with Debbie, making sure she has the love and support she needs to get through this ordeal. But you go ahead and do what you feel led to do. I'm sure the Lord knows where your heart is."

"Peter!" Julia mouthed in a loud whisper. "Give me that phone!"

He grinned at her. Then he turned back to the receiver. "We sure wouldn't want you to shortchange any of those youngsters who need to hear about the missionary work in Africa."

"Well, we only have those two sessions a day," his father said.

"But who would take our time slot if we left, Don?" Mom let out a deep breath. "Peter, has Deborah taken a turn for the worse? Do you think she needs us there?"

"I wouldn't know what to tell you, Mom and Dad. You're just going to have to follow the Lord's leading in this. If you need to stay there and fulfill your speaking engagement, that's fine. Or if you feel like you ought to come and spend time with your children, then that's what you should do. The main thing is just to seek God's will."

"Well, thank you, Peter." His dad sounded strange. "We'll certainly pray about this. Won't we, Olive?"

"Yes, we will. Peter, it's very good to hear your voice. We love you, honey."

"I love you, too. Bye, now."

As he hung up the phone, he saw Debbie draw her two thin hands together and begin to clap. "Yay, Peter!" She laughed. "You didn't get mad."

"He completely messed up their minds, is what he did," Julia said. Then she gave a reluctant giggle. "Peter, what was all that 'God's will' stuff about, anyway? That didn't sound like you at all."

"Just giving our loving parents a little dose of their own medicine." He shrugged. "You told me the anger route wouldn't work, so I decided to try the old reliable — guilt."

"Oh, Peter!" Julia shook her head. "You are a naughty boy."

"He's smart," Debbie countered. "You know, I'm pretty good at the guilt thing myself. Watch this. Ralph, you aren't thinking of leaving us now, are you? We're enjoying your company so much."

Ralph chuckled. "I do hate to go. You people could keep a fellow entertained for hours."

"But what will we do without you? You've been such a great help, adjusting the IV and checking my feeding tube. Surely you don't have anything to do that's more important than we are, do you?"

"You're good," Ralph said. "If I weren't afraid of getting fired, I'd sit here with you all night. Of course, making me feel guilty about leaving will only get you so far. And I might even resent you while I'm sitting here."

"It always worked on us," Peter said. "Our parents used it with great results. And if you throw 'God's will' on top of it, you can get people to do anything you want."

Ralph grasped the ends of the stethoscope draped around his neck. "I imagine you're right. But in the long run, there's something a lot more effective than guilt. And that's love." He gave the three of them a nod as he left the room.

Peter looked from one sister to the other. "Love?" he said. "What's that?"

"Oh, Peter, you know our parents loved us." Julia propped her feet on the end of Debbie's bed. "They loved us very much. But you might be right about guilt being their primary motivator."

"No kidding," Debbie said. "I could almost hear Mom's voice when Pete was talking. You sounded just like her, Pete! It was great."

"It was pretty slick," Julia admitted. "They're probably twisted up in knots right now, trying to decide what to do. Of course, Pete's always been able to talk his way in and out of things."

"Yeah," Debbie said. "Remember how he could bargain with the vendors on the beach until they were practically giving him shells for free? And what about the way he used to talk the train conductor into moving us to First Class when we were on our way to boarding school every term?"

"That was great," Julia agreed. "But you have to admit he was at his best, his very best, the time he saved us from the crazy man."

Peter rolled his eyes. Was Julia going to recount that silly story again? Although he had to admit, he had been pretty proud of his quick thinking that day in Nairobi.

"It almost cost me Baby," Julia was remembering, "but as usual, Peter managed to work everything out . . ."

julia • africa • 1975

I love the long drive from our house in Maasailand to the big city of Nairobi. Every two weeks, Mommy and Daddy have to make the trip to buy groceries. When Peter, Debbie, and I are home from boarding school for the holidays, we get to go with them. We pile into the Land Rover, all five of us together, and we set off down the dry riverbed that is our main road to the highway.

As we drive along, a fine red dust begins to sift up through every seam in the gray metal. After a while, the dust billows into the car like smoke, and in the beams of sunlight, it hangs suspended, sparkling and magical. By the time we get to Nairobi, our white socks will be a pale pink and our faces will be powdered with dust. Our mouths will taste like dirt, and when we blow our noses, it's disgusting. But we never care about that. We're having way too much fun.

Whenever it's my turn to sit by the window, that is my favorite time of all. Even better than Christmas. I hold Baby tightly in my arms, and I show her all the things we're passing as we drive along. I know we live in the most beautiful place in the whole world, because I have been to Europe and America, and this is much better.

When we finally get to Nairobi, the landscape changes all at once. Presto! Suddenly, the vast grasslands vanish and skyscrapers loom on the horizon. In the city, millions and jillions of people scurry around, walking down sidewalks or maneuvering their bicycles through traffic. The cars are all ancient and rusty, and the smell of diesel fumes hangs thick in the air. We can feel the excitement as Daddy pulls the Land Rover into a parking space near the old City Market.

On most days, Daddy has to go to the bank while Mommy does the shopping. We love to go into the market with her, to smell the ripe pineapples and gaze at pyramids of fruit and vegetables. But this time, she tells us to wait in the car. Even though I am nearly twelve, and Peter and Debbie aren't much younger, Mommy says it's too much trouble to manage all three of us. Peter always wants to go exploring. And several times Debbie has gotten lost in the market. In fact, we have discovered that Debbie gets lost almost everywhere we go. We're very disappointed to be left behind in the Land Rover, because often the African ladies will give us a banana or a tangerine to eat.

Our parents set out, each in a different direction, and Peter climbs into Mommy's seat in the front. He tells us he's thinking about getting out of the car and looking at the wood carvings for sale along the sidewalk. Debbie and I plead with him not to go. Sometimes Peter does naughty things, and then usually we all get into trouble.

The three of us are sitting in the car making up verses to a silly song we invented a long time ago, when we notice a disturbance down the street. A crowd of people is moving toward us, and at the front strides an African man wearing a long blue wool coat, the kind soldiers wear in the Kenya army. We know right away that this man is a Mau Mau.

Even though the war against the British colonists was over a long time ago, a few Mau Maus still hide out in the forests. Some of them think the war is still going on. They have sworn terrible vows and drunk poisonous potions to seal their commitment that they will kill all white people. Once in a while, they come down out of the forests to walk around in town, and even the other Africans stare at them in fear. But this Mau Mau is clearly crazier than most. He's jabbering about something, and even though we all know Swahili better than our parents do, we can't understand what he's saying.

"He's naked!" Debbie shouts. "Under his coat, he's naked, and he's all splattered with white paint!"

"Don't look!" I warn her, while at the same time trying to see if she's right. "He *is* naked! Oh, close your eyes, Debs."

I squeeze my eyes shut, and I grab Debbie's hand to make sure she feels safe. But as I'm peeking out the corner of my eye, I realize the crazy man has spotted us — three white people! He takes off toward the Land Rover on a dead run, screaming at the top of his lungs and waving a huge panga. I am terrified of pangas. The long machetes are used to cut grass and brush. But I have read in the newspaper that they're also used for murder, hacking people to death, blood flying everywhere!

Peter yells at us to duck just as the crazy man leaps onto the hood of the Land Rover. Debbie bursts into tears, and I throw my arms over her head. The Mau Mau squats down, puts his panga between his teeth, and starts slapping the windshield of our car with his palms like a drum, spattering white paint over the glass. Peter scrambles into the backseat with Debbie and me. His face is pale, and he looks like he might vomit. All the same, he scrunches us behind him as best he can, sitting on us and putting his arms around us for protection.

I can hear myself screaming, and Peter is shouting for help. Hundreds and thousands of Africans are all around the Land

Rover, but they're all too afraid of the crazy man and his panga. Just as we think he's going to break our windshield, he discovers that the driver's seat window is open. How could we have been so stupid not to lock the car and roll up the windows? Oh, we're sure all three of us are going to die a bloody death as the Mau Mau grabs the radio antenna and swings himself right through the front window and into the car.

"Stop!" Peter shouts in Swahili. "Don't hurt us!"

The man leans over the front seat, leering at us as we cower in the back. His two lower front teeth are missing, and his hair hangs down in long dreadlocks all around his white-painted face.

"We are only children," Peter says. "And we are *wananchi* — natives of this country, just like you."

"But you are white!"

"So are you. Look at yourself!"

The man stares down at the white paint, as though he never noticed it before.

"We are Africans." Peter is jabbering. His eyes keep darting to the sides, looking for our parents. "See how we speak Swahili? See how we wear our beaded bracelets?"

At this, Peter pulls Debbie's chubby little

arm out from behind him. I'm terrified that the Mau Mau will cut off my sister's hand!

Instead, the man grabs her arm and examines it. His face grows very solemn. "Two eggs daily," he announces suddenly in English, his prescription for Debbie's health.

"I will tell my mother," says Peter in Swahili. "Two eggs daily for this *mtoto* — this child."

The Mau Mau smiles, and we can see that most of his teeth are rotten. His eyes are red, too. That tells us he's probably been drinking African honey beer. He smells worse than anything I've ever smelled before — and I have smelled a lot of bad things in my life in Africa.

"Who is this?" the Mau Mau asks in Swahili. He takes my arm and pulls me out from under Peter. "Oh, she is very pretty."

"This is my sister," Peter says. "You must leave her alone."

The man looks me up and down. Finally, he speaks in English again, pointing at me and then at himself. "You, for the wife, for me!"

He grins, as if this marriage proposal is a great idea. By now, I can see three policemen have arrived, pushing back the crowd and trying to take control. But they aren't willing to come up close to the Land Rover, in case the Mau Mau decides to use his panga.

"This girl has no dowry," Peter informs the man. "You will not want her for your wife. She is worthless."

"Your father has no cows?"

"None. My father is a poor man."

"But he has a car."

"This is not his car. This car belongs to God. Our father has nothing, not even a small spotted goat."

The Mau Mau looks disappointed. Then he notices Baby. I'm still clutching her tightly in my arms. He stares at her for a moment in confusion. Finally, he reaches out and touches her face. His big, white-painted fingers cover her soft blonde hair and comb through it.

"Your sister has a child already?"

"This is not a child," Peter says. "This is a . . ."

He looks at us, and we know he doesn't remember the Swahili word for *doll*. Is there such a word? None of us can remember! I think I'm going to cry when the Mau Mau takes Baby out of my arms. He cradles her as though she is a newborn and stares down at her face. She has eyes that shut when you lay her down, and he moves her up and down, watching her eyes open and close. He pats her hair some more.

"I will take this baby," he says in Swahili. "She will be my child, and I will take good care of her."

"Oh!" I gasp out loud.

The Mau Mau scowls at me through his bloodshot eyes. He grips his panga and shakes it a little to frighten me.

"That baby," Peter says, "you will not want."

"Why not? It is a good baby!"

Peter is trembling a little bit. I put my hand around his. "You will not want the baby because . . ." He is trying to think of something. "Because it has been cursed. See how stiff it is? Its skin is like a stone. It is like dead, that baby."

The Mau Mau studies the doll. I can tell he really loves Baby, and this makes me feel a little bit soft toward him. He is nothing but a poor, crazy man who wants a wife and children to love. I am trying to get up the courage to give him Baby, when Peter starts to untie his shoelaces.

"I have something better for you than that cursed child," Peter says. "I am going to give you these shoes, so that when you run through the forest, you will not have to worry about stepping on a thorn."

"Ah," the Mau Mau says, eyes wide.

He studies Peter's feet as the shoes come off one at a time. They are almost brand-new — Bata safari boots, "the boots that say you know Africa," as the advertisement goes. They are dark brown suede, and Peter is proud of them. But now he is giving his boots to the Mau Mau.

"I want those, too," the man says, pointing at my dusty white kneesocks.

Without even thinking about what Mommy will say when she gets back and finds us without our shoes and socks, I peel right out of mine. The next thing I know, the crazy man is sticking his bare feet through the gap between the two front seats. I carefully pull my socks over his big, hard, scaly toes and up his ankles. He seems very happy about this. He wiggles his toes up and down. Then I take Peter's shoes and slip them on him. To our relief, they fit just right.

I tie up the laces nice and tight. Then I untie them, and I show the Mau Mau how to tie a bow. It takes him a little while to learn, but he finally gets it down.

"If you come to the forest of Mount Kenya, near the waterfall of the two buffalo," he says to me, "I will bring a man who can take the curse from your child. He is a good witch doctor."

He hands Baby back to me, gives a final rotten-tooth smile, and opens the Land Rover's front door. As he steps out onto the pavement, he gives a few little hops, trying out his new shoes. Then he goes marching away, his navy wool coat swinging wide open as if it were the most normal thing in the world to be naked as a jaybird and painted all white.

As the crowd parts and the three policemen start after him, Peter and Debbie and I look at each other and let out a long breath. We thought we were going to die, but we didn't! Finally, Mommy and Daddy come back from their errands, and we tell them what happened. They are very concerned and ask us lots of questions, but we can't seem to make them realize how terrible it was.

Daddy gives Peter some old flip-flops from the back of the car. After that, we all go eat dinner and then to a movie. The Nairobi Cinema has shown almost every film that has anything to do with Africa. We have seen *The Jungle Book*, *Tarzan the Ape Man*, *Hatari!*, *The African Queen*, and lots of others. On this night, we only make it through the first few minutes of *Shaft in*

Africa before Mommy signals us all to get up out of our seats. We follow her and Daddy as they go stomping out of the theater in disgust.

As Peter and Debbie and I snuggle into the backseat for the long ride home to Maasailand, we all put our arms around each other. It has been a long day, and nobody but us really knows what we went through. Peter whispers that he is angry with Mommy and Daddy for leaving us alone in the Land Rover. They shouldn't have done that. I nod, but I don't really care. I don't care that we didn't get to see the whole movie, or that Baby nearly got kidnapped, or even that I almost had to marry a Mau Mau. All I know is that Peter was smart and brave and wonderful. He took care of us, and I'm really, really glad he's my brother.

---

chapter five

"How'd you sleep?" Peter asked as he and Julia walked across the hospital parking lot the next morning.

She sighed. She should have known her brother would notice the dark circles under her eyes. "Not very well. I'm so worried about Debbie. I keep thinking about those children we used to see during the famine years in Kenya. Last night I thought of the name we called their malnutrition — *kwashiorkor.* Peter, most of those children died."

"I know. The ones that didn't had brain damage."

"Oh, great." She laid her hand on her stomach. "I hope we can talk to Debbie's doctor this morning. I want some information. Did you think she seemed any better by the end of the day?"

"Not really."

"She was pretty perky around that nurse, though," Julia reminded him. "I think she kind of likes the guy."

"Ralph?" Peter looked surprised. "But he didn't know New Mexico was in the United States. Even when you explained it to him, he kept saying *olé* and *cha-cha-cha* and talking about his honeymoon trip to Cancun. He's weird."

"He's not weird, Peter. He's like a lot of people around here. Sure, he hasn't traveled the world like we have, but he's a good person. He was gentle with Debbie. He said she reminded him of his wife. Did you see how she held his hand?"

They stepped into the lobby and were greeted by the now-familiar smell of antiseptic. "I thought Debbie had a boyfriend," Peter said. "That Dave fellow."

"Yeah, they've been dating off and on for years."

"Some boyfriend. He never showed up the whole day. Never even called to check on her. What is it with Debbie and men? I can't figure out why she's never gotten married. She's pretty. Well, she was before the *kwashiorkor*."

"Oh, Peter, don't even call it that. Last night, I remembered how those starving children had frizzy reddish hair. Have you looked at Debbie's hair? It's the same!"

Her brother put his arm around her. "Relax, Jules," he said. "Debbie's not a starving kid in Africa. She's here in the States with all the latest medical technology. Is something else bothering you?" He stopped and looked at her.

She let out a deep breath. Peter would probably laugh if he knew what was really bothering her. "To tell you the truth, I was thinking about Baby."

"Your doll?"

She nodded. "She meant so much to me when I was a little girl. She still does. I keep her on a shelf in my bedroom."

"At least you still have her. I have no idea what happened to my spear." He fell silent for a moment. Did Peter's spear have the same significance for him that Baby had for her? Memories of a long-ago, faraway home they could never return to? As they reached the door to Debbie's room, he held Julia back. "So, what's the deal with Baby? Why were you awake last night thinking about your doll?"

"I don't know." She hung her head. "I just kept wondering why I never took her to boarding school. Why didn't Mom and Dad let me take her? But even more important, why didn't I fight to keep her with me? I never argued with them about it, even though it nearly killed me to leave her behind each time we left home. Last night I kept thinking over what you said about me — *conform, conform, conform.* The perfect little girl who's always obedient. Is that who I am, Peter? Is that who I've always been?"

"Well, it's . . . just that you were the oldest, Jules. You wanted to keep peace, but I kept stirring things up."

"I *became* that conformist, Peter. I've always done the right thing, even as an adult. I do what everyone else wants, and I don't even let myself think about what I want. Why am I like that?"

"Because you're a Christian?"

"Do Christians have to be doormats? I'm a doormat, Pete!"

"You're not a doormat. You're a kind, loving, gentle person. A pregnant person. I wish you'd calm down."

"I'm calm. I'm just distressed."

"Well, look at it this way. You turned out the best of the three of us, so maybe doormat-hood has advantages."

"Doormat-hood?"

"It's a thought." He shrugged and chucked her chin with his finger. "Come on; let's go see if we can find the missing

111

doctor and figure out what's up with little sister."

When they walked into Debbie's room, they immediately knew things had taken a turn for the worse. Two unfamiliar nurses hovered over Debbie, adjusting tubes and working to arrange their patient in the bed. She looked terrible, her eyes bright and feverish, her hands shaking. She had been crying, and when she saw Peter and Julia, she reached out to them with scrawny, clawlike fingers.

"They're not going to let me go home!" she moaned. "I just want to go home. I'm lost here. I'm lost."

"Debbie?" Julia hurried to her sister's bedside. "I'm here now. Peter's with me. What's the matter?"

"Her temperature has gone up," one of the nurses explained. "She's a little bit delirious. The doctor's on his way."

"I'm not delirious." Debbie took Julia's hand and held it to her cheek. "I just want to go home. Please, take me home."

"The doctor's coming to see you," Julia said, glancing at her brother. "She's really hot, Peter."

"What's the matter with my sister?" he demanded of the nurses. "Why does she have a fever?"

They studied him. "We're not sure," one of them said. "That's why we called for the doctor."

"Is it her doctor, or just some generic guy?"

"Yes, it's her doctor — Dr. Bryant. He'll be here in a few minutes. Don't worry, we're watching her."

"Watching her? What about getting that temperature down?"

"Peter, please," Julia said. "Take it easy."

"Press this button if you need us," one of the nurses said. "We're right down the hall at the nurses' station."

As they walked out of the room, Julia pulled a chair to her sister's bedside and sat down, still holding tightly to Debbie's hand. Peter walked over to the window and drew one curtain aside. Debbie moaned as a beam of sunlight crossed the bed.

"Hey, Debs," Julia murmured. "Everything's going to be all right. You just need to get some rest."

"I want to go home." Her blue eyes focused on Julia. "I feel lost."

"You're not lost. You used to get lost when you were a little girl, but you're not lost now. You're with us. Peter and I are right here beside you in the hospital in Bolivar."

She shook her head. "It's just like that time I got lost in the African market, and I didn't know where to go or what to do. I'm so scared, Julia. I think I have cancer."

"You don't have cancer, Debbie. You have a fever, that's all. The doctor's going to come and look at you. He'll give you aspirin or something, and then you'll feel a lot better."

"I haven't run on my treadmill in days. I'm way behind in my schedule. I haven't marked my calendar."

"Your treadmill is in your house, and it'll be there when you get home from the hospital. Right now, you need to rest. If you don't rest —"

The telephone's ring cut off her words. She glanced at Peter.

"That'll be Mom and Dad," he said. "Let me take it."

But when he lifted the phone and began to speak, Julia could tell her brother had been wrong. He held out the receiver to her. "It's your husband."

"Mike?" she spoke into the phone. "Hi, honey. What's going on?"

"Hey, sweetheart. Well, I thought I'd better give you a call. Heather's sick."

"Oh no."

"You know, I told you she's had a runny

114

nose for a couple of days, and she woke up this morning with her ear hurting."

"I bet she's got another ear infection. Oh, dear." Julia rubbed her hand across her stomach. "You'd better call Dr. Bennett."

"I did, but I can't get her in until late this afternoon." He paused. "There's something else."

"What?" She felt her heart tighten. "What's the matter, Mike?"

"Well, Danny told Jessica that since they're going to different colleges, he thought they ought to date around. She's a wreck. Basically, she just fell apart last night. I thought about calling you, but it was really late when I found her crying in the bedroom."

"You found her crying? You couldn't tell she was upset by the way she was acting when she came in after being with Danny? You didn't ask her what was wrong?"

"I'm not her mother, Julia." He sounded hurt. "I don't have your intuition for these things. I wish you would just come on home."

"Is Jessica there? Let me talk to her."

"She went to work this morning. I told her to take the day off, but she wouldn't listen to me."

"Oh, this is awful." Julia tried to take a deep breath. She looked up at Peter. He wore a look of concern on his face. "Just a second, Mike."

She cradled the phone as she spoke to her brother. "Mike is asking me to come home. Heather's got a bad cold — maybe an ear infection — and Jessica's boyfriend told her he wants to date around."

Surprise crossed Peter's face. "That's it? The way you were going on, I thought someone had been in a wreck or something."

She stared at him. Julia's motherly instincts told her to rush back to Santa Fe and protect her children. These incidents might sound like nothing to Peter, but they were serious to her daughters. Not life threatening, of course. Peter's mockery drifted back into her thoughts — *conform, conform, conform.*

Should she race back home? She couldn't shield her children forever. Jessica was going to have to learn to deal with disappointments soon enough. In college, there would be new boyfriends to manage and a whole variety of unpredictable heartbreaks to come.

But what about Heather? Well, it wasn't as though Heather's illness was some kind of mystery. She had suffered from ear infections most of her early childhood, and even as a teenager, she had the occasional bout. She just needed to go to the doctor and start taking an antibiotic. That was it.

Julia thought of her big, strong husband — so intelligent, so capable of handling one crisis after another among members of the church youth group. He could handle this one, too.

She lifted the receiver to her ear. "Listen, Mike. It's probably a good thing Jessica went to work this morning. It'll keep her mind off things. Tonight she's got choir practice, and tomorrow night is the youth group's party at the roller rink. I've seen this coming on for a while, and I think she has, too. She'll just have to adjust."

As she spoke the words, Julia could hardly believe they were coming out of her mouth. She had always been there for her children. Always. Maybe Peter had been right about more than one thing. Maybe that urge to hover over her daughters came from the losses she had suffered in her own life. The thought of abandoning her daughters almost sent her into a panic. But they were nearly grown now. It was past time to start letting go.

"I don't know," Mike was saying. "I'm really not sure what to say to Jessica. She'd do a lot better if you were here."

"You can talk to her, Mike. You're her dad. Give her some of that great advice you're always sharing with the kids in the youth group. She'd love that. I think it would mean a lot to her."

"Really?"

"Sure. As I recall, you said you got dumped a couple of times in high school. How did you make it through? Tell Jessica about your own experiences. You're a great dad, and you've always been so wonderful with teenagers."

He was silent, and Julia could feel a sense of euphoria sweeping through her. She was letting go! She was empowering herself *and* her husband. "Dr. Bennett will have you and Heather in and out of his office in no time," she went on. "He knows exactly which antibiotic works best on her ear infections. She'll be feeling better by this evening. Just give her a little Tylenol right now. Put that six-hour *Pride and Prejudice* series in the VCR, and fix her a Coke and a bowl of popcorn. She'll be fine."

"Well . . . ," Mike said. Julia could feel his hesitation. "How's your sister?"

"She's struggling right now. We're

waiting for the doctor." It hurt her that he hadn't asked about Debbie until now. But that was the way it had been for so long — his focus was always on his work. She had grown used to taking care of their family and all the little details of their lives. Again Peter's words rang in her head: *"Conform, conform, conform."* Maybe it was time to make some changes. She swallowed her reservations and stepped out into un-known territory. "Mike, I'm going to stay here with Debbie until the end of this week, at least."

"The end of this week?"

"Yes." She glanced up at Peter. He was eyeing her appraisingly. "Maybe a little longer, if I need to. As long as nothing is seriously wrong at home, my family needs me here."

"Are you sure?"

"I'm positive."

"Well, okay."

"Love you, honey."

"Love you, too, sweetheart."

Mike sounded a little down as Julia hung up the phone, but she knew she had done the right thing. It hadn't been selfish or thoughtless — or even unchristian — to make a choice that was appropriate for the situation. She gave Peter a smile.

"I'm staying here," she said.

He laughed. "You hear that, Debbie? Your big sister just stood up on her own two feet for the first time."

"Not the *first* time," Julia protested.

"No," Debbie agreed. "Julia was the one who found me almost every time I got lost. She would go right out into the market or the beach or wherever and look for me."

"That's true," Peter said. "And when we were really little, she used to buy roasted corn for us from those ragged men on the street, remember? I was terrified of those guys, but she wasn't a bit afraid. And how about the time we got on the train to head home from boarding school, and the conductor tried to make us get off in Nairobi? Jules told him we were planning to stay on until Konza Station, but he said there was nobody out in the bush. He grabbed me to make me get off, but she told him our parents were missionaries, and she promised they'd meet us. So, he let us stay on the train."

"Then they *weren't* there," Debbie reminded him.

"Yeah, the train was early for the first time in its whole history. So, Jules talked the man into letting us get out and wait all by ourselves at the station in the middle of nowhere. And then Mom and Dad finally showed up before we could get eaten by a lion." Peter smiled at his older sister. "But the time I remember the best, Jules — the time you really stood up for yourself and us — was the time you tried to fix up the school."

"Oh no," she said. "Don't remind me. That was one of my worst decisions ever!"

"No it wasn't." Peter leaned back in his chair. "You were great, Jules. You were a champion, the time you tried to change the school. It all started with that worthless social studies class . . ."

peter • africa • 1977

Even though I'm a grade level lower than Julia, we're in the same social studies class. It's taught by the cockiest little son of a gun at the school, Mr. Vincent DaGama. I hate him. I don't even know why they let somebody like that be a teacher.

Besides teaching a class or two, he's head coach of the varsity soccer, rugby, and basketball teams, and he directs the school choir. If you go to Kenya Christian Academy and you don't play sports or sing in the choir, you're nobody. And Mr. DaGama makes sure you know it. I didn't make the soccer team, and I can't sing a note on key. I'm scum.

I've been dreading this class, but as it turns out, it's a joke. Right now we're studying democracy — yeah, right. What do we care about democracy? All us missionary kids stuck at KCA have been brought up in a country with a single-party system, ongoing tribal warfare, and a government that runs by corruption. Kenya has problems, sure. We've got diseases like leprosy and tuberculosis. We've got lousy roads, intermittent electrical service, and water that runs brown. We've got malarial mosquitoes and tsetse flies. We've even got rampaging elephants and the occasional crocodile attack. We don't get worked up about these things, because they're part of our normal everyday existence. But what does democracy have to do with us?

Oh yeah.

We all have to go back to America after we graduate. We have to try to live there like we belong. We have to pretend to know what we're doing.

So, Mr. DaGama has ordered a few copies of the international edition of *Time* magazine for his class. We're supposed to read it and discuss the problems of democracy we find in there. So, we sit in class and talk about the president of the United States and the Congress and the national debt. We talk about the U.S. defense system — stuff like billion-dollar radar-evading warplanes. I sit at the back of the room and try to calculate how many bags of cornmeal a billion dollars would have bought for the kids who starved during the most recent famine in Kenya. It turns out to be quite a lot, but of course, nobody's going to turn over that money to feed African kids. After all, a world power like the United States of America needs a strong defense system. And that — as we learn in social studies — is one of the problems of democracy.

Mostly, I sit in class and daydream. I think about sneaking out of the dorm at night and going hunting with my friends. What we do is poaching, really. Hunting isn't allowed in Kenya these days, but we don't care. I also spend a lot of class time thinking about girls. I have been dating Monica, but I really like Rachel. And last week, we got this new girl whose parents are missionaries from Sweden. Her name's Marita, or something. Whoo. Now, that is one good-looking blonde. If I can get my mind off girls, I usually think about lunch and supper, and I wonder whether we'll be having something edible. Usually, we don't. I'm always hungry. Most days, I fill up on bread.

While I daydream, Julia sits up at the front of the class and absorbs every word out of Mr. DaGama's mouth. She's the perfect student, always taking notes, always asking pertinent questions, always interested in any topic he's covering. She actually reads the *Time* magazine each week. But on the first day of class this term, Mr. DaGama announced something very distressing to Julia. He said everyone who comes to class and participates at all gets a B. Bad news. Julia's on the eighth-grade honor roll, and she doesn't want a B. She wants an A.

So, Mr. DaGama has finally come up with a solution to the problem. Anyone who wants an A has to write a report. What kind of a report? Any kind, says Mr. DaGama, who is much more concerned that his rugby team beats the snot out of every school in Nairobi.

"What are you going to write your report about?" Julia asks me, as we trudge through the mud to the cafeteria. There's

124

only one sidewalk at KCA, and it runs from the cafeteria to the chapel. If you want to get to your dorm or classroom, you have to hoof it down a bare footpath. During third term, which starts in April, Kenya has a long rainy spell — that is, if we're not having a drought. When it rains, all the paths at the school turn to mud, which cakes an inch or two thick on the soles of our tennis shoes.

"What report?" I ask.

"The one for social studies — so you can get an A," Julia says.

I don't get to talk to either of my sisters at school very often. It's not like the administration thinks of us as a family or anything. When I do talk to Julia, I always wonder how we happened to be born from the same set of parents. Even though we both have thick, wavy blond hair and blue eyes, we're nothing alike. She obeys every rule that was ever invented. I break them.

"Hey, I'm happy with a B," I tell her. "If I can get that just for showing up, I'm not complaining."

"You know, Peter, you might put out a little effort once in a while."

"It takes a lot of effort for me just to make it to class."

"Oh, never mind." She shakes her head,

disappointed in me the way Mom and Dad always are. But Julia never lets it last long. She looks for things about me to love. "What kind of a sketch are you working on these days? Or are you painting something?"

"I'm doing a buffalo."

"Really? When can I see it?" Her smile radiates. "You know, I bet the yearbook staff would love to have a picture of a buffalo, since it's our school mascot. They might use it on a full page."

"They wouldn't print anything a seventh grader drew. Besides, it's not that good."

"I bet it is. Let me see it, Peter. Will you?"

Julia likes my art. She keeps piles and piles of my pictures in the black steel trunk in her dorm room. Sometimes she writes poetry to go with my sketches. She shows my work to her friends, and they all agree I've got talent. If I could, I'd draw and paint all day. I know the tests all say I'm smart, but I hate school. I'd rather be an artist.

"I'll show you the buffalo when I'm done," I tell Julia.

"You know," she says, "I've been thinking about the report I'm going to write for Mr. DaGama's class. Would you be interested in illustrating it for me?"

"Illustrating a school report? Come on,

Jules. Mr. DaGama doesn't care what you write about. He's probably not even going to read your report. Why go to all the effort?"

We have arrived at the cafeteria, and we pause for a moment, our feet slowly sinking into the mud. In spite of the overcast day and drizzling rain, Julia's eyes are bright. "I'm thinking of doing a study of the school," she whispers. "You know, I'll examine all the buildings, the classes, the cafeteria, and the dorms. I'll take a look at the staff and the structure of the student-teacher relationships. Things like that. And then I'll make a list of suggested ways to improve KCA!"

I stare at my sister, wondering if she's gone completely bananas. She's grinning at me like this is the coolest idea anyone ever had. I try to figure out what she's so excited about, but I can't see it. We've been going to this boarding school since first grade, and KCA has never changed. Not in all those years. We're wearing the same uniforms, eating the same food, slogging through the same mud, and sleeping in the same gray concrete-block dorms we always have. One little report — a report that won't even get read — is not going to change this dump.

"I was thinking it would be so great if you could illustrate each section," she says. "You know, you could draw the school buildings, only instead of being gray, they'd have paint on them. And you could show sidewalks and landscaped gardens —"

"Gardens? Jules, get a grip."

"And in the cafeteria, you could draw vases of flowers on the tables and a mural on the wall. You could design the mural, Peter! They might even let us really paint one!"

My sister drives me crazy. Where does she come up with these ideas? Why is she always wanting to make things better? Things are the way they are, I want to tell her. Don't bother to try to make changes. Nothing will happen. It's a lost cause.

But she lays her hand on my arm. "Please, Peter! We can make such a difference here. We really can!"

Before I have time to answer, she heads off to join the line of girls snaking out of the cafeteria. I saunter around to join the boys' line, and I'm thinking about this big project of Julia's. The weird thing is, I'm wondering if I illustrated her report, would Mr. DaGama give me an A?

For the next few weeks, I mostly forget about Julia's project. It's been raining like crazy at KCA, and everyone's getting sick. Somehow dirt gets into the water pipes during the rainy season, and every year most of us come down with amoebic dysentery or hepatitis A or something nasty like that. Brown water pours out of every faucet, and it's hardly worth the trouble of taking a bath or brushing your teeth. When you wash your hair, you figure you're putting in about as much dirt as you wash out, so it's kind of break even. Most of us seventh grade boys have worked up a pretty good stink by the end of third term.

I'm cruising around as usual, flirting with the girls, trying to round up enough slices of bread to fill my stomach, sneaking out at night to hunt. And then one day after social studies, here comes my sister with a thick stack of papers covered in her neat handwriting.

"You won't believe what I found out," she says in a conspiratorial whisper. She takes me to one side of the classroom while everyone files out for lunch. "I interviewed Cookie!"

I envision the enormous, lumbering, buzz-headed ex-Marine who runs our cafeteria. Cookie retired from the military and probably felt the call of God to come to Africa and torture a bunch of missionary kids. It's the only explanation for the treatment we get.

"Cookie sat for an interview?"

"Well, he didn't exactly sit. I followed him around the kitchen." She looks very proud of herself. "And get this — I found out there's no nutritional plan for our meals!"

"And the pope's Catholic. Surprise!"

"Seriously, Pete. Wouldn't you think Cookie would at least make some attempt at providing balanced menus? I mean, years ago when we were *titchies,* we learned about the food pyramid, and the four major food groups and all that."

She's talking about when we were in grade school. As bad a place to live as KCA is, we've learned a lot in our years from *titchie swot* to junior high. The point is, Julia *cares* about all the stuff she's learned. I don't.

"Cookie doesn't even try to balance our meals!" she goes on, as if she has discovered a new planet. "He says it's too hard to know what kinds of food he's going to be able to get from town, so he never plans ahead. That's why we'll sometimes have macaroni and potatoes and bread in the same meal. All starches!"

"Jules, this is not a revelation."

"I think it is. We're malnourished! I bet

some of us are bordering on kwashiorkor!"

I try to read the message behind this excitement. It's never been a mystery to me that the students at KCA live on a mostly carbohydrate diet. And when we have the occasional cauliflower or broccoli dish, it's usually infested with worms or tiny black bugs. The meat tastes like Cookie boiled a batch of old leather shoes for a couple of hours and then put them out on a platter. And the gelatin desserts are always studded with flies. One time I even found a long, curly piece of metal in my macaroni. At KCA, things are always exciting.

"So, get this," Julia whispers. "I gave Cookie a whole bunch of tips on how to make our meals more appetizing. Like I suggested he could put parsley on the boiled potatoes. Or try to get shipments of tangerines from the coast. And I told him there were plenty of local farmers who would love to sell him their fresh corn, beans, and potatoes. He actually seemed to be listening to me, Peter."

"That's great." I really do feel happy for her. She's acting like this is the best thing to happen in years, like she's really doing something important.

"And he gave approval for flower vases on the tables!" Julia throws her arms around me, she's so excited. "A whole group of us girls are going out this afternoon to pick flowers. We promised not to go off campus. We've collected all kinds of soda and medicine bottles to put them in. Isn't that wonderful?"

"It is, Jules. The cafeteria's going to look like a whole new place."

"I know. And I think Cookie will work harder on the nutritional plan, Pete. I really do."

"That would be tremendous."

"So, will you do the sketches?" Before I can make an escape, she has dumped her report in my arms and is showing me exactly what she wants me to draw. I try really hard to think up a reason not to do this for my sister. The best excuse I can come up with is that I mostly don't draw landscapes and buildings. I really prefer doing animals and people. But when I try this on her, she tells me I'm the best artist in the whole school, and if I do these sketches, the teachers will be so impressed they'll want to make all the changes.

I am thinking of telling Julia that no one will make any changes, because no one cares. Instead, I look into her hopeful blue eyes, and I tell her I'll be glad to do the sketches.

So, night after night, I read through Julia's report and make detailed drawings of all her ideas on how to improve the school. By the time I'm finished, the two of us have turned KCA into a model learning environment. We have curved cement walkways lined with — as Julia puts it — "bountiful gardens overflowing with a lush array of flowers." We have a cafeteria painted in "shades of soothing blue and green," colorful tablecloths and napkins, and vases filled with bouquets of flowers from the aforementioned gardens. Teachers monitor the cafeteria at every meal, mingling with the students and sharing the nutritious, well-balanced menu. Gone are the metal army trays. We have plates! Gone are the food fights. We all behave ourselves because the cafeteria is so beautiful.

Our student center is no longer a huge empty room lined with plain wooden benches. Now we have a place to play music and buy soft drinks. Bright cushions cover the benches. Game tables are scattered around the room. There's a television set, too. We actually have something to do in our spare time!

Following Julia's directions, I transform the school on paper. We have calculators in the classrooms, telephones in the dorms, and lush lawns with picnic tables. The teachers float around monitoring the huge array of after-school activities, and it appears they actually care about us. There's an art club, a drama club, a science club, and a group of mentors to help the kids at KCA through troubled times. All in all, Julia's report is brilliant.

I tell her this as I hand over my sketches. She's so excited about the drawings, I'm afraid she's going to have a heart attack. Plus, she's already putting some of her ideas into practice. Her team of friends is sewing cushions for the student center, and they've been keeping their little Coke-bottle vases filled with fresh flowers in the cafeteria. Her roommate's dad is a missionary at a seminary someplace in Kenya, and he found a few cans of extra paint in a storage locker there. He's going to bring them the next time he comes up to KCA to visit his daughter. The cafeteria mural is in the planning stages, and it's beginning to look like Julia has started a revolution.

One night we're all in the student center, sitting around staring at our feet or trying to get girls to notice us, when Julia and her team march in with the new cushions they've sewn. This is pretty exciting stuff. But even more amazing — my sister has rounded up a tape player and some cassettes. While the music starts to play, Julia and her friends arrange the new cushions on the benches. People start laughing and talking, and pretty soon a few of us get to our feet and sort of start boogying in place. Before long, somebody has organized a line dance down the middle of the room. We're kicking up our heels and swinging the girls around and feeling like this is the most fun we've ever had in our lives.

And then the lights go off. When they come back on, a whole squadron of angry staff members floods the room, taking down the names of all us violent offenders and ordering us back to our dorms. Dancing, as it turns out, is an illegal activity at KCA. We are in major trouble.

The next morning, about twenty of us get suspended, including me. Miraculously, Julia avoids punishment because at the time of the dance, she was back in the dorm rounding up the cinnamon toast she and her team had grilled over the fire for us. Since Mom and Dad live so far out in the bush, it takes a while to get messages to them. So I have to spend three days doing stupid stuff like washing walls and painting the boys' bathrooms. Finally Mom and Dad get here to pick me up. They're pretty upset about the whole incident. I spend two weeks at home, having a great time hanging out in the kraal with my Maasai friends.

When I get back to school, I notice that the cushions have been removed from the student center. So has the tape player. As I sit down to a meal of boiled potatoes, I realize there's not a sprig of parsley anywhere in sight. And the Coke-bottle flower vases are gone.

Julia and I stand outside in the mud one day after social studies. She tells me that Mr. DaGama is going to give her an A in the class. But she doesn't think he even read the report she turned in. She tells me none of the teachers wanted to sponsor an art or drama or science club. They told her that with all the sports and music activities, there's plenty for the students to do. And when the cans of paint arrived from the seminary, the girls opened them and found that they were all dried up.

Julia shrugs. "You were right, Pete. It was a dumb idea to try to change the school."

Even though all around us kids are heading for lunch, I give my sister a hug.

"Your ideas weren't dumb. Your ideas were great. And my drawings were good, too. Maybe you didn't change the school, Jules. But you tried. You really tried. And that's the most important thing."

She wipes a tear off her cheek. "I'm sorry I got you suspended, Pete."

"Hey, I had fun. It was the nicest thing you could have done for me." I chuck her on the chin, and then I hurry off toward the cafeteria, hoping nobody notices the tear that ran down my own cheek. Before long, I'm standing in line pounding the walls with everyone else, chanting for Cookie to open the iron gate so we can get in and get some slop. I'm hoping we don't have cauliflower.

chapter six

"Oh, Peter," Julia said, shaking her head. "I still can't believe I got you suspended. It's a wonder Mom and Dad didn't kill you."

"Jules, I'm telling you, those were two of the best weeks of my life! I wished I never had to go back to school." Remembering those two bonus weeks with his friends in the kraal had lifted Peter's spirits considerably.

"Still . . . that turned out so badly, it's no wonder I gave up being assertive. It was a complete disaster," Julia insisted.

"Well, I think the important thing was that you didn't conform. You worked for change and improvement, even when it threatened the peace. See, you do have a bit of the rebel in you."

"You know what I remember about KCA, Peter?" Debbie inserted. She seemed more cheerful and alert, though a nurse had come in during the past few minutes and confirmed that her temperature was still elevated. "I remember the infirmary at school. There was a boys' ward and a girls' ward, each with a row of beds along the wall. It was so bleak."

"No kidding." Peter recalled a time he'd been kicked in the stomach during a fight with one of his classmates. He had vomited up a bunch of black stuff, and they thought his liver might have been damaged. So they put him in the infirmary for almost two weeks. "I hated that place."

"But you did those great cartoons, Pete," Julia reminded him. "Remember all the posters of Snoopy and Charlie Brown you drew? The school nurse hung them in the infirmary, and it really brightened up the place."

"Yeah," Debbie said, "but it was still lonely. There was nothing worse than being sick at boarding school. I remember the time I got malaria."

"Oh, that was awful." Julia reached over and patted her sister's forehead with a damp washcloth. "You were so sick, Debs. And I remember I kept having to go up to the infirmary to get medicine for some kind of amoeba."

"You were basically green through the whole sixth grade, Jules," Peter said.

"I was, wasn't I? You know, I bet that to this day we're all carrying around some kind of nasty African bug."

"But the time I got malaria was the worst." Debbie closed her eyes. "I thought I was going to die."

debbie • africa • 1977

I feel hot and sweaty. But it's not even the dry season. My bed feels wet from my sweat. My three roommates are rushing around getting dressed, and they don't notice I can't seem to get out of bed. It's almost time for inspection, so the prefect will be coming down the hall any minute. She will check our uniforms and make sure we haven't rolled our skirts up too short. I'm really scared of the prefect —

"Knock, knock!" A tall man stepped into the hospital room. "Hey there, Deb, how are you feeling today?"

"Oh, Dave. Hi." As Debbie looked across the room at him, Julia noticed that her sister's eyes were still bright with fever.

Dressed in a white shirt, dark suit, and striped tie, the man had dark brown hair that had been trimmed short to minimize the hint of curls. He glanced at Julia, then at Peter, and gave them a polite smile. "You must be Debbie's sister and brother."

"Yes, I'm sorry," Debbie said. "Dave Hornburg, this is my sister, Julia Chappell, and my brother, Peter Mossman. They got here yesterday."

"Nice to meet you both. I'm a good friend of Debbie's."

Good friend, Julia thought. Although Julia had never met him, she knew from Debbie that the two had been dating for years. Yet Dave never got around to asking Debbie to marry him. In spite of herself, Julia took an instant disliking to the man. What was his problem? Couldn't he see Debbie was the sweetest, most beautiful woman he was ever likely to meet?

When she turned back to her sister, of course, Julia was reminded that Debbie was not exactly beautiful at the moment. Maybe her constantly foundering relationship with Dave had initiated this problem with anorexia. Peter would have an opinion on that.

"I'm sorry I haven't been to see you for

the past couple days," Dave said. He seemed to hesitate, then approached the bed. "I had to go to Springfield on business."

"Dave works at a bank on the town square," Debbie explained. "He's a loan officer."

"So, what does the doctor have to say about you? Have you been able to eat anything?"

She looked away. "I've got a tube, you know."

"Well, you ought to try to eat." He turned to Julia. "Up until recently, Deb took really good care of herself. She exercises all the time. In fact, she was in great shape before she started having problems. To tell you the truth, I didn't even notice at first."

"You didn't?" Peter's eyes were narrowed. A bad sign. Julia hoped he wouldn't make a scene. "I mean, had you looked at her?"

"Well, yeah. But she's always been thin."

"Not like this."

Dave stared at Debbie as if he were looking for a clue. "I just didn't notice," he said finally.

"It's okay." Debbie weakly waved her hand, dismissing the issue. "Dave's so busy. I get lost trying to keep up with all the projects he has going on."

"I do care about you, Deb. You know that."

"Sure." She smiled through her dry lips.

"So, eat. Got it?"

"Aye, aye, captain." She reached for his hand, but he was already turning to go. "Wait! Can you come back tonight, Dave?"

"I'm not sure. I'll try." He shrugged at Julia and Peter. "I belong to the Evening Lions."

"He's involved in a lot of civic activities," Debbie explained. "City council, chamber of commerce, that kind of thing. Dave is director of the singles department at church. That's how we met."

"Wow, you are busy," Peter said.

Dave eyed him curiously. Julia suspected he was weighing Peter's sincerity. "As a matter of fact," he said, "I'm about to be late for a meeting at the bank."

"You'd better hurry," Debbie said.

He pointed a finger at her. "Eat, you hear me?"

She nodded as he hurried out into the hall. Julia felt the tension in the room seep away like water down a drain. What on earth did Debbie see in the man? She was so precious and gentle and loving — and he was clearly too driven by his own ambition to pay her much attention. *I didn't notice*, he'd said. Didn't notice! What kind of a man could let his girlfriend slip to the brink of death and never notice? And Debbie seemed perfectly comfortable with the idea of being lost among all his projects. Julia had to admit she felt both of them were behaving a bit oddly.

As Peter went to wring out the damp washcloth, Julia thought about her own relationship with her husband. Had she chosen a man any different from Dave? Mike was loving, of course, but he rarely had time to be romantic or attentive. The youth group kept him running, and when he did come home, he was so worn out that he just wanted to read the newspaper or watch a ball game. She instinctively ran her hand over the swell beneath her maternity shirt.

What kind of a home would these babies grow up in? What plans had God made for the children developing inside Julia? To her and Mike, the pregnancy seemed like an accident. But to God, these children were already intimately known, lovingly knit by his heavenly hand. Her thoughts drifted to verses of Scripture she had memorized as a girl at boarding school. Psalm 139 had been smack-dab in the middle of the old green *Living Bible* she had nearly worn out by reading so much. "You were there while I was being formed in utter seclusion! You saw me before I was born and scheduled each day of my life before I began to breathe. Every day was recorded in your book!"

Each moment of these unborn children's lives was known to God. The babies were already precious and valuable, just as Julia and her brother and sister were deeply loved by their Father in heaven. What had the three of them done with the days that were recorded in God's book? Was he pleased with them? Did they have the right to blame their parents for the mistakes and pain in their past? And, more important, what would they make of their future? What could she and Mike provide their new babies? These unexpected — but marvelously complex and beloved — lives were growing inside Julia. "How precious it is, Lord, to realize that you are thinking about me constantly!"

She looked across at her brother, who was arranging the pillow behind their sister's head. Certainly, the past lived inside each of them to this day. In Peter, that pain was still raw. He felt abandoned, and maybe he had been. In some sense, he had been set aside by their parents as they poured themselves into their labors on behalf of the kingdom of God. Maybe she and Debbie had been abandoned, too. But what each of them had done with their adult lives had been their *own* choice. Hadn't it? Julia had chosen to conform. Peter had chosen to rebel. And Debbie was still lost.

"We're stuck," she said out loud. Surprised, both her siblings turned and waited for her to continue. "In our childhood, we got trapped in certain patterns, and even now we act them out again and again."

"What are you talking about?" Peter crossed his arms. "I'm not stuck. The only one who's stuck around here is Debbie. Stuck with that cold fish, Dave Hornbill."

"Pete!" Debbie scowled at him. "It's Dave Horn*burg,* and he's a wonderful person."

"So wonderful he didn't quite notice you were on the brink of death."

"I wish you would quit saying that, Pete. I am not on the brink of death."

"Yeah? Then why don't you get up and skip-to-my-lou out of this hospital? You haven't even been out of bed since we got here."

"That's because I can't get out of bed." Debbie's eyes suddenly filled with tears. She swallowed twice before she could bring herself to speak. "When I fell at church . . . I broke my pelvis."

Julia sucked down a deep breath. "Debs? You didn't tell us that."

"I asked the doctor to keep it confidential." Tears began rolling down Debbie's cheeks, and Julia grabbed a tissue. "I didn't want people at church making a big deal out of things. You and Peter, either. I wish everyone would just leave me alone. I can take care of myself."

"You can't take care of yourself!" Peter exploded. "By taking care of yourself, you've wound up in a hospital with a broken pelvis, a feeding tube, and who knows what else!"

"Pete," Julia snapped, "stop yelling at Debbie."

"I'm not yelling at her! Why does everyone always think I'm yelling?"

"Because you yell!"

"No, I don't! I say what I'm thinking —"

"Excuse me?" The door opened and a young man in a white coat stepped into the room. "I hope I'm not interrupting anything. I'm Dr. Bryant."

Julia pasted on a smile. "Hi, I'm Debbie's sister, Julia. This is our brother, Peter."

"Nice to meet you both. Listen, if you two wouldn't mind stepping outside for just a minute, I'd like to take a look at our patient here." He approached the bed. A couple of nurses entered the room behind him. "I hear your temperature's a little elevated, Deborah. Can you tell me how you're feeling this morning?"

"We'll head down to the cafeteria for a cup of coffee," Julia said, beckoning Peter. As the doctor began his examination, they hurried out into the hall. Julia could hardly walk fast enough to stay ahead of her brother.

Peter caught her arm and swung her around. "How come you've got a bee in your bonnet all of a sudden?"

"I do not have a bee in my bonnet," she said. "I have an obnoxious brother in my life. You don't seem to be aware of how sick our little sister really is. We find out she has a broken pelvis, and you instantly start castigating her. Don't you realize she needs peace and quiet? She needs to heal — not to be thrown in the middle of all your ranting and raving."

"I do not rant and rave."

"Yes, Peter, you do."

As he stared at Julia, he felt angry yet aware that this argument seemed uncomfortably familiar. This was exactly what Maria and others had told him time and time again. He maintained he was expressing his opinions. They insisted he was yelling.

"If Debbie didn't tell us her pelvis was broken," Julia said, starting down the hall again, "then maybe there are other things she hasn't told us. Did you think about that?"

"All I know is, my little sister is lying there dying, and there's nothing I can do to help."

"Well, you could start by being nicer."

"Nice? You're the one who's nice. You're always nice, nice, nice."

"What's wrong with that?"

"It's fake!"

Julia's eyes flashed, and Peter could tell he'd stepped over the line. "I — am — not — fake." She pronounced each word with seething clarity. *"Being nice* is part of how I live out my faith in Jesus Christ. And don't start telling me my faith is fake. Because, *guess what?* It's *not!"*

She stomped into the cafeteria, her hips doing that maternity waddle. He watched from the doorway as she tore open a tea bag and slam-dunked it into a Styrofoam cup. As she filled the cup with hot water, he sidled into the room and poured himself some coffee. Before she could get to the register, he produced a few bills and paid the cashier. *Peace?* He wanted to beg his sister. *Please, can we have peace?*

Julia did her waddle-stomp over to a table and dropped into a chair. "Why don't they ever have milk?" she asked the ceiling. "I hate putting this creamer junk in my tea. It's fake, just like you think I am."

"Okay, you're not fake, and you're not nice. I've changed my mind. You're real, and you're mean. You're real mean."

Her blue eyes darted up. "Shut up, Peter."

"Is this how you live out your faith in Jesus Christ? Talking like that to your brother?"

She stirred her tea and took a sip. Even though she was angry, it felt kind of good. How long had it been since she'd stated who she was and what she believed in? She didn't do it often enough. Instead, she lived in her insulated little Christian world where no one ever questioned her faith. The book in which God had recorded her days was probably the most boring reading in history. In fact, the thought had occurred to her recently that she might be one of those lukewarm people — like the church at Laodicea whom God would spew out of his mouth in the end times.

"The main thing here is to be supportive of Debbie," she told Peter, lowering her voice. "The least we can do is help her try to get better."

"How can we do that?"

"We can start by talking to her doctor. Trying to get some answers. Then maybe we can come up with a plan. But let's not fight, Peter. Okay?"

"I'm not fighting. I'm just saying what I feel."

"When you criticize my faith or Debbie's boyfriend — anything that really matters to us — it makes us feel bad, Pete. Yesterday on the phone you did really well talking to Mom and Dad without getting hostile. You said what you felt — but you didn't turn it into a battle."

"What good did it do? They're not here, are they?"

"They might be on their way. I wouldn't be surprised."

"And desert Vacation Bible School?"

"There you go with the sarcasm." She set her cup on the table and leaned forward. It had been years since she'd confronted her brother, but he had pushed her just far enough. "It's like a sharp thorn is buried deep inside you, all infected, filled with anger and hate and unforgiveness and bitterness. That raw pus just keeps seeping out all over the place in the things you say, in your relationships with your family — probably in your marriage, Pete. You need to get in there and get that thorn out. I mean, really deal with this stuff once and for all. Otherwise, you're just going to keep festering and making yourself and everybody else sick."

Peter studied his sister, her wavy golden hair spilling over her shoulders, her cheeks flushed from her pregnancy. Julia couldn't see that the same thorn of abandonment had dug its way into her own heart. That she, too, suffered the lingering effects of that wound. He smiled gently at her. "Thank you very much for that lovely image."

"You know I wouldn't have said it if I didn't love you. I'm too *nice*, remember?"

He gave a reluctant grin. "And how do you suggest I get rid of this festering thorn, O Queen of Niceness?"

"You'll say I'm giving you a trite answer, but I'm not. The only way to be washed clean inside, Peter, is to surrender your life to Christ. Let him do it."

"Washed in the blood of the Lamb."

"That's right."

"Okay, I'm sorry. I realize I'm angry a lot. I know about that thorn, because I feel it inside me. I'm just not sure your solution is the right one. If I surrender to Christ, I might suddenly have to start running around teaching Vacation Bible School."

She shot him a look. "Give me a break."

"I'm serious, Jules. I don't want to be like our parents. I don't want to be judgmental and rigid and intolerant."

"Well, some people might say you already have those qualities down pat." She laid her hand on his. "Listen, Peter. God doesn't want you to be like our parents. He wants you to be like *him*. Follow Christ. Mold yourself in his image. Then you'll find some real healing."

Peter regarded his sister. Maybe he had been too harsh on her. Maybe this faith of hers was the real thing. She certainly defended her position well. And if she was right — if following Christ would really heal him — Peter thought it might be worth the risk.

What risk? he wondered as he watched Julia carry their empty cups to the trash can. What kept him so far from God? What made him want to run and hide at the thought of Sunday school and prayer meetings and all the rigmarole that went with being a Christian? The only thing he risked by surrendering to Christ was the pleasure of running his own life. And he'd done such a dandy job of it so far, hadn't he?

"Come on." Julia was beckoning from the door. "Let's go find the doctor. I want to know how Debbie broke her pelvis."

As they hurried down the hall, they spotted the physician coming out of another patient's room. Julia called his name, and he paused.

"Dr. Bryant, please," she said. "What can you tell us about our sister's condition? Why does she have a fever?"

"I'm not completely sure. I've ordered some tests. Listen, would you mind if we discussed this in the waiting room?" He led the way into a small area off the corridor. "Have a seat. First let me tell you that even though your sister is choosing to deny the gravity of her condition, it is quite serious."

"Is she going to die?" Peter asked, wanting to get to the bottom line.

"I'm certainly doing all I can to prevent

that, but I could use any information you're able to give me. As you may know, anorexia nervosa is both a psychological and physical disorder. I'm beginning to gather that Debbie's struggle with it has been going on for several years, maybe even as far back as her teens. Would you agree with that?"

"Well, she's always tried to stay thin," Julia said. "But she exercises a lot. I mean, she's literally worn out a couple of treadmills, and she really keeps her body toned. I'm worried it might be something else, Dr. Bryant. Debbie said her stomach had been hurting; she'd been feeling bloated. She told me that when the accident happened at church, she was trying some different kinds of laxatives."

"Obsessive exercise, a refusal to eat, and the use of laxatives are all characteristic behaviors of anorexia nervosa." He selected a pamphlet from a rack on the wall and handed it to Julia. "This might help explain it. The important thing for you and your brother —" he nodded at Peter — "to understand is that Debbie's body has undergone extreme malnutrition for a long period of time. She shows all the symptoms of the latter stages of this disorder — her menstrual periods stopped some time ago; her breathing, blood pressure, and pulse rates are very low; and her hair, nails, and skin are brittle and dry. More significant is the fact that Debbie has developed severe osteoporosis. Her bones are very thin and weak, hardly able to support her."

"Is that how she broke her pelvis?" Peter asked.

The doctor's eyebrows rose in surprise. Apparently he hadn't expected Debbie to tell them about that. He cleared his throat before replying. "It's hard to know exactly what happened there. Debbie may have fainted, and the fall snapped the bone. Or the pelvis may have broken and caused her to faint. Either way, the area is badly damaged, and her bones are so porous that it's going to be hard for her to rebuild a healthy pelvis."

"You mean she might never walk again?"

He shook his head. "Right now, physical therapy is not a high priority. It's more important that we stabilize Debbie and try to get some nutrients into her system so she can begin to work her way back toward health. The elevated temperature is very troubling. I'm concerned we may have an infection in the pelvic area — or maybe a urinary tract infection. I've ordered an antibiotic, but we're having some trouble keeping an IV line open. Her veins are very fragile. We may need to insert a central line — a minor surgical procedure — for longer-term service."

Peter jammed his hands deeper into the pockets of his jeans.

"What you need to understand," the doctor continued, "is that your sister is in such a weakened condition, it's hard for her to fight off anything. Her immune system isn't functioning well. Nothing's functioning terribly well."

"So she really might die," Julia whispered.

No! Peter wanted to shout. There had to be something more that could be done. "Do you think this hospital is capable of the care Debbie needs?" he asked. "Should we have her moved?"

"Well, that's a possibility. I've consulted with a physician at Cox Medical Center in Springfield who specializes in eating disorders. I asked Debbie if Dr. Baines could have a look at her. But your sister still doesn't want to admit there's anything seriously wrong with her."

"How can that be?" Julia spoke up. "Just looking at her, it's so obvious. And now we find out her pelvis is broken. Surely she knows it's bad."

"A major component of anorexia is denial."

"The Mossmans are really good at that," Peter said. "Our family's been living in denial for years."

The doctor smiled. "The Mossmans and a lot of other families. Denial is a coping strategy. It can be a part of dealing with loss and grief. Unfortunately, in the anorexia patient, denial is extreme. Debbie has a distorted image of herself. In fact, she has told me she thinks she's fat."

"Fat?" Julia's voice was edging toward hysteria, Peter realized. He put a hand on her shoulder and squeezed.

"You know," he said, "I was looking for a towel last night, Jules, and I found a bunch of girdle-type things in one of Debbie's drawers. Elastic thigh slimmers and tummy tuckers and all. Does she think she needs to wear those, Dr. Bryant?"

"Undoubtedly." He set his hands on his knees. "Believe me, if I feel the situation is beyond our ability to handle here, I'll have Debbie taken to Cox Medical Center in Springfield. We'll airlift her if we need to. But I don't think it's going to get that bad. Your sister's been through a lot in her life. She's a pretty tough young lady." He stood as if to leave.

"Is there anything we can do, Dr. Bryant?" Julia asked. "Anything to help her?"

"I'd like for Debbie to speak with a psychologist. Psychotherapy could help her deal with her morbid fear of gaining weight. We may need to get her to a psychiatrist and put her on medication to deal with her obsessive thinking and compulsive behaviors. But at this point, your sister's not willing to see anyone except me. Maybe you could encourage her to think about expanding her horizons."

Peter struggled to contain his anger, realizing the doctor was doing everything he could to help Debbie. How could this have happened? How could his beautiful little sister be in such a desperate condition? And how could they get her to listen to reason?

"There is one thing I would discourage," Dr. Bryant said as he turned to go. "Don't belittle Debbie or reveal too much of your frustration with her. You're probably not going to be able to talk her into eating — arguing, pleading, anger, none of that works." Peter wondered if the doctor had read his mind. "The main thing is just to love your sister. Stick together, and love each other."

As he vanished down the hall, Julia buried her face in her hands. Peter moved to the couch beside her and draped his arm around her shoulders. "Remember what Ko-ko-o told us?" he said. "*Love each other. Take care of each other.* That's what we're doing, Julia. And I never knew that old Maasai woman to be wrong about anything."

chapter seven

Julia stretched out in the mauve chair in Debbie's room and propped her feet on the bed. She didn't know how she had made it through the day. Her body felt like a massive lump of unformed lead. Her fingers and toes had swollen into plump sausages, and she was so exhausted she knew she could sleep ten or twelve hours without wakening. What she had written off as indigestion in the past was now clearly the movement of the babies inside her. And those children could wiggle! There were moments Julia was sure her offspring were performing synchronized somersaults in her stomach.

"I don't know why Mom and Dad haven't called," Peter said. "They need to know about this infection."

"Oh, don't worry them with it." Debbie shifted in the bed. She had taken to plucking at the sheets, as though they

161

weighed too much against her translucent skin. "I think there was a banquet tonight. Mom mentioned it."

"A banquet? Why would a Vacation Bible School have a banquet?"

"They're having an international missions festival to go along with it. Food from foreign countries, exhibits, missionaries in native dress. The usual."

"I remember going to those deals. Fifty million people walking by the booth, commenting on how sweet the bananas were — as if they'd never tasted a banana before in their lives. As if those bananas really had come all the way from Africa and not from South America by way of the corner grocery store."

"Well, it's not like our parents could have put any of the other African foods out for tasting," Debbie said. "Can you imagine the reaction they'd get to *posho?*"

Peter laughed, recalling the pastelike concoction made of white cornmeal — the primary food of many tribes in Kenya. *Posho* had no seasonings, and therefore almost no flavor. And it had the consistency of overcooked grits.

"What about goat stew?" he asked. "Don't you think the church folks would like to try that?"

"Okay, people, let's change the subject." Julia rubbed her stomach. "I know I'm past the stage for morning sickness, but you're about to get me going, Peter."

"Goat stew," he continued, "with nice chunks of fat floating around in it. And how about a warm Coke to top it off?"

"Peter!" Julia was so cute when she got upset. Peter had forgotten how much he liked teasing his big sister.

"That's what they ought to serve at the banquet. Goat stew, *posho*, and warm Coke. Give those people a real taste of Africa."

"I never liked those missions conferences," Debbie said softly. "I felt so weird — all dressed up in Maasai beads and fabrics and being paraded in front of the congregation."

"Furlough was the pits, no matter how you looked at it," Peter agreed. "There we'd be, the three of us kids standing in front of some church full of strangers. And Dad would hold up one thing after another and say, 'Now here's a basket woven of sisal by the Kikuyu tribe. And here's a carving of an elephant made by the Wakamba people. This is a python skin from a snake we killed right outside our house. And this is our son, Peter.' It was like I was one of the objects on display. 'Speak some Swahili, Peter.' 'Sing one of your little Maasai songs, Peter.' I remember I used to grin from ear to ear like an organ grinder's monkey, and inside I was thinking how much I hated America, and I hated all those stupid people who didn't know how to speak any language but English and didn't even have a clue where Kenya was on the map. All I wanted to do was get back home to Africa where I belonged."

"Yep." Julia shook her head as her own bleak memories of their yearlong sabbaticals in the United States flooded back. "But don't forget — furlough was also when we got to eat Fritos and Dubble Bubble gum, and when we played in the snow, and when we got to see our grandparents and our aunts and uncles."

"Yeah, right." Peter studied the uneaten dinner on Debbie's tray. So far, he and Julia hadn't managed to get more than a bite or two down their sister. "Mom and Dad always said our relatives were supposed to be so special to us. But honestly, Jules, did you ever feel like you really knew Grandma and Grandpa? And what about our cousins? They were almost as foreign as all those people in the churches where we did our presentations. The relatives were nice, and they drove huge cars, and they fed us big meals. But did you really love them? I mean, like family?"

"Oh, probably not. But only because I didn't really *know* them."

"I never understood anybody in America," Debbie said. "The music they listened to, the clothes they wore. It was all so strange. Every time we came to America, we got fat, remember? We ate all that rich food. We'd gain tons of weight, and then we'd get back to Africa and lose the weight right away, and then none of our new clothes would fit. I never felt like I was wearing the right thing, no matter where I lived. I was always out of place."

"No, you weren't, Debs," Julia said. "You were really popular at KCA."

"Popular? Are you kidding? The boys liked me, but I never had any close girl-friends. Not like you did, Julia. I changed roommates every term."

"I don't remember that."

"The worst time I ever had at boarding school was the time I got malaria. No one came to see me."

"I did."

"You're my sister. My roommates never came at all. I think the unhappiest days I ever spent were during the time I got malaria at boarding school. I'll never forget how awful I felt the morning I woke up sick . . ."

I feel hot and sweaty. But it's not even the dry season. My bed feels wet from my sweat. My three roommates are rushing around getting dressed, and they don't notice I can't seem to get out of bed. It's almost time for inspection, so the prefect will be coming down the hall any minute —

"Sorry to interrupt." Ralph, the nurse they had met the night before, stepped into the room. "Time to check your vitals, Miss Deborah. And what's this I hear about an infection?"

Debbie's face softened as Ralph took her wrist and began to time her pulse. "It was just a little fever this morning," she said. "I'm better now."

"You've got some pretty strong antibiotics flowing into you, so you ought to be feeling dandy. If not, we'd be in trouble."

He laid her arm back on the bed. "Have you had a pretty good day?"

"Dave came by this morning. The pastor from my church visited this afternoon. And Dr. Bryant checked on me twice."

"Let me check a few things out here, how about?"

At the realization that Ralph was preparing to tend to Debbie, Julia decided it was time to call it a day. "Hold it!" She swung her feet to the floor and pushed herself out of the chair. "Come on, Pete. Let's go back to Deb's house. These babies and I need a good night's sleep."

"I figured you were pregnant, Miss Julia," Ralph said. "When are you due?"

"I'm not exactly sure. Probably another three months or so."

"She's keeping it a surprise," Peter put in, "even from herself."

"No, I just didn't find out right away, and then I had to leave town before I could meet with my doctor to get the results of the ultrasound. This was very unexpected."

"Even though she's already given birth to two kids, and she was gaining weight, and all the other signs of pregnancy, Julia managed to live in denial for months."

"Months? How many?" Ralph asked.

"I was probably about four months along before I did the home pregnancy test."

"Hot dog." He smiled and gave her a thumbs-up. "Well, if you need anything while you're here, you could make an appointment with one of our OBs. Considering the situation, they'd probably work you in."

"I'll think about it."

"You do that."

Julia and Peter hovered over their sister for a moment. "I'm sure Mom and Dad will call soon," Julia said. "Please tell them about your fever, Debs. They need to know."

"I'll think about it," she said, echoing her sister's vague response. "Tell you what. You agree to check in with an OB, and I'll talk to our parents about the fever."

"Deal." Julia bent down and kissed Debbie's cheek. "Please," she whispered. "Please get better."

Peter stroked his finger across her chin. "Sleep good, Debs. We love you."

As Debbie waved good-bye, Ralph walked them toward the door. Peter pulled him out into the hall for a moment. "Hey, what's all that peach fuzz on Debbie's face? Is she growing a new batch of hair?"

"That's called lanugo," Ralph explained in a low voice. "It's kind of a downy growth that occurs during severe anorexia. You also see it on premature babies."

Stricken all over again with the horrible reality of her sister's condition, Julia felt her eyes well with tears. She bit her lower lip as Ralph returned to the room. As she and Peter walked down the hall, she heard the nurse pick up with his friendly chatter. "So, what was that big story you were telling when I walked in? One of your African tales, I bet . . ."

debbie • africa • 1977

I feel hot and sweaty. But it's not even the dry season. My bed feels wet from my sweat. My three roommates are rushing around getting dressed, and they don't notice I can't seem to get out of bed. It's almost time for inspection, so the prefect will be coming down the hall any minute. She will check our uniforms and make sure we haven't rolled our skirts up too short.

I'm really scared of the prefect, because she's mean to me all the time. I've tried to figure out why she hates me, but I just can't. Is it because my parents work for a different mission than hers do? Maybe she thinks her parents' mission is better than ours. Or is it because I beat her in a spelling bee a long time ago in second grade? Or maybe it's because I have wavy blonde hair and the boys like me. The prefect has friends, but none of the boys like her. She's pudgy.

Anyway, I'm still lying in bed when the prefect appears. I'm so hot I feel like someone could fry an egg on me. The prefect glares at me.

"Deborah Mossman, what are you doing still in bed?"

Right then, I lean over and throw up. It goes all over the floor. My roommates will be mad. They just swept that floor for inspection. Everyone starts screaming and yelling, "Oh, gross!" "Debbie Mossman just puked!" "Eeew!" "Disgusting!"

I wish I could crawl under the blanket and die. Instead, I throw up some more. Then our dorm mom comes in. She's even scarier than our prefect. Miss Weir has never been married, and I can see why. She has a long pointed nose, and she looks like she just got hit by a train. At night in the dorm, she has devotions with us girls. After she tells us all about how much God loves us, she announces who lost points during inspection that day, and she tells what their punishment will be. Usually, it's something like washing walls or cleaning toilets. I have never lost points, but I think today might be the day.

Miss Weir stands at the edge of our partition and stares at the vomit on the floor. "Oh, good heavens, Debbie," she says. "You need to get up to the infirmary before everyone catches that."

I imagine the whole dorm full of girls throwing up left and right. Somehow I haul myself out of bed and find a pair of jeans. The prefect has brought over a bucket and a mop. While my roommates and everyone else head out to breakfast, I clean up the floor.

I really think I am going to die. I wish someone would call Julia. She would help me mop, and she wouldn't even complain about the smell. I wish someone would call Peter. He would hold me up during the long walk to the infirmary. But no one thinks of this, and I am just too sick to say a word. Every time I open my mouth, I suck down a breath of air and pray that I won't puke again.

The walk up the hill to the infirmary feels like ten miles. My legs hardly move, and I see black spots moving around in front of my face. I decide they must be some kind of black birds, vultures circling overhead, just waiting to swoop down the minute I keel over. They'll peck out my eyes and eat them, just like they do to the dead zebras the lions kill out in the bush. Then they'll wait until the hyenas show up and tear me to pieces, and the vultures will dance around, plucking strips of my intestines to take back to their nestlings.

I really don't care. In fact, I am thinking of sitting right down on the hillside and letting them go to work. So, I do. I keel over in the tall golden grass and lie there, waiting for the vultures. I pray a little bit, because I know God is with me even during this moment of death, and I'm grateful. I decided a long time ago that I would rather be in heaven than anywhere else. So, I wish he would just come and get me. As a matter of fact, I wish he would come before the hyenas get here.

Then I start thinking about the three-legged leopard who lives in the forests here at KCA. All the kids live in terror of that leopard. It comes out at night and kills the dogs of the missionaries who work at the school. That leopard has lived at KCA for so many years that it has probably turned into a legend by now. In fact, some kids think there never was a three-legged leopard at all. They say the story was invented by the teachers to keep the students from wandering off campus. Peter's always off campus, and he's never seen the three-legged leopard.

Still, the more I lie there in the grass and think about that spotted cat leaping out of a tree and tearing open my throat, the less happy I feel about dying that way. So, I roll over onto my stomach, and I start to crawl toward the infirmary. It takes me at least another ten years, and I'm sure the vultures are going to start dropping on me any minute, but I finally reach the steps. The cool concrete feels good, so I lie down and stretch out.

When I wake up, I'm in a narrow bed in the girls' ward of the infirmary. The school nurse is really nice. Whenever I have been sick before, she has always given me hugs and grilled cheese sandwiches. Her name is Miss Bellows, and she's in love with Mr. Williams, who teaches biology. They're probably going to get married, and I think they make just the cutest couple. Miss Bellows comes into the ward and checks on me. She asks all kinds of questions. I try to answer, but I keep puking. She cleans it up.

I love her for that.

Finally, she decides that I probably don't have amoebic dysentery or hepatitis A or the flu. When I tell her that our family went to the coast for a week during the last holidays, Miss Bellows decides I might have caught malaria there. Malaria comes from mosquitoes. Every time we go to the coast, we all have to take the nastiest medicine in the world. It tastes just like earwax. I took mine, but you can still catch malaria. If you get malaria, you will probably get over it, but you better hope it's not cerebral malaria. If you get that kind, you're going to be insane for the rest of your life.

So, I lie there in the infirmary, staring at a white wall and wondering if it might not have been better to let the three-legged leopard drag me off into a tree. One afternoon, my sister, Julia, shows up. She is all upset, because no one told her I was sick. She fusses all around me, pushing on my pillows, wiping my forehead, bringing me slices of bread she has toasted over the fire in the dorm. I really love Julia.

She comes to see me every day, and I give her poems I have written. Julia is supposed to take them to Peter. Mostly, my poems tell Peter to come and get me! Save me! Rescue me! But he doesn't come up to the infirmary at all. Julia tells me he's just a boy, and that's how they are.

But then one afternoon, there's a rugby game down at the field, and a player gets hurt. He's so popular — the captain of the team. Pretty soon people start showing up in droves to visit him. I watch them hurry past the girls' ward, headed for their hero in the room next door. He gets so many visitors that Miss Bellows finally has to put a sign on his door. She's worried because girls like to come and sit on his bed, and that's not proper.

One day, to my surprise and amazement, my parents walk into the infirmary! Wow! How did that happen? How did they find me? How did they know? My mom has a whole bagful of homemade cinnamon rolls she made just for me. My dad has an armful of books off the shelf in my bedroom at home. I feel like I'm in heaven. They sit down by me and talk, talk, talk. They tell me all about their work, mainly the big pastors' conference they're getting ready for. They say the Maasai are finally responding to the gospel, and it's just the greatest blessing in the world. My parents ask how I'm feeling — which isn't that great. But I try to pretend I'm better than I am. I don't want them to worry.

I find out how they knew I was sick. Julia went over to the school office and called the head of our mission on the telephone. Then he called somebody, who called somebody else, who drove all the way out to our house in Maasailand to tell my parents how sick I was. I just can't believe they made that long trip all the way up here to KCA to see me. I feel so special and wonderful inside, like it's Christmas. I want them to stay and stay, so I hold their hands and try to get them to keep talking.

Pretty soon, Julia shows up and so does Peter! We're all together, the whole family, right here in the infirmary. Peter says the room is the most disgusting thing he's ever seen, and he decides he will sketch some cartoons of Lucy and Snoopy and Charlie Brown to hang on the bare walls. Julia tells us all about a report she is writing for one of her classes. It's a report that will change the school, Julia says. She's very excited, because she and her friends have been putting flowers in the cafeteria to make everything look pretty. Our parents give her a big hug.

I've never been so happy in all my life. Here we are, all five of us. I love my mom with all my heart. She's the prettiest woman in the world. She has soft blue eyes and pretty blonde hair, and she just smiles and smiles. My dad is the best father a girl could ever have. He keeps patting my hand and telling me how much he loves me. And then he starts cleaning his glasses, which is what he does when things get to be too much for him. I think he's just the perfect missionary, and I'm so proud of the work he's doing with the Maasai. They are all turning into Christians like crazy. My dad is starting churches in all the far-off places where the gospel has never been preached. It's wonderful to hear.

But before I barely have a chance to soak it all in, my parents hug and kiss me, and Julia and Peter wave at me, and then everyone walks out the door. They're gone! They leave me behind! I'm left in the girls' ward of the infirmary with the three-legged leopard haunting the forest outside my room at night.

I lie there and cry. Miss Bellows tries to get me to eat the cinnamon rolls, but I just can't. Not even for Miss Bellows, who is the nicest lady in the whole school. I send them over to the rugby star in the boys' ward next door, and I never see them again. For days and days, I lie in that bed and feel like the loneliest person in the world. I miss my family so much. I love them so much it hurts.

Before I really feel strong enough, Miss Bellows says I am well. She packs up the books my dad brought, and the clothes Julia brought, and the Bible I have been reading day and night. I climb out of bed and stand there trying not to fall over. My legs feel like spaghetti. Carrying my bag, I start down the hill to the dorm. I pass the place where I lay waiting for the leopard and the hyenas and the vultures. Something deep inside me wishes I had never gotten up and crawled to the infirmary. I think it would be better right now to be a pile of bones, bleaching in the sun.

Back in my room, I find out that I missed three tests and pages and pages of homework. My roommates tell me the smell of my puke hung around for days, and it was just disgusting. The prefect stops by to tell me there's a new rule now. None of the girls are allowed to roll up our skirts and make them short.

"By the way," she says, "it did you good to get sick. You lost weight."

I look at myself in the little mirror. She's right. My skin is white, and I have dark circles around my eyes. I look like a ghost. I feel like one, too. I think about that for a long time, and I decide that the best thing . . . the very best thing in the whole world . . . would be to fade away. Disappear. Just like a puff of steam from the nose of the three-legged leopard.

---

chapter eight

"I'll bet they didn't call." Peter slammed the car door and started toward the hospital. "How much you want to bet she never heard a word from them?"

"I don't want to bet at all," Julia said. She was wearing one of her new maternity dresses, and she felt as big as a hot air balloon floating down the sidewalk. Why had she ever let her daughters talk her into buying this thing? Pink flowers and bows and storks danced across fabric that seemed to billow all the way to her ankles.

"You won't bet me because you know you'd lose, right?" Peter said. "You don't think they bothered to call either."

"They probably didn't, Peter. If they had a banquet last night, I'm sure it ended late, and they must have been exhausted. They *are* retired, you know. Our parents aren't spring chickens anymore."

"Were they ever?"

"Of course. When they went off to Africa, they were a lot younger than we are now."

"Are you sure?"

"You hadn't realized that? Dad and Mom were just a couple of kids with three little babies, called out on a difficult mission to a remote area of Africa. They'd grown up in rural Missouri and Kentucky, Pete. It's not like they knew what they were doing or had any idea of what they were getting into. They were actually very brave. It took a lot of courage for them to do what they did."

"Or selfishness."

"How can you say that? You know God called our parents to the mission field, Peter."

"Oh, rang them up out of the blue, did he? Sounds like schizophrenia to me — hearing voices and all that."

"Good grief, Peter. If you don't understand our parents' call to missions, you're so in the dark I can't even begin to explain." She pushed open the hospital's front door and started down the hallway, feeling like an Arab dhow with pink-flowered sails. "God spoke to our parents when they were both very young. He called them to become missionaries. Don't you remember them telling the story?"

"I don't know." He felt dispirited suddenly. Stupid. How could this "call" be such an obvious thing to Julia but such a mystery to him? He'd never heard God's voice in his life. For that matter, he hoped he never would. If God ever started talking to Peter, he'd know he was in deep trouble.

"Well, I just hope they did phone from Joplin," Julia was saying. "They need to know how serious this is. I could hardly sleep thinking about how awful Debbie looked yesterday. Dr. Bryant's words kept racing around inside my head. *The latter stage of anorexia,* that's what he called it. *Latter stage.* I mean, what's after that, Peter? Is there another stage after the latter stage? Or do you die?"

She turned the doorknob and stepped into her sister's room. At the sound of laughter, she paused. Ralph was sitting in the mauve chair, his feet on the bed. Debbie lay propped up on a stack of pillows, and she was giggling helplessly.

"Oh, come in, you guys!" She waved a hand at her brother and sister. "Ralph's been telling me about when he was a rodeo clown. Do that thing! Show them that thing you used to do, Ralph."

He gave a sheepish grin and stood from the chair. "Aw, it was just something dumb I was telling Miss Deborah. Back in my younger days, I worked the rodeos, and we used to have a time keeping those bulls from stompin' on the cowboys. Anyhow, I'd better get back to the nurses' station. My shift's about up."

"Oh, don't go," Debbie said. "Stay with us. We could all talk."

Ralph chuckled and looked at Julia. "I do believe your sister could talk the legs off a chair, Miss Julia. And by the way, her fever's about gone. Pulse and blood pressure are up a little bit, too."

"Ralph did my hair." Debbie tilted her head to one side to display a curly topknot perched on her head. "He got it from the oncology ward. Cancer, you know. It's practically the same color as my real hair. Isn't it cute?"

Julia gawked at the hairpiece Ralph had pinned to Debbie's brittle hair. It really did look like the original texture and color. She forced a smile onto her lips. "Wow, that's amazing, Debs."

"Yeah," Peter managed.

"I've taken her up and down the hall in a wheelchair a couple of times, too," Ralph said. "If she's up to it, you could push her outside. It's a beautiful day."

"What about all the tubes?" Julia stepped to her sister's bedside.

"I'll unhook the IV for you. The feeding tube goes with her."

"Sitting in the wheelchair doesn't hurt her pelvis too much?"

"I can handle it for a little while," Debbie said. "It would be great to get outdoors. I can't wait until I'm able to go for a run. Or at least get back on my treadmill."

Peter glanced at Julia. "Maybe it's a good idea to take a break from all that exercise, Debs. Dr. Bryant told us you don't need to be so obsessed with it."

"I'm not obsessed. I'm conscientious." She gave him a grin. "So, go find that wheelchair, Pete. Let's go on safari!"

As he and Ralph went into the hall, Julia sat down beside Debbie. "You look so much better this morning, Debs. Did you sleep well?"

"Not bad. How about you?"

"Mmmm . . . I'm a little uncomfortable with the babies." She lowered her head for a moment. "Debbie, I'm so worried about you. Dr. Bryant is really concerned. He wants to bring in a specialist."

"A shrink."

"He'd like for you to talk to a psychiatrist. And also a doctor working with patients who have eating disorders. I think you should agree, Debs. It can only help."

"What's everyone at work going to think if they find out I'm seeing a psychiatrist? It's embarrassing enough to be in here in the first place. And then there's all this anorexia talk. Look, Jules, I'm in a really good mood right now. Can we drop this?"

"Just say you'll let Dr. Bryant bring in the eating disorders guy. Please, Debbie?"

"Look, I fainted and cracked my pelvis, that's all. I do not have anorexia or depression or obsessive thoughts or anything like that. Dr. Bryant is a great doctor, but he tends to be an alarmist. I know I'm thin, but I eat when I'm hungry, and I exercise to stay in shape. I need to look good, Julia. I'm in the clothing business. You can't go around to those trade shows looking like a hippopotamus."

"You don't look like a hippo, Debs."

"Remember that song we used to chant in a British accent?

Fatsy Bumbola
sitting on a roller
drinking Pepsi Cola.
The roller tipped over and over and over,
and that was the end of Fatsy Bumbola."

"You're no Fatsy Bumbola," Julia said. "In fact, you're way too thin. Your bones —"

"Hey, there it is!" Debbie shifted her focus to Peter, who was rolling in the wheelchair. "Where did Ralph go?"

"He had to go check on some other patients before he leaves."

"Well, be careful when you lift me into the chair, okay?"

Peter and Julia gathered beside their sister. As they moved her slowly out of the bed, she grimaced in pain. Julia could hardly believe how little Debbie weighed. She felt like a baby bird, all scrawny bones and loose skin. It was as though everything about her was crying out for nourishment — everything except her voice.

How had this happened, Julia wondered as Peter pushed the wheelchair out into the hall. Ralph lifted a hand and waved when they rolled past the nurses' station. How had Debbie fallen into such a destructive pattern? And what could bring her out of it? For the thousandth time, Julia lifted up a desperate plea to God to rescue her sister. Debbie couldn't die. She had to get better. *Dear Lord, please let her get well!*

"And here we go," Peter said, pushing the chair through the open front doors.

"Out into the big, wide world."

"Oh, it's so pretty!" Debbie leaned back and drank down a deep breath. "Everything smells fresh and new."

Peter stared at the artificial hairpiece pinned to his sister's head. He clenched his fists. A wig? How could she be wearing a wig? Debbie used to have the most beautiful hair he'd ever seen. It rippled down her back in long golden waves. It bounced around her pretty face.

Frustrated, he tipped back the chair into a wheelie. Debbie let out a gasp and then began to laugh with more strength than Peter had seen her demonstrate since they'd arrived. "Go, Peter!" she cried. "Faster! Go faster!"

He set off in a lope down the sidewalk, Debbie giggling in the wheelchair and Julia trotting along beside them. Peter wished he could push his little sister straight out of the parking lot. Right down the streets of Bolivar. Across the whole state of Missouri.

He rolled the wheelchair around a corner, barely keeping it from tipping. If he could, he'd take both his sisters soaring over the Atlantic Ocean and across the endless sands of the Sahara. Then he'd slow to a stop out in the middle of a grassy plain under the shadow of Mount Kilimanjaro. Back to Africa where things made sense, where life was simple, where they could all begin again.

"Whee!" Debbie cried as the wheelchair rolled along. "Whoopee!"

"Go Pete!" Julia was keeping up as well as she could, her flowery dress dancing around her ankles. *"Harambee! Harambee!"*

Peter laughed at the Swahili word that urged unity, pulling together, oneness. Many times when they were kids, they had heard crowds at political rallies cry out the word as their leaders challenged them — *harambee!* On the old rope-drawn ferries that plied the water between the mainland and the coastal islands, workers chanted the word again and again as they pulled on the heavy cables — *harambee!* Teams of laborers building roads with pickaxes and shovels shouted the word back and forth, encouraging each other to press on, not give up — *harambee, harambee!*

"Went to Mombasa," Peter began to sing loudly, "for a holiday!"

"Great big fish," Julia and Debbie joined in. "Swimming in the water, frightened me away!"

"Doo I doo I doo!"

"Uh-huh!"

"Doo I doo I day!"

"That's right!"

"Great big fish, swimming in the water, frightened me away!"

Short of breath, Peter slowed the wheelchair as the sidewalk ended in a parking lot. Julia bent over, hands on her thighs, gasping for air.

Debbie clapped her hands. "Went on up to the station," she sang. "Took a little look behind. Saw that fish coming after me; oh, I think I'm gonna lose my mind!" They all joined in on the chorus as they paraded back down the sidewalk toward the hospital, Julia and Peter singing at the top of their lungs, Debbie more softly but with real enthusiasm.

"Hey, Debs, you ought to sing that one for Ralph," Peter said. "Then you can tell him stories about our family vacations in Mombasa."

"I already did."

"Aha!" He tugged on her hairpiece. "What's going on with you and that guy, huh? You better watch out, little sister. I think he's got his eye on you."

"Oh, hush, Pete."

"Seriously, Debs, I think Ralph really likes you," Julia chipped in. "And he seems so nice."

"He is. He's wonderful." She paused for a moment, breathing rapidly. "He makes me laugh."

"You ought to drop that Hornbill jerk and get to know Ralph better," Peter said.

"Horn*burg*. Dave Hornburg, and he's not a jerk."

"Then why didn't he come over this morning?"

"He's busy."

"Ralph's not too busy to sit with you for hours."

"Ralph gets paid to take care of me."

"To tell you all about his rodeo days? To make you blush and giggle? I don't think so. I think Ralph likes you. And I think that's great." Peter pushed the wheelchair into a spin. "Ralph and Debbie sitting in a tree, k-i-s-s-i-n-g!"

"Stop that, Pete!" She clutched the arms of the chair as he turned her around and around. "You're making me dizzy!"

"First comes love, then comes marriage —"

"Be quiet, you nut! People are going to hear you."

Debbie was laughing as he stopped the spinning and rolled the chair over to a bench. "Then comes Ralphy with the baby carriage."

"Peter Mossman, you are such a pain, you know that?"

"I know that."

"Wow, I feel like I'm about ten years old." Debbie grinned up at her siblings. "I feel so silly!"

"But you look really pretty this morning, Debbie." Julia took her hand. "Your cheeks are pink."

"Oh, I wish you guys didn't have to go back to New Mexico. I wish you could just stay here. We could all live near each other and visit back and forth. Wouldn't that be fun?"

"It would be great." Julia gazed at her brother and sister, realizing how very deeply she loved both of them. How much she had missed them. There was an empty place in her heart, something inside that ached to hold them close, to never let them go.

"Hey, here comes Ralph," Peter whispered, prodding Debbie with his elbow. "He's looking for you."

"He is not. He's going out to his car."

"He sees you. He veers to the left. He lifts his hand to wave. He heads this direction —"

"Hi!" Ralph called as he neared the bench.

"The look of love," Peter sang softly, "is in his eye —"

"Peter, hush!" Debbie weakly smacked him on the arm. "Hi, Ralph. Heading home?"

"Yeah, but I was hoping to find you first."

"Oh, really?" Peter said. He'd been half teasing his little sister, but maybe there was more truth to his suggestion than he realized. He liked the thought of Debbie being cared for by someone as genuine and loving as Ralph seemed to be. She deserved that, and more.

"You had a phone call, Miss Deborah," Ralph was saying. "Your parents left a message at the nurses' station saying they're on their way here from Joplin. They ought to be in by two or three this afternoon. I thought you'd want to know."

"Oh, that's good news," Julia said. "Thanks for coming out here to tell us."

"No problem. I've been a nurse for about ten years, and I can tell you, things almost always perk up when a family gets together. Somehow they bring a support and love that's better than any medicine."

"But they have to be here to give it," Peter said.

Julia read the bitterness in his voice. "It

192

was very good of them to leave early. I'm sure it wasn't easy for the VBS director to replace them."

"Yep," Ralph said, his brown eyes focused on Debbie. "I know how much your family means to you, Miss Deborah. Well, I'll see you tomorrow."

"What about this evening? Don't you have the night shift?"

"I'm not on duty. It's my night off."

"You could stop by, though," she said. Then she looked away. "If you wanted to, I mean."

"I might just do that." He gave the three of them a thumbs-up. "You all have fun now."

As Ralph walked away, Peter picked up a small twig from the sidewalk and snapped it in two. Debbie tapped her fingers on the arms of the wheelchair. "My hip hurts."

"You're going to be nice to our parents, right?" Julia asked Peter.

"No, I was planning to be as nasty as possible."

"I'm just asking. Try not to get angry."

"I'm not angry."

"Yeah, and Debbie's not really sick." Julia regretted the words the instant they were out of her mouth. She laced her fingers together and let out a breath. "I'm sorry, Debs. I shouldn't have said that."

"It's okay." Her voice sounded fragile. "You guys have said it enough that I'm starting to believe it might be true."

"People who are sick get well." Julia's eyes flooded with tears. "You have to try harder, Debbie. You can't just fade away. We need you."

For a moment they all sat beneath the shade of a small oak tree, Peter and Julia on the bench and Debbie in her wheelchair. A squirrel darted out from behind the tree and scampered across the sidewalk. Pausing at the edge of the grass, it cocked its head and studied the three people. Then the squirrel leaped onto the trunk of a walnut and vanished in the canopy of bright green leaves.

"Ring, ring!" Peter said suddenly, sitting up straight. "Ring, ring!"

Julia frowned at her brother, wondering momentarily if he'd lost his grip on sanity. But when he picked up a pretend telephone receiver, the memories flooded back through her. The three of them had played this game since they were barely able to speak.

"Hello?" Peter said into the imaginary phone. "This is Peter Mossman. Who's this?"

Debbie chuckled. "It's the glue lady," she whispered to Julia. Debbie remembered, too.

"The glue lady?" Peter said angrily into his empty hand. "No, we don't want to buy any glue! How did you find us?"

He listened for a moment. Then he turned to his sisters. "The glue lady tracked us down. It doesn't matter where we go, she always finds us. Julia, do you want to buy any glue?"

"No!" Julia said loudly.

"My sister doesn't want any glue," Peter snarled into the imaginary phone. "I don't care how cheap it is. We don't want your glue. We don't need your glue."

"Let me talk to her," Debbie said. She took the phone from her brother and held it to her ear. "Listen, glue lady, we're sick and tired of you following us around. We don't want any glue, and that's final."

She pretended to listen as her brother and sister watched intently. Finally she growled. "No, we do not want your glue. We hate your glue. Stop following us!"

"I'll tell her," Julia said, taking the imaginary receiver. She listened for a moment. Then she turned to Peter and Debbie. "She says she has new glue. Better glue than ever. And it's very cheap.

She'll give us a good price."

"Nope," Peter said.

"Uh-uh." Debbie shook her head. "No glue!"

"She says she's been looking all over for us. She thought we might have moved to Morocco, because she says there's no glue in Morocco."

"Tell her we're not in Morocco, and we don't want her glue." Peter glared at the pretend phone. "Tell her we're moving to Pakistan."

"Glue lady, we're moving to Pakistan," Julia said into her empty hand. "And after that, we'll be living in Namibia."

"And then Guatemala," Debbie whispered.

"Guatemala and Antarctica and Guam." Julia grinned. "You'll never find us, glue lady. So, go away, and don't bother us again!"

She slammed down the phone and dusted off her hands. "There! That takes care of that."

"She'll find us," Debbie said.

"She always does," Peter added.

Then they looked at each other and laughed. Peter leaned over and kissed Debbie on the cheek. He gave Julia's rounded stomach a gentle poke. She ruffled his hair.

"Good grief," Julia murmured. "Why did we always do that? Who was the glue lady, anyhow?"

"I don't know," Debbie said. "One of you invented her. I remember when I was little I used to believe she was really talking to you guys."

"She was." Peter nodded. "She was."

"The best thing about the glue lady," Julia said, "was that we could yell at her. I loved yelling at the glue lady. I could just tell her exactly how I felt. Really let her have it!"

"You ought to yell at a few people besides the glue lady." Peter gave her a wink. "Yelling's good for the soul once in a while. Lets some of that pus out of the ol' infected, festering wound."

"Yuck," Debbie said. "What are you talking about, Pete?"

"Just reminding our big sister that I'm not the only one who needs some soul cleansing."

Debbie looked back and forth in confusion between her brother and sister. Then she shrugged. "Well, the thing that always amazed me about the glue lady was how she could find us anywhere in the whole world. She phoned us in Amsterdam one time, remember? We were on our way to

Africa after furlough, and we were staying in that tiny hotel room at the top of a narrow flight of winding stairs. We had left our friends and relatives behind, and I didn't have a clue where Amsterdam was. I thought we were completely lost. But then the glue lady called. She knew where we were."

"She always knew," Peter said.

"We were never lost," Debbie went on, "because the glue lady could find us. No matter where our parents took us or how confused we got, just when we thought things were hopeless, she'd give us a call."

"I liked that, too," Peter said. "But the trouble was, she always wanted us to buy her stupid glue. Like she could stick us down, you know? I figured if we had ever agreed to buy her glue, she'd have us for sure. But we refused to get stuck. We were too smart for her."

"Yeah." Debbie knotted her bony fist. "We're the Mossmans."

"We're tough," Julia said. *"Harambee!"*

Then she burst out laughing, and Peter and Debbie joined in, and from the branches of the nearby tree, the little squirrel studied the three humans as it gnawed on a walnut.

chapter nine

Debbie ate a whole bowlful of Jell-O for lunch. And two crackers. She drank a diet soda and put on makeup and asked Julia to tie a pink ribbon in her hairpiece. Her conversation revolved mostly around Ralph. Peter wondered if she realized how much she cared about the man. Though Dave Hornburg called, they didn't talk long. In the course of the morning, three visitors had stopped by — two from the church and one from the office where Debbie worked.

"She's better," Julia whispered as Debbie dozed in her hospital bed after lunch. "I think she's going to be okay, Peter."

"I don't know. Dr. Bryant said she's done a lot of damage to her body over the years." He thought about the short discussion they'd had in the hall that morning. The doctor had said that although the fever was fading, Debbie still was under a great deal of physical stress due to the effects of malnutrition. It would be difficult to repair the bone deterioration caused by her osteoporosis, and the recovery of her body's systems would take time. Peter was feeling more and more doubtful as to Debbie's prospects for recovery.

"Did you hear him say she might not be able to have children?" he asked. "And I'd been teasing her about Ralph and the baby carriage."

"You didn't know."

"We're going to have to tell Mom and Dad."

"Why? They don't need all the details. It would just upset them."

"Look, you and I aren't going to be here in Missouri forever, Jules. When we leave, our parents will be Debbie's main support." Ha. As if that would help Debbie. Still, it was worth trying to convince their parents how much their youngest daughter needed them.

"I don't know if they can handle it."

"They have to. Anyway, they need to face the truth for once in their lives." He rubbed the back of his neck. "I'm tired."

"Me, too. But we don't need to take it out on Mom and Dad."

"I just want them to face the facts," he

told her, struggling to keep his voice quiet so as not to disturb Debbie. "They need to know what Debbie's been going through while they went off to their VBS gig and abandoned her. They've been doing that to us all our lives! You heard what Debs said about her childhood. She's always felt like a nobody. Like she was lost. I think our parents need to know that!"

"Why? What purpose will it serve?"

"You're the one who said I have a festering thorn wound. Well, I'm not the only one, Julia. I think we're all infected. Maybe if we talk about the past we'll be able to do something about it. Find some healing."

"Peter, some of Debbie's problems do go back to her childhood. I'm sure of that. But not all of them." She studied the flowers on her dress for a moment. "I'm willing to admit you were right when you said our upbringing was unusual. And it's possible . . . maybe . . . that our parents might have neglected us a little bit."

"A little bit?"

"Yes, a *little bit*. But you have to admit what I said was right, too. Mom and Dad made the choices they did because they felt they were under a direct commission from God to be working out there in the bush with the Africans. Both of them."

"The call of God."

"That's right." She smoothed her dress over the swell of her stomach. "So, confronting and belittling them is not going to accomplish a thing. It would be like telling Joan of Arc she'd been wrong to lead the French armies into battle."

"Yeah, but our parents weren't the ones who got burned at the stake. We were."

"We were not."

"Were too."

"What's going on?" Debbie said, rubbing her eyes. "Are you guys arguing again?"

"Oh, Peter thinks we had this miserable childhood where we were abandoned like little orphans," Julia said. "We had more happy times than sad ones, Peter. We were a good family. Our parents loved us very much, and they still do."

"Yeah, right."

"You just choose to remember all the bad stuff. What about the times we went to the beach, Pete? We always had fun at the beach. We would go in August right before the new school year started, remember?"

"I remember."

"What about the time Dad paid for us to stay at that fancy hotel?" Debbie said.

"Oh, that was great." Peter closed his eyes and let the memories wash over him.

"I'll never forget the time at the beach when we stayed in the fancy hotel . . ."

peter • africa • 1978

August is the month when the Mossman family heads for the coast for a whole week of vacation. That's the month we have off at the end of the school year. The first term of the new year starts in September, but Julia, Debbie, and I always try our best not to think about that while we're at the ocean.

We pile into our Land Rover, the three of us fighting for the window seats, while Dad and Mom finish loading the car. Mom tries to take everything valuable, because while we're gone our house usually gets burglarized. Mostly, the thieves take sugar and rice, stuff like that. Mom used to have a few pieces of fancy silverware that she got at her wedding, but those are long gone. One time they stole all our blankets. Now sometimes we'll be sitting in one of Dad's churches way out in the boonies, and we'll notice some old Maasai man wearing one of our blankets as a robe. Mom says she doesn't mind, but I think it kind of bugs her.

Mom packs lots of food for our road trips. We have little cans of Vienna sausages we brought in our suitcases from America a long time ago. Also Beanee Weenees. You can eat them right out of the can, and even though they're cold, they taste pretty good. The potato chips they make in Kenya are real greasy, but I like them that way. Usually we have a big bag of tangerines that drip all over us in the Land Rover. By the time we get to the beach, we're covered in red dust and sticky juice.

The trip to the coast takes almost eight hours. The roads are mostly dirt until we get to the Mombasa Highway. It might as well be unpaved, too. It's full of potholes, and the pavement is so soft that when the sun hits it, the painted lines start to melt. If Dad tried to keep the Land Rover inside the lines, we'd crash for sure. They weave and squiggle all over the place.

Dad's a good driver. He has to be. There's no telling what we'll pass on the road to Mombasa. We see elephants and elands and all kinds of gazelles. One time we pass a crazy lady walking down the middle of the highway. She doesn't have any clothes on, and Dad runs off the road into the bush and nearly hits a baobab tree. We see accidents, too. People drive like maniacs in Kenya, and they have wrecks all the time. Dead bodies lie out there by the side of the road until someone comes along and scoops them up. There's one hill named Killemalorry because it's so steep that the trucks — called lorries — lose their brakes and crash.

Overloaded buses with people hanging from the windows and roofs roar by our Land Rover. We wave and honk. Big trucks filled with imported goods struggle to climb the hills. While they're heaving upward, thieves climb on the back, pry open the boxes inside, and toss the cargo to their accomplices waiting on the road below. We have bought Hershey's chocolate syrup at a little shop way out in Maasailand. The cans are always bent from being dropped on the highway. One time Mom found a whole stack of Chicken of the Sea tuna fish cans in a shop in the middle of nowhere. She went into a frenzy of happiness. You'd have thought she'd discovered gold.

We stop and eat under a big thorn tree on the way to the beach. The girls go hide behind an anthill when they need a bathroom. There aren't many gas stations along the road, and the rest rooms they have could make you barf. Usually it's just a hole in the ground, and you have to pray you don't fall in. I prefer the anthills myself.

About suppertime we realize we're in Mombasa, the main city on the coast. We can smell the Indian Ocean. The salt hangs heavy in the air. We wrinkle our noses at the scent of drying fish. We maneuver through the old town built by Portuguese and Arab traders as we head for the ferry that will take us to our favorite place, Diani Beach. But while we're crossing the water — munching on cashews and roasted ears of corn we bought from roadside vendors — Dad makes a big announcement.

We're not going to our usual little beach cottage this time. He has reserved two rooms at one of the big, fancy hotels! Julia and Debbie go nuts over this news. I'm pretty excited, too. I can't figure out how our family can afford this, but Dad says he's been saving up for a long time. I start thinking my dad might be cooler than I used to believe. That he would do something like this for us . . . wow. By the time the ferry gets us over to the other side, and we find the hotel, and we stand in the lobby to register, we are feeling like the richest people on earth.

The lobby has a polished red concrete floor and big cage with a parrot inside. The parrot says swearwords in English, one right after the other. None of the Africans who run the hotel seem to realize this might be a problem. I think it's hilarious, but Mom gives me the eye, so I stop laughing.

Julia, Debbie, and I have the most amazing room looking out over the ocean. I stand on the balcony for a minute and just stare, wishing I hadn't packed my pencils and watercolors at the bottom of my suitcase. The color of the sea always amazes me — green, turquoise, bright blue, even purple all mixed together. Waves wash up onto the white sandy beaches, and the bright green leaves of the palm trees whisper overhead. But there's no time to think about drawing a picture. Julia and Debbie have pulled on their bikinis — yes, Mom finally agreed to their pleading and sewed a couple of the most awful-looking bathing suits anyone ever laid eyes on.

I try not to snicker as we race out of the room, across the swimming pool area, and down the beach. I'm the fastest, of course, so I beat my sisters into the water. I do a shallow dive right into a huge wave. The water swooshes over my head, washing away the grime and the tangerine juice. Seaweed swirls around my feet, and sand filters between my toes. Of all the places I have been to in the world — and, believe me, I have been to a lot of places — this is where I'm the happiest.

The days go by like some kind of magic. Every morning we wake up to the sound of monkeys playing tag on the roof of the hotel. We all head down to breakfast. At this hotel we have a feast every meal. Breakfast is a huge buffet with cold cereals, scrambled eggs, omelets, sausages, fresh milk, and fruit. The fruit is what really gets me. We have our choice of mangoes, papayas, oranges, tangerines, bananas, pineapples, and even grapes! We drink gallons of passion fruit juice. The only problem is the monkeys. They like to swing down off the thatched roof, dart across the table, and grab your toast. It's funny to me. But Debbie is scared to death of those monkeys.

At lunchtime, we have something more simple. Ha ha. Roast beef, chicken, fifteen kinds of vegetables, a whole tableful of bread, and salad — which Mom won't let us eat because she's not sure it's clean enough. At home, she always washes our salad and vegetables in this liquid called Milton, which is mostly bleach. It adds an interesting flavor. I guess she doesn't have any idea the kind of food we eat at KCA. She would have a heart attack.

Dinner could feed two armies. All us tourists — and there are people from Germany, England, and Switzerland at the hotel, too — descend on the long tables, where we find enough food to make a twelve-course meal. There's soup, fish, beef, chicken, shrimp, crab, lobster, every kind of vegetable, fruit, salad, rolls, and at least seven different desserts. A chef is carving huge slabs of pork off a pig he has been roasting all day. While we eat, Africans come out to show off their tribal dancing around the swimming pool. The Giriama tribe lives at the coast, and their women dance in grass skirts and nothing else. I am very interested in this, but Mom makes us leave right after the meal.

After a few days of this kind of eating, we all feel as healthy as horses. I'm sure I could run a marathon and not get tired. Debbie has bright pink cheeks and a constant smile on her face. Julia, of course, is in love. She always falls in love at the beach. She meets some handsome young British tourist or gets to know the assistant hotel manager or somebody like that. And then — boom — she's in love. I don't understand that about Julia at all. Even in her ugly bikini, the guys seem to like her. They look at Debbie, too, but she's kind of shy. Sometimes she's so quiet I forget she's even around.

In between all the eating, we have a great time. I like to swim out in the ocean. Body surfing is fantastic on Diani Beach. I talk to the vendors who walk up and down the beach selling shells, and I trade with them. They show me how to find octopuses in the coral pools at low tide, and they take me out to the reef in their dugout canoes. Sometimes Julia and Debbie go with me, but lately they think lying around the swimming pool and baking themselves in the sun is great entertainment. We're all as tan as the bark on the palm trees already, but my sisters get some kind of thrill out of lolling around in their bikinis. I think it has to do with the tourists from Germany. Male tourists.

Anyway, Dad spends most of his time by the pool, too. He must be trying to keep an eye on my sisters. He sits under an umbrella and reads books like *The Winds of War* and *The Rise and Fall of the Third Reich.* At mealtimes, he launches into big discussions about World War II, which Julia seems to think is the most fascinating subject she ever heard of. She's such a goody-goody.

When Dad's not reading about war, he's got his nose buried in some Bible commentary or language study book. He's pretty good at speaking Swahili, and he's trying to learn Maasai. Compared to me, he's pretty hopeless. He makes really goofy mistakes sometimes. Like once he preached a whole sermon on Jesus' mother, and all the way through, instead of calling her a *bikira,* which means a virgin, he called her a *birika* — a teapot. But I've got to give him credit for trying. On the other hand, how come he doesn't ever take a break from all that studying? There's lots to do on the beach. What's his problem? I don't understand my dad.

Mom is more of a mystery than Dad. I don't even know where she is most of the time. She takes naps and reads Victoria Holt and Mary Stewart books. They're full of romance and mystery and junk like that. Mom won't go in the water, because she never learned how to swim when she was a kid — and besides, it would mess up her hairdo. As if anyone cares. She has wavy blonde hair like the rest of us, and she

211

spends hours trying to make it look like something out of a magazine. Doesn't she realize we're in the middle of Africa?

Anyhow, we do a couple of things all together as a family — and I've got to say those are the best times of all. Once Dad rents a big dugout, and the African owner takes us out to the reef to snorkel. Dad and the girls and I swim all over the place, looking through our goggles at the amazing stuff underwater. Big coral heads are home to all kinds of tropical fish — angelfish, zebra fish, neon-colored fish, and hundreds of varieties I can't even name. We see deadly stonefish and lionfish, too. And once we swim right over a bed of eels, their tails buried down in the sand and their heads floating upward with their toothy grins just waiting to nab some prey. That sight sends Debbie straight back into the boat.

Another day, the whole family heads to Mombasa town. We drive over to Fort Jesus, the huge Portuguese bastion built out of coral. The walls are kind of a whitish gray, and when the light hits it just right, it looks pink. When we're at the coast, we always visit Fort Jesus, and I always love it. The walls are sort of broken down now, but I like to imagine what the place was like when soldiers roamed the ramparts watching for enemy ships in the harbor. Old cannons and stacks of cannonballs line the perimeter of the fort. I always pretend I'm a Portuguese captain, and I try to send Debbie and Julia to the dungeon. But they always escape. Except for Debbie, who gets lost and sends everyone into a panic. Julia finds her, of course.

After the fort, we walk around in Old Town. This is the most awesome place, and I have tried to draw it a hundred times or more. The Arabs built the town hundreds of years ago — tiny little alleys and narrow streets, two-story white houses with iron balconies sagging overhead, fantastic wooden doors with geometric carvings and huge brass studs. Way back inside each house, there's a courtyard full of laundry and naked babies and women in their long, black, hooded robes called *burkahs.*

We drink tiny cups of strong black Arab coffee that we buy on the street corners from men with big cone-shaped brass pots. Old Town smells like curry, cinnamon, and cloves. It also smells like dead fish, raw sewage, and rotting food. It smells like the sea and dirty people and incense and coconuts. I love Old Town. I am pretty sure I have the greatest life of any kid in the whole world.

But then Mom and Dad pull a really sneaky trick on us. It makes me think of all the times they have suddenly parked in front of a doctor's office — without any warning at all — and marched us three young Mossmans inside for a whole array of shots. Yellow fever, tetanus, typhoid, cholera, smallpox — you name it, we got it. If you're going to live in Africa, you've got to have vaccinations all the time. Of course, we scream bloody murder over these shots, so I guess I can't blame our parents for not announcing them in advance. Today it's needles of a different sort. They parade the three of us into a little tailor shop right there in the middle of Old Town. It's time for new school uniforms.

We have been trying not to think about school. Trying really hard. See, we get three months off a year, but each of those vacations is divided by three months of school. Three months without being at home. Three months without hanging out in the Maasai kraal with my friends. Three months eating the worms and metal chunks in Cookie's food. Even Mom's bleach-flavored salads are a whole lot better than that. And she usually makes cinnamon rolls, and allows us to sleep in as late as we want, and lets me paint and draw until all hours of the night.

I hate school. I hate wearing a uniform.

I try making a U-turn and heading out of the tailor shop. But Mom is standing there with her fists planted on her hips, and I realize any escape attempts are useless. Before I know it, I'm being stripped down to the undie-gags by a couple of Indians with yellow measuring tapes draped around their necks. One of them measures me all over — lengths, widths, circumferences — while the other one records the numbers in his little notebook. The two of them make a big show out of this, sounding real professional, while Mom looks through bolts of fabric for just the right khaki-colored cotton to fashion my uniforms. This year, she informs me, I will have the best-looking set of uniforms of any boy at KCA. She instructs the tailors to make pleats in my trousers, cuffs on the legs, epaulets on the shoulders of my shirts, and ample pockets everywhere.

I begin to hold out some hope — like I do every August — that things might be different at school this new year. I'll have a new set of teachers. There might be some new kids who've moved to Africa in the last month and have been sent to KCA. Maybe Cookie will have gotten fired. Maybe I can make myself care about my grades, and Mom and Dad will finally be proud of me. Maybe I'll look so great in my new khaki uniform that I'll actually be one of the popular kids. I might be popular enough to make it onto the rugby team or into the choir.

In the fitting room next to mine, I hear my sisters griping about the length of their skirts. They want shorter skirts. But Mom has the KCA handbook right in her purse, and there's no arguing with that. It's like the Bible. Pretty soon Julia and Debbie have been measured for gray skirts, white blouses, bright red ties, and red blazers. Julia keeps assuring Debbie that everything's going to be all right. They'll have fun this year at school.

Why is my sister like this? Why am I? Why do we keep hoping things will change?

After this major dip in the enjoyment factor of our vacation, we all head back to the fancy hotel. We have a few more great days digging up clams, body surfing, exploring the reef, and eating all that good food.

One day when I'm walking down the beach with the wind whipping at my hair, it suddenly hits me how much I love my parents. I'm really thankful God gave them to me. In fact, I feel so good about my life that I start to cry. This is very embarrassing, and I hope nobody sees me. I decide I'd better get out of the tourist traffic — which isn't much, but there are some pretty German girls strolling around — so I head up to the line of coconut palms along the beach.

I sit down under a palm tree and just cry until I can't cry anymore. The thing is this: I want so much to tell my parents I love them, but I don't know how. I want them to know that I'm glad I'm their son, and I would do just about anything I could for them. I want them to know that I love God — I love Jesus — and I'm proud of the fact that my parents are missionaries. I know it's a great thing they've done to give up their easy lives in America and come all the way out to Africa to live.

I pray really long and hard under that palm tree. I really want to be a Christian. I want to tell my parents that even though I don't always show it, I really do believe in God. How can I tell them? How can I show them? I cry and pray about this for a long time. Finally, I figure out the answer. I'm going to paint them a picture. Once they see it, they'll understand.

All excited, I head back to the fancy hotel. After dinner, I go to the room and take out my watercolors, pencils, and paper. I spend the evening sitting on the balcony sketching a picture of our family — all five of us — standing on the African beach with the sun coming up out of the water behind us. The sun is supposed to be like Jesus, always looking over us and keeping his hands on us.

"It's a sunset!" Julia says, looking over my shoulder.

"No, it's not, goombah. It's a sunrise. In Kenya, the sun doesn't set over the Indian Ocean. The ocean faces east. This is a sunrise picture."

"I look like a potato," Debbie says over my other shoulder.

"It's just a sketch!"

"Well, how come I look like a potato?"

"I haven't painted it yet. You won't look like a potato when it's done."

"I hope not. Don't make me look fat, Peter."

"If you do, blame your stupid bikini." I glance up at her, and she blinks like she's about to burst into tears. "Oh, just forget it!"

I toss the sketchbook down in my chair and head outside to watch the Giriama ladies dancing in their grass skirts. Why couldn't I have had a brother? That's what I'd like to know.

The next morning, while Mom and Dad pack up the Land Rover, the three of us kids head down to the beach. Julia started a tradition a long time ago, and even though it seems kind of silly to me now that I'm older, I still go along with it. We take off our shoes and wade out into the ocean. Then we all bend down and kiss the water good-bye. This is our way of promising that we'll come back. Someday . . . someday . . . we'll return.

Once the car is loaded, we settle in for the long ride home. But to our surprise, Dad stops in Old Town. We all pile out and head for the little tailor shop. There, Mom pays for three packages of brand-new uniforms all wrapped in brown paper and tied with twine.

Later, when we're packing our trunks for school, we'll discover that the fine tailor in Mombasa has done some interesting things with his careful calculations. The neat cuffs of my khaki slacks hit me about mid-shin. The waistline has a set of pleats — in the back. And the girls' skirts could be worn by nuns. Mom will lengthen hems and shorten hems and do all the alterations as she usually does.

Then we'll pile in the Land Rover for our long ride to boarding school. Somewhere in the bottom of my trunk I have packed the picture of my family standing together on the beach at sunrise. Maybe one day I'll finish it.

Peter stared down at his laced fingers, his blue jeans, his running shoes. How vivid the memories of that special beach vacation were. Funny — he hadn't thought of it in years. He'd shared a few of the memories aloud, but he knew he would never tell his sisters about the time he cried under the palm tree. They wouldn't understand. *He* didn't understand. Who had he been? And what had happened to him in the years since then?

He thought of Maria and Angelo. Twice since coming to Missouri he'd called the house where they were staying. Maria's mother always said the same thing: her daughter never wanted to speak to him again.

Never again? Had he been that bad a husband? His arms ached for the solid weight of his son — the wiggling, squirming, babbling child he had fathered. Was he never to see his precious Angel again? But what was the point of seeing the boy, anyway? Peter had nothing to offer as a father. He didn't even know how to be a father. Not really. His own dad had sent him off to boarding school. During the holidays, Don Mossman was usually away preaching or conducting pastor-training sessions. How was a father supposed to act? Peter wondered. What was a father supposed to say to his son? What were they supposed to do together?

"Were our bikinis that bad?" Julia asked. "I thought they were kind of cute."

"They were bad." Peter glanced across the room and saw that Debbie was dozing again. "You know," he whispered, "I think I made fun of Debs. I told her she looked fat in her bathing suit."

"Don't blame yourself for the situation she's in, Peter."

"Didn't we all contribute? I teased her."

"Well, I know I used to talk to her for hours about looking beautiful. We thought it was the only way to attract the boys, and somehow that seemed like the most important thing in the world." She let out her breath. "I remember one time, right before

Debbie started ninth grade, we were looking through all those old Sears catalogs that somebody had sent us from America. We were evaluating the women on the pages, saying whether we thought they were pretty or not. That's when Debbie told me she had made a big decision."

"What was it?"

"She said she was going to be tan and thin and have long blonde hair. And that's when it all started. Right then, she started growing her hair out. She began spending hours in the sun trying to get as brown as she could. And she stopped eating."

"I never knew that."

"See? It's my fault. If I hadn't been so fixated on looking good, on that shallow stupidity, Debbie wouldn't be in this shape."

"You didn't do this to her, Jules. If you won't let me take some of the blame, I'm not letting you blame yourself, either."

"I did my part." She grabbed a Kleenex and pressed it against her eyes. "Oh, Peter, I'm so scared for her."

"You'd better talk to Mom and Dad. Tell them the whole truth."

She lifted her head. "It would just kill them."

"Don't say that. You're the Bible person, remember? What was that verse we had to memorize — 'You will know the truth, and the truth will set you free'? Well, maybe a good dose of the truth is what we need here. I'm starting to wonder if it's the secrets and lies and denial of the truth that are destroying Debbie. And maybe —" he paused — "maybe me, too. Talk to our parents, Jules. Tell them everything — not just the details of Debbie's disease, but tell them that they played a part in the problem. I agree we had a lot of good times in Africa. But our parents were wrong to let a boarding school raise us! They were wrong to put their work before their family!"

"It was God's work, Peter, not theirs."

"*We* were God's work."

"We were children. Mom and Dad were trying to win people to Christ. Build churches."

"But what about us, Julia? Shouldn't we have been our parents' first church work? Before all those other lost souls, before all those empty church buildings, they had three little lost children. Julia, Peter, and Debbie Mossman."

Julia blotted her cheek. "Oh, Peter."

"You've got to do it, Jules." Now that the

idea had occurred to him, he latched on to it like a life preserver. Maybe it was their last hope. For Debbie, for him, for the family they once had been. "Confront Mom and Dad with what they did by abandoning us. Maybe if they finally acknowledge the truth, then Debbie will get well." He paused for a moment. "Maybe we all will."

She bent over, sniffling. "Peter, I just can't do this. I hate fighting."

"It's not a fight. It's the truth. Tell the truth."

"Why don't you do it? You love confrontation."

He shook his head. That would be a sure course to disaster. "It wouldn't work. You know that. When I get mad, things just go south. I don't know how to express anger without hurting the people I love the most."

She wadded the tissue into a ball. Peter was right. Even more than confronting her parents, she feared having Peter do it. "Okay," she whispered. "I'll do it. I'll talk to them."

"Good. You can do it, Jules."

"But you have to promise not to butt in. If you get mad —"

"Hello, hello!" The door inched open

and their mother slipped into the room.

Behind her came their dad, the light from the hallway making his white hair glow like a halo. He smiled. "Hey there, you three rascals."

"Oh, Don," Mom said softly, taking her husband's hand, "isn't this just the most precious sight you ever saw in your life?"

chapter ten

"Is Deborah asleep?" their mother asked, approaching the bed on tiptoe. "I don't want to wake her up."

"I think she's napping." Julia rose and slipped her arms around her mother in greeting. How small and fragile she seemed! When had her hair gotten so white?

Her mom gave Julia's tummy a gentle pat. "Hello, there, little ones! This is your meemaw speaking!"

Julia glanced across the room to see her father giving Peter a stiff handshake. Moving away from her mother, she edged into her dad's warm embrace. "Honey, how're you feeling these days?" he asked, his arms holding her tightly. "How're those new babies coming along?"

"We're fine, Dad. How are you and Mom?"

"Well, to tell you the truth, we're tired," Mom whispered. "Just plain old tired. It's a long drive up here from Joplin, you know. How's Deborah feeling today?"

"I'm glad she's resting," Julia said. "Maybe we ought to go down to the cafeteria and get something to drink. I could use a cup of tea."

"Yeah," Peter said. "That's a good idea."

As they left the room, Peter draped his arm around Julia's shoulders. He knew it was going to be rough for her to be honest with their parents. Julia had worked her whole life to please them. Upsetting their carefully constructed view of the world would be the last thing she'd want to do.

It was strange to be walking down the hospital corridor with his mom and dad, Peter thought. They both looked older to him. And smaller. His mother used to have blonde hair, didn't she? And where were the old tortoiseshell glasses his dad used to wear? The wire-framed lenses perched on his nose looked nearly an inch thick, and they were trifocals! Good grief, how long had it been since he'd seen them? They had come out to New Mexico right after Angelo was born. That was only a little more than a year ago. How had they aged so much?

"She's very thin, isn't she?" Mom was saying to Julia as they moved down the hall. "I can see it now that she's lying there in her nightgown. But you know, I don't think any of us realized she was on the verge of a problem. I'd never even heard of anorectica, myself. Had you?"

"Yes, Mom. Anorexia."

"Her hair did seem a little thin the last time we were together. I thought maybe she'd had a bad perm."

"Debbie has naturally wavy hair. She never gets a perm."

"Well, you just don't know what somebody's going to do. I mean, look at you! This is such a surprise, Julia. Not that we're unhappy about it. Of course not. But I just wonder how these new babies are going to affect the rest of the family."

What about how they're going to affect me? Julia wanted to ask as she glanced into the cafeteria. *What about my life? What about all the things I wanted to do after I raised my two daughters?* But she swallowed the thoughts.

"It's crowded in here," she said. "Peter, what do you think?"

"Let's grab some Cokes and see if we can find an empty waiting area."

"Maybe we should go back up to

Deborah's room," Mom suggested. "She might wake up and wonder where everybody's gone."

"We'd like to talk to you privately, Mom and Dad," Peter said. "Julia wants to talk to you."

Thanks a lot, Peter, she felt like saying. Her heart was pounding so hard that she'd just about decided not to say anything.

"Talk to us?" Mom patted her hair. "Well, this does sound serious."

"Yes, it does," Dad said. He took off his trifocals, pulled out the end of his shirt, and began to clean the lenses. "I suppose it's a good idea, Olive. Maybe there's something we need to know about Deborah."

Pursing her lips in response, Mom made a beeline for the soda machine. Julia looked to her brother for reassurance, and he gave her a wink. *You can do this,* he seemed to be saying. *Be strong. Tell the truth.* But, oh, it was going to be so hard!

She drew a cup of hot water and dipped a tea bag into it. If only she had a fortifying cup of Kenya chai right now. Her thoughts slipped home, as they frequently did. She and Mike had been talking on the phone every day — sometimes twice a day. As it turned out, the girls were doing fine without her. Jessica seemed to be surviving the breakup with Danny. She was in the anger stage of grieving, Mike pointed out, and Danny had become the stupidest, most selfish jerk in the history of mankind. Heather's ears had stopped hurting once she started the antibiotic. And the three of them had discovered the joys of Taco Bell takeout.

Julia took a sip of her tea as Peter led the family down a corridor. Through the glass doors to the outside, she noticed boiling gray clouds and streaks of lightning. A distant roll of thunder foretold a typical Missouri storm. She hoped it wouldn't wake Debbie.

"This floor has the ER waiting room, and upstairs is oncology," Peter said, reading a sign by the elevator. "Let's see what's in the basement."

Julia clutched her Styrofoam cup as the elevator sank beneath the level of the ground. She could see her mother sipping away at a Diet Coke while giving disapproving looks at Dad, who had bought himself not only a soda but also a little snack cake. Julia wondered, Had their family always been concerned about weight gain? Or was she just more sensitive now because of Debbie's situation?

They followed Peter down a semidark corridor until he found a small sitting area with two ground-level windows. Julia placed a protective arm over her stomach as she settled into a chair. Was she going to be able to go through with this? Wasn't there another way?

"I'll tell you what," Mom said, letting out a breath. "That was the best-organized Vacation Bible School I've ever seen. Didn't you think so, Don?"

"It sure was. Lots of kids."

"Hundreds." Mom gave Julia a smile as a peal of thunder rattled the windowpanes. "We were supposed to speak this afternoon, but we thought it would be better if we came back here to check on Debbie. Your father was going to talk to the children about the Maasai rites of passage. He always does such a wonderful job on that subject, you know. I guess all your Maasai friends are probably elders by now, Peter, don't you imagine? They've already had their time as warriors, and they'll have wives and children. Do you ever hear from any of them, honey?"

Peter shook his head. "I don't think the Maasai are really into writing letters, Mom."

"Well, your father hears from the pastors

a couple of times a year when they get together for training. I think Brother Lemeikoki actually does the writing. But they all sign the letter."

"How are things with the churches, Dad?" Julia asked, deliberately avoiding Peter's steady gaze. She noticed that raindrops had begun to spatter mud on the ground-level windows near the ceiling.

"Still going along."

"Dad wishes he could be there, of course," Mom said. "Tell them what you're worried about, honey. You know, the sacrifices."

"I'm just a little concerned they'll get their Maasai sacrifice rituals mixed up with their Christian Communion rituals. They drink blood, as you know, and I taught them about Christ holding the cup at the Last Supper and saying, 'This is my blood.' I just wish I could make sure they understood the symbolism in the whole thing."

Mom nodded. "You know Christian rituals got all confused with pagan Indian rites in South America after the missionaries left. Your father and I just don't want that to happen to the Maasai."

"Aren't there any missionaries out there right now, Mom?" Julia asked. So relieved to be discussing anything but their personal relationship, she leaned back and let out a breath. Outside, the rain had begun to fall in sheets, streaking the small windows and blurring any view of the outside.

"Not in our area. It's so remote, I don't think anyone would even want to try it. Sometimes I wonder how we survived all those years out in that little tin house. Besides, there's so much political and social unrest in Kenya right now, it's hard to get anyone to go there as missionaries."

"We just have to pray that the Lord will touch hearts," Dad said. "The fields are ripe unto harvest, but where are the reapers? I never have understood why the mission board would force retirement on a young fellow like me."

He grinned, and Julia reached out to pat his knee. "You *are* still young, Dad, and I'm glad you're keeping busy with things like that VBS engagement."

At this, Peter let out a sigh. Julia stiffened, aware she wasn't getting anywhere with her assignment. Instead, she'd fallen right back into her old patterns — loving, affirming, doing everything she could to please her parents. And why not? She adored them. She was so proud of their years of hard work.

"Staying active is really important," she began. She wished the rain weren't so loud. It was hard enough to talk about this. "But you know there are times to rest. Times when your family needs you around."

"Yes, honey, how are Jessica and Heather managing while you're away?" Mom asked. "We got that lovely photo of Jessica at her graduation. My stars, how that child has grown!"

"She's so pretty," Dad put in.

"Thank you. The girls are fine." She turned the cup around in her hands. "It was hard to leave them, but I really felt like Debbie needed me."

"It was so good of both you and Peter to come all this way to be with your sister." Mom beamed. "Peter, tell us how our little Angelo is doing. Is he walking yet?"

"Not yet. Well, I don't think so." He tilted his head toward Julia. "But about Debbie."

"Just a minute on Debbie," Mom said. "You don't know whether Angelo's walking or not? How could that be?"

Peter leaned back in his chair and hooked his thumbs in the belt loops of his jeans. Why wasn't Julia telling their parents about Debbie? Why wasn't she confronting them with their part in the illness their sister was suffering? Though the basement room was humid and dank, he could feel his blood beginning to boil. Right now was not the time to talk to his parents about his troubled marriage. But he realized his mother wasn't going to be put off.

"I can tell by that look on your face, Peter," she said. "Something has happened. Oh, dear. Julia, what's going on? If Peter won't talk, you'd better tell us."

"Maria and I are separated," Peter said. "But that's not the point of this conversation."

"Oh yes it is. Peter, Maria is your wife. You *cannot* let us down by failing to honor your marriage vows."

"It's my marriage, Mom. It's my life. I can do what I choose."

"What did I tell you, Don?" Mom shook her head. "I just knew this was going to happen. Peter, didn't your father and I warn you about marrying outside your own culture? It doesn't bother us in the least that Maria is Hispanic. All races are equal in the sight of the Lord. But her culture is so foreign to ours."

"Mom, *everybody's* culture is foreign to ours. I mean, get serious here. Who shares a culture with me? What woman could I ever find who grew up in the middle of the African bush, went to boarding school all her life, and then got catapulted across the Atlantic Ocean to some American college where she didn't know anybody? There's not a single person in this world who shares my culture — except my sisters. And I can't very well marry them, can I?"

"Peter." Breathing hard, Julia swallowed down her dread. "Mom, what Pete is trying to say is that things have been a little difficult for all of us. Us three kids, I mean. But anyway . . . right now . . . well, we need to talk about Debbie's condition, because that's really what's most important. We're very concerned about her. The doctor, Dr. Bryant, has shared some serious things with us in the past few days, and we wanted to tell you about that."

Before anyone could interrupt, Julia launched into a detailed account of the physician's assessment. She explained about Debbie's obsessiveness, her refusal to speak with a counselor, and her unwillingness to admit that she actually was suffering from anorexia.

She had barely started when her father took off his glasses and began cleaning them again — blowing at specks of imaginary dust, adjusting the earpieces,

236

checking the screws, holding them up to the light to make sure the lenses were free of fingerprints. Mom had clamped her mouth shut and was staring blankly at Julia. Finally, she dug around in her purse, found a pair of clippers, and began to trim her fingernails.

"So," Julia said, "we all need to be prepared for a long process here. Debbie's not just going to snap out of this. And Peter and I feel like it would help her a lot if we all supported her through her recovery. I mean, we hope she can recover. We think she'll have a better chance if we give her lots of love and assurance."

"Of course," Mom agreed. "We've always done our best to let you children know how much we care about you. We'll certainly be available for Debbie. But I'm sure she doesn't need a psychiatrist. This seems to be a physical problem, not a mental one. Every time I talk to Debbie, she's perfectly clear in her thinking."

Julia glanced at Peter. He gave her a nod.

"Well, that may be," she said, "but a lot of things have contributed to her condition. Not just physical things. I think Debbie's always felt kind of . . . sort of lost, you know?"

"What do you mean by that?" Mom

folded her clippers and dropped them into her purse. "Lost?"

"Abandoned." Julia said it and then pushed herself up out of her chair. For a moment, she stared out at the rain. "*Abandoned*. It's an awful word, but it's the right word. She felt somehow forsaken by you —"

"By *us?*"

Julia took a few paces and then turned. "Yes, by you. By all of us, in a way. But you know, being abandoned wouldn't be so terrible if she didn't love — truly love and need — the people who keep deserting her."

"I don't know why you're talking like this, Julia. Your father and I never deserted or abandoned our children. We did everything we could for you three. We fed you, we clothed you, we brought you up in a Christian home, we loved you — loved you very much. And we still do!"

"I know that, Mom. And we love you." She walked across the tiny room, wishing she could somehow get out.

"Then I don't see the problem. It's as though you and Peter are accusing us of causing this situation with Debbie."

"I'm saying we're all partly responsible. Peter and I, too."

"Don, do you hear your daughter? And,

Julia, I wish you would keep your voice down. There are lots of people in this hospital. We know so many members of the churches here in Bolivar, and if they heard —"

"But I'm not saying anything bad."

"You said we abandoned Deborah! Didn't she say that, Don?"

"Mom and Dad," Julia implored, "please try to hear me."

"We're listening. Just say it quietly." Mom set her jaw. "But I really think we ought to get back to Deborah's room. We have been down here a long time."

"It might be a good idea to let Julia explain herself a little better, Olive," Dad said. "She and Peter are trying to tell us how they feel."

"Peter, do you have something to say?" Mom asked. "I believe you've put your sister up to this, just the way you always got her involved in your pranks."

"No, Mom," Julia said. "I want to say this." And strangely enough, she did. She'd started this ordeal for Peter's sake, but the more she spoke the truth, the stronger she felt. "I'm trying to tell you that Peter and Debbie and I . . . we love you. We've always loved you." She sat down beside her brother and took his hand. "We've loved you, and we've *needed* you," she said firmly.

"The best way I can explain what I'm trying to say is to tell you about KCA. About what it was like for us there."

"Most of the other missionary kids we know just loved KCA," her mother said. Julia could tell by the shrill tone in her voice that she was feeling a bit defensive. "And as you recall, you had lots of happy times there — all three of you. Julia, you were so popular with all your friends. You were in the National Honor Society, and you were on the student council. Peter had no trouble entertaining himself — getting into all kinds of trouble. And Deborah was the homecoming queen, if you'll remember. She had lots of boyfriends, and she was so pretty during high school. You don't get to be homecoming queen if you're walking around miserable all the time. KCA was a good school, and the three of you were happy there whether you choose to remember it that way or not."

Julia nodded. "We did have some good times at KCA. But you know what? We were kids. We needed more than friends and clubs and school pranks. We needed hugs and kisses. We needed to be tucked into bed at night. We needed someone to talk to and explain the world to us. We needed parents."

"Well." Mom looked into her purse again.

"It's true that you were great parents," Julia went on, speaking in a low voice, "when we had you. We just needed you more often. The hardest times of all were when you took us up to KCA and left us there."

"That was hard for us, too, Julia," Dad said.

"Do you remember the year you took us back to school and Debbie decided to run away? That's sort of how we all felt. Every year."

"Run away?" Mom looked up. "Deborah? I don't remember that, dear. Are you sure? She would have been suspended for something like that, and Deborah was always such a good little girl."

"She was good, but inside she was screaming for help. I didn't realize how much she was struggling all those years. Not until the time she decided to run away from school. It was the beginning of her freshman year in high school . . ."

As Peter, Debbie, and I get ready to go back to boarding school, I feel like a death-row prisoner on the way to execution. Mom and Dad try to make the most of the last few hours we have together. Mom fixes us a fantastic breakfast — usually an omelet with ham and cheese. Then she fills three big bags with gooey homemade cinnamon rolls. Dad helps us carry our black metal trunks out to the Land Rover.

Debbie drives me crazy during the time we pack the car. Instead of helping, she sits on her bed and writes poems. Does she think we're her slaves or something? This is going to be her first year of high school, so she's all moody like it's the biggest tragedy in the world. I'm always as patient as I can be with her, but this time I can't stand it anymore.

"You could help with your own trunk!" I snap at her.

She folds her notebook and slips it down into her trunk. That's when I notice she's been crying. I really do want to comfort her, but we're trying to get on the road.

"It's not that big a deal to go to high school," I tell her. "It's the same old place, the same buildings, the same teachers and kids. You'll just be in a different dorm, that's all."

"Okay," she says, her voice barely above a whisper. She looks as though it's the end of the world. "My stomach hurts."

"Why don't you eat something? You hardly ate a bite at breakfast."

"I'm not hungry."

"You need to eat, Debs. Go get one of Mom's cinnamon rolls."

"I'm too fat anyway."

"You're not fat. Don't be dumb." She really isn't fat, but she is getting very shapely. Even though she's younger, she is a lot more developed than I am. No wonder all the boys at school are after her.

"My uniforms don't fit anymore," she says.

"Our uniforms never fit right in the first place. Come on, Debs."

I manage to get her up off the bed, and we lift her trunk and carry it to the Land Rover. It takes us a while to find Peter, who has gone down to the kraal to spend a few minutes with his friends. His friends have given him something to drink out of a calabash, so when he finally gets into the car, he has that awful smell on his breath. No doubt it was the mixture of cow's blood and milk the Maasai always drink. I don't know why Peter likes that stuff. It's so nasty.

We drive for hours toward Nairobi, and I try to imagine good things that might happen at school. I might get asked to the junior-senior banquet. I might get a boyfriend. I might make straight A's. If nothing else, at least it's my last year at that stupid place.

To keep myself from thinking too much about school, I let my mind wander back to how I spent my school break. Almost every day, I walked over to the kraal to sit with the women who make beautiful beaded necklaces and earrings. They keep their best work and send the rest of it away to a game park hotel to sell to tourists. I'm not as good at understanding the Maasai language as Peter is, but I love to spend time with these ladies and listen to their stories.

My favorite thing of all about vacations is when the British farmer who lives nearby comes over for a visit. After Mr. Wilson talks to our parents for a while, he lets us three Mossman kids pile into the bed of his truck with his big dogs, Hercules and Theseus. We hang on for dear life as he drives all over creation inspecting the fences on his farm and talking to the employees who watch his herds of cattle. We see all kinds of wild animals, get covered with dust, and have a total blast. We love Mr. Wilson. Someday, I hope I can marry someone just like him.

After all my daydreaming in the Land Rover, we finally get to Nairobi and pull into the parking lot of the Intercontinental Hotel. This is our family tradition. We walk inside the air-conditioned lobby and head straight for the dining room. The walls are covered with huge photographs of wildlife — lions roaring, rhinos charging, buffaloes staring malevolently.

Peter calls it "the last supper." We each order our favorite dishes. I have a club sandwich and French fries and a glass of Coke loaded with ice cubes, and these taste better than anything imaginable. Again, Debbie doesn't eat much, so I'm starting to worry about her. Is she sick, or what? She had malaria a few years ago, and it can come back on you sometimes. I wish she would cheer up.

I look around the table. Dad is planning a big pastors' meeting next week. After they leave us at school, he and Mom have to do some major grocery shopping, so she can cook for all the men. They're writing out their supply list and discussing whether they ought to buy a goat to roast. Peter is sticking fries on the tines of his fork, pretending they're fingers, and trying to scare us. No one else seems to notice how crummy Debbie is feeling, so I don't say anything.

After "the last supper," our gloom begins to set in for sure. The Land Rover makes its way along the winding roads that edge the escarpment of the Great Rift Valley. The huge fault in the earth sweeps down into a massive valley dotted with volcanoes and lakes. We make the turn off the main highway onto the school road, and that's when we often run into mud so deep even the Land Rover can barely make it through. Finally, we see the long wooden sign that lets us know we're back at good old Kenya Christian Academy.

Dad pulls the Land Rover up to the boys' dorm and unloads Peter and his trunk. Before we know it, my brother has vanished with a bunch of his friends. I'm pretty sure his bag of cinnamon rolls will be empty before supper. He doesn't even bother to kiss Mom and Dad good-bye.

When Dad parks over by the girls' dorm, I spot one of my roommates. I hop out, and before I can say anything, she tells me she got three letters from her boyfriend over the vacation. I'm so jealous I can hardly stand it. What's wrong with me? Why don't I have a boyfriend? I give her a big hug and tell her how happy I am for her.

Debbie, Dad, and I unload our two trunks and carry them into the dorm. Debbie's roommates are already there, and they've taken the upper bunks. I can tell she's disappointed, but that's how it goes. We walk over to my room, and I pick out a bunk near the window. I visit with my roommates for a couple of minutes, and then I walk down the hall to find my parents again. It's time to say good-bye.

I've decided I'm going to make this last year the best ever. I'm going to wear my new red blazer a lot, because it looks really good on me. It's the one piece of my uniform that those tailors didn't mess up at the shop in Mombasa. I'm going to read the whole Old Testament straight through, and I'm not going to get bogged down in the "begats" the way I usually do. I'm also going to flirt. In the bathroom at home, I practiced a lot, and I think I'm getting the hang of it. Maybe I can get a boyfriend this year.

But as I walk out of the dorm with its gray concrete blocks and barred windows, I start feeling pretty bad. I can see Mom and Dad over at the Land Rover hugging Debbie. I don't want to cry. I'm not going to cry. Haven't I been at this school forever and ever? What's the matter with me?

Mom and Dad give me big hugs and kisses. They say they'll be praying for me. They promise they'll write lots of letters. Then they climb into the Land Rover and shut their doors and drive away.

Debbie and I stand there watching until we can't see the car anymore. We stand until we're sure they are completely, totally gone. We stand until we know, beyond a shadow of a doubt, that they're not coming back. Not today. Not for three months.

Then Debbie gives a shrug and starts walking away from the dorm. "Bye, Jules," she says.

"Where are you going?" I call. "Supper isn't for an hour."

"I'm not going to the cafeteria."

I jog after her. She heads up the sidewalk, past the cafeteria, past the boys' dorm, and makes straight for the forest.

"Hey, Debs," I call. She's moving really fast now. "Stop. What are you doing?"

She keeps walking. I catch up to her and grab her by the arm. She turns around, and I can see she's crying.

"What's the matter, Debbie?" I ask. "It's

going to be all right. You'll like high school. You're going to do great."

She pulls away from me and walks into the forest. The jungle lands that surround KCA are very scary, and I can't believe my chickenhearted sister is going in. For one thing, the forest is off campus, and that means if you get caught, you'll get detention or even be suspended. But it's not just that. We have heard there's a three-legged leopard in there, and it might attack you if you wander away from the school. There are bush babies that sound like lost children when they cry at night. And there are Mau Maus.

KCA is smack-dab in the middle of what used to be Mau Mau territory. Every night in the old days, the faculty in the houses and dorms rang bells to let each other know they hadn't been slaughtered in their beds. The Mau Maus made people swear horrible oaths, and they killed Christians and white immigrants. They killed Africans, too, the ones who refused to participate in the tribal oathing. One time Peter was hunting off campus, and he saw a dead body lying near the railroad tracks. The man's eyeballs had been gouged out and his lips cut off. Peter didn't recognize the man at first, but later he realized it had been one of the African cooks who worked for Cookie in the cafeteria.

"Where are you going?" I yell to Debbie. "You can't leave campus!"

"Leave me alone. I'm going to the railroad tracks."

"The railroad tracks!" This is about as bad as anything you can do at KCA. I glance left and right to make sure no one is looking, and then I plunge into the forest after Debbie. I have never been in trouble at school, and I hope I never am. But this is my sister, and I can't leave her alone. She's trudging through long tangled vines, slipping in the mud, and not caring at all that her blue jeans won't get washed until the next laundry day.

"Debbie!" I call as loudly as I dare. "Please stop, Debbie."

She keeps plodding along. Finally I catch up with her, and I work my way through the tangle, trying to catch my breath. What is she thinking? Is she crazy? Peter is the Mossman kid who's always bad. Not Debbie and me. Why would she want to go to the railroad tracks?

Scared half out of my wits, I walk beside my sister up the steep hill. I'm trying not to fall down, and I'm scanning the trees for a three-legged leopard. Or a four-legged one. Debbie has stopped crying. As she marches forward, her face looks like it's carved out of wood.

"You're going to get lost," I warn her. "We'll both be lost."

"I didn't ask you to come."

"You're my sister."

"I don't care. I don't need you."

"Yes, you do. You always get lost. If you get lost out here, something will eat you."

"I hope the three-legged leopard gets me."

"Debs!" Now I'm really worried. I consider running back to the school and telling one of the teachers. I also consider picking up a rock and knocking my sister out. But I couldn't drag her back through all that jungle. And if I leave her for even a minute, she'll get lost. I'm totally sure of that.

Just when the sun starts to sink, and it's probably dinnertime, we emerge into a clearing near the top of the ridge. Straight ahead lie the railroad tracks. We stare at them. Debbie walks over and sits down right on a rail. I say my fifteen-thousandth prayer of this crazy adventure and sit down beside her.

"What are you going to do now?" I ask.

"I'm going to walk down the tracks to a station," she says. "Dad gave me some spending money. I'm going to buy a ticket and get on the train and go home."

I look at her for a long time. I know we are both thinking the same thing. This is a really good idea. A wonderful idea. There's only one problem with it. We'll get in huge trouble, and then Mom and Dad will just bring us right back to school.

"I'll go with you," I tell her.

"No," she says. "You can't. This is my journey."

"You're my sister. We're almost the same. I'm not going to leave you up here."

"I'll be fine. I'll walk down the tracks."

"Something will attack you."

She looks at me. "Don't you see, Julia?" Her voice is low and her eyes are dark blue. "I don't care. I don't care what happens to me. I don't care if the train runs right over me."

"Debbie!" I take her hand and hold it really tightly. "Please don't say stuff like that."

The moment I stop talking, we hear the train coming. The rail starts to shiver under us. Then the tracks begin to hum. And finally, in the distance, we can hear the train whistle blow.

At that very instant, just when I think Debbie is going to throw herself onto the tracks, Peter and two of his friends step out of the forest. I didn't think anything could really surprise Peter. But he is so shocked to see us that his mouth drops open.

"What are you doing here?" he exclaims.

"We're waiting for the train," Debbie replies.

"Why?"

We stare at Peter, neither of us saying a word. Now I can see the steam from the old locomotive spilling out over the tops of the trees. I hold Debbie's hand tighter.

Peter looks from me to Debbie and then back at me again. I have the most terrible feeling that he knows what is going on. He has figured it out. Leaving his friends at the edge of the clearing, he trots toward us. As the train chugs around the bend, he puts his arm around Debbie.

"You got any money?" he shouts.

She nods. He holds out his hand. She digs in her pockets and gets the change Dad gave her, the money she was going to use to buy her train ticket. Peter takes it, bends over, and sets three silver shillings on the rail. Then he grabs our hands and pulls us off the tracks, just in time.

The train blasts by us. The whole forest shakes. Steam and cinders float down on top of us. I hold on to Debbie's hand. Peter keeps his arm around her. The cars go by, one after the other, rattling the rails and shaking the ground. It is so loud, the only other thing I am aware of is the throbbing of my heartbeat.

Finally, the last car rumbles past. Peter bends over and picks up the three silver shillings. They're flat and smooth and very warm from the train wheels' running over them. He gives each of us one.

"Well," he says, "that's that."

The sun is setting as we all tromp down through the forest. Peter, Debbie, and I link our arms around each other's shoulders, and he begins an old chant we used to say when we were little kids.

"We walk straight, so you'd better get out of the way," he sings out. Then I join in, and finally Debbie starts chanting, too. We say the words over and over again. As though nothing in this whole world can stand in our path. As though we are invincible.

We make it to the cafeteria just in time for supper. It's cauliflower.

---

chapter eleven

Peter studied his parents, watching for some sign that they understood Julia's words. She had spoken so well, so perfectly. Her voice hadn't held a single note of accusation, but she had told the truth.

As rain lashed the windows, their father sat with his hands folded and his head down. Peter couldn't tell if he was asleep or praying or crying or just wishing he could clean his glasses one more time. Their mother had waited, her face set like a rock, through Julia's reminiscence. Peter knew his mom always hardened her lips when she didn't want anyone to guess how she was feeling. It was an effort to convey lack of emotion, but the Mossman kids recognized it as anger.

So, Mom was mad and Dad was . . . something. He probably wouldn't say a word until he was sure where his wife stood on the issue at hand. Then he'd come in behind her, backing up her every word. One thing you could say for Don and Olive Mossman. They made quite a team.

Peter glanced at Julia sitting beside him. She looked like she'd been put through a wringer. Her face had grown pale and her eyes sunken. Even her hair seemed kind of flat. As though she was wilting.

Peter had urged his sister to tell the truth. *The truth will set you free,* he'd promised her. But nobody in this group looked free. They were mad and sad and scared. They were resentful and confused and upset. But they weren't free.

What had made him think he could rely on a Bible verse? To this point in his life, he'd seen nothing but broken promises out of the Bible. He thought of all the Scriptures he'd been required to learn during religion class at KCA. He could still quote them. Deuteronomy 31:8 said, "Don't be afraid, for the Lord will go before you and will be with you; he will not fail nor forsake you." Yeah, right. If God wasn't forsaking them, then why had he sent Peter and his sisters off to boarding school?

Proverbs 2:7–8 promised, "He grants good sense to the godly — his saints. He is their shield, protecting them and guarding their pathway." Protecting? Guarding? Sure, that's why Debbie was lying in the hospital so sick she couldn't even walk. Peter figured he could go on and on. The whole book was nothing but a bunch of pithy sayings, and he couldn't understand why his parents had devoted their entire lives to pushing it on people.

"I had no idea Deborah would do such a thing as run away." Mom spoke up finally. "She never said a word about being unhappy at KCA."

"No, she never did," Dad agreed. "Not to us."

"We've certainly all had difficult moments in our lives." As Mom spoke, she was double-checking, looking around for her purse, making sure no one had stolen it. A habit. She seemed impervious to the loud booms of thunder, as though not even a bolt of lightning could crack that rock-hard exterior. "Your father and I can tell you it was not easy living in the bush all those years. We rarely had running water and electricity, and our food was always so hard to prepare. I used to just crave fresh meat, you know, but we rarely had any. Plus, the bugs and things kept raiding our supplies of flour and sugar. And what about the people? We never could fully trust anyone out there, not even our neighbors in the kraal. And that's not mentioning the filth and disease we had to face on a daily basis. If anyone would know that life can be quite a struggle, it would be your father and me."

"But that's really not the point," Julia said.

Peter stared at her, amazed at the firmness in her voice.

"The point isn't *you*. It's Debbie." She lifted her chin. "When she was a child, when she was struggling, Debbie needed you. But you — her parents — you weren't there for her. You left her at KCA. You left all of us."

"What other choice did we have?" Mom retorted. "I couldn't home-school you. I wasn't trained for that. I had no skill in that area whatsoever. But more important, the Lord had called me to women's work among the Maasai. And whether you remember it or not, the women were the key to our reaching that tribe. Most of the time — especially in those early years — the men wouldn't even show up at our services. They considered religion a woman's matter. My role in our work was essential."

"That is very true," Dad said. "Your

mother played an important part in everything the Lord led us to do out there."

"I don't want to get into an argument with you about the past," Julia said. "I know what God had called you to do. And I know you suffered in many ways. What I want us to focus on is right now. This time in Debbie's life, this hospital, this disease — it's her boarding school. She needs you now. Don't abandon her. She needs your love."

"We do love Debbie," Mom said. "I would hope she knows that."

"Peter and I need your love, too." Julia's voice was almost a whisper. "We still need your love . . . and sometimes we don't feel it."

Peter felt like cheering. *Way to go, sis!* Julia had really come through. But would their parents get the message?

"There you are!" Ralph stuck his head through the waiting room door. He was dressed in jeans and was carrying a dripping umbrella. "I stopped by to visit Miss Deborah, and I noticed she wasn't responding real well. I got one of the nurses on duty to come over and check on her, and it turns out her fever's spiking again. We've called Dr. Bryant. He's on his way over. I thought you ought to know."

"What's wrong with her?" Mom pushed out of her chair. "Why does she have a fever? And who are you?"

"We're not sure why she has a fever, ma'am." Ralph nodded politely. "I'm one of the nurses who has been caring for your daughter. I'm off tonight, but I promised her I would try to stop by and see how she was doing. I don't know if you were aware that she'd had trouble before, and the doctor put her on an IV antibiotic. It should have worked, and we thought it did. But it looks like the trouble's back."

By now, everyone in the room was standing. Julia had started crying, the whole episode clearly too much for her. Peter put his arm around his sister and gave her a hug. Their father stood awkwardly, looking from his wife to his children.

"Well," Mom said, "what are we standing around here for? Let's get up to her room."

As they followed Ralph's damp, squeaking tennis shoes through the maze of hallways toward the elevator, Peter felt Julia give a deep, shuddering sigh. He squeezed her shoulder again. "Hey, Jules, it's going to be okay," he whispered. "You did good with Mom and Dad."

"No, no, I shouldn't have said anything." She pressed a tissue to her cheek. "Now I've just made them angry and hurt their feelings — and it won't do Debbie any good. Peter, I'm so scared for her!"

"Don't panic. This is America. They've got all kinds of medicine here." For some reason, he reached back for one of those useless promises to hand his sister. "Remember that verse we learned when we were kids? Proverbs 2:7 and 8 says, 'He grants good sense to the godly — his saints. He is their shield, protecting them and guarding their pathway.' Debbie's pretty godly. God is going to protect her."

"Oh, Peter, don't be dumb. That verse isn't talking about protection from sickness and death. Satan is the ruler of this earth, and people are going to have all kinds of trouble."

"Well, what does it mean then?"

"It's talking about how God is just. He's not going to let anyone pluck a Christian out of his hands. That verse means a believer's salvation is secure, and God is protecting us from Satan's power."

"Are you sure? I thought it meant he would protect us . . . like from sickness and stuff."

"Peter, how could you have sat through

as many sermons as I did and still believe God is going to protect you from every bad thing? Bad stuff happens to Christians all the time. That's why he tells us to run to the Rock of our salvation. He tells us to hide in his name. God is here for us right now, Peter. He's going to protect us from Satan's attempts to own our souls. But he's not promising to always keep harmful things from happening to us."

"Well, why not?"

She stared at him as if he were the densest human being on the face of the earth. "Because that's how we grow. Pain is part of it. You won't protect Angelo from everything bad that comes along, or he'll become a complete wimp. He won't be worth anything as an adult. You'll let him have bumps and scrapes; you'll make him go to school and learn; you'll give him consequences when he does wrong. None of that will be fun for him. Or for you. But you'll do it because you love him. Don't you get it?"

Peter tried to process what she was telling him. If only he could go somewhere and sort it all out. Maybe to the NFD. Then the realization hit him for the millionth time in the past twenty years. Never again would he see a Kenyan sunrise through a tent flap in the Northern Frontier District. As he followed his sister into Debbie's room, he felt an unexpected craving inside. *Make it make sense for me, Julia,* he wanted to cry out. *I have all the verses and all the sermons inside me. But I don't get it. I'm like Angelo when Maria tells him not to throw food off his high chair. He knows. He's been told a hundred times. But he doesn't want to hear it. He still throws the food right onto the floor again and again.*

The only solution Peter and Maria had figured out was to smack his little hand. Peter had hated that! Punishing his son was the last thing he wanted to do. But how was Angelo ever going to learn unless doing wrong brought on something bad?

Something bad. Was that what it would take to make Peter learn? Something really, really terrible?

"She's not here," Mom said, swinging around to face Ralph. "Where's my daughter?"

"I'll check at the nurses' station."

He was gone for only a moment, long enough for Peter to walk to the rain-streaked window and stare out at the bench where he had sat with Debbie and Julia just that morning. Was the loss of his little sister going to be his punishment? His wake-up call? Was God saying, as Julia had said, "Oh, Peter, don't be dumb"? Had he been so dumb, so stupid, that God needed to slap him to get him on track?

"She's been taken down to the surgery department," Ralph said, slipping back into the room. "Dr. Bryant's going to insert a jugular central line for delivering IV fluids. It won't take too long."

"A jugular line?" Mom took Dad's hand.

"That sounds pretty serious," Dad said. "Is it going to help her to get enough nourishment?"

"That is one thing the central line can be used for," Ralph said. "I hope you folks don't mind, but I'm going to head over to the OR and find out how it's going. You're welcome to wait in here, or there's a visitors' room down there."

Dad squared his shoulders. "We'll wait here. We need some privacy so we can pray about this. Would you tell Deborah we're praying? I mean, tell her if she's awake?"

"I'll be glad to." Ralph vanished, and the rest of them sat down.

Julia let out a shaky breath. She felt as though she were in the midst of a huge inner storm, just like the one booming and crackling outside Debbie's window. Confusion, fear, and regret swirled through her.

She looked at her parents and a wave of guilt swept over her. Had she hurt them with her words? She hadn't meant to! She loved her parents, loved them so very much. Her brother had said — and it had seemed to make sense — that she ought to confront them. But now she felt like Judas Iscariot. Or the apostle Peter when he denied knowing Christ. Oh, why had she said anything?

And now, right in the midst of the turmoil she had caused, Debbie had been whisked off to surgery. A thousand things she needed to say to her sister rushed through Julia's thoughts. Had she hugged Debbie enough? Had she been too judgmental about the anorexia? What about Debbie's choice of a boyfriend? Julia and Peter had dismissed him in favor of Ralph, who hardly knew their sister. Dave Hornburg was busy, but did that make him the wrong man for Debbie? He had been her loyal friend for years.

Oh, why hadn't she just sat quietly and let Peter step out on the limb? But maybe Peter shouldn't have been allowed to say anything either. After all, life was so short, so fragile. What was the point in dredging up the pain the Mossman children had felt? It was over anyway. Confronting their parents with it, especially when they were old and tired from their years of labor for the Lord, would do no good at all.

For some reason, all she could think about was the fun they used to have at home in Africa. They had pretty lace curtains in the windows, and on cool days Dad would build a fire in the fireplace. Whenever he turned on the diesel generator, they would have electricity for a few hours. That was when Julia liked to listen to music or sew. Usually, she tried to help Mom with the cooking, too, because it wasn't easy making meals with a gas refrigerator that didn't always work, a rickety old stove, and safari ants in the storage room. Julia loved it when giraffes passed by their house. Once a family of cheetahs came and took a nap in the front yard.

Julia tried to concentrate as her father led the family in prayer for Debbie. Filling the small room, his voice was a warm and familiar sound, a comforting sound. Every morning that Julia could recall, he had prayed for his children in this way, calling on the Lord for strength, wisdom, courage. He loved his son and daughters; there could be no doubt about that.

"Amen," he said, lifting his head at the conclusion of his prayer. "Let's not forget that God is watching over Deborah right now. His loving hand is on her. We can take comfort in that."

"Yes," Mom agreed.

There was a long silence in the room, and Julia fought the urge to apologize to her parents for recounting the story of Debbie's attempt to run away from school. It was a true story, something they needed to know perhaps. But what good would it do if Debbie got worse? What if they lost Debbie? The thought was too terrible. Julia dug in her pocket for the damp tissues she'd been using off and on all day.

"Debbie might die," Peter said suddenly. "She might."

"Peter!" Mom shot him a warning look. "Don't say such things."

"Why not? We need to look this thing in the eye. Debbie might die, and we have to face that."

"I'm not going to face any such thing. My daughter is not going to die."

"How do you know?"

"Well . . ." She sat without speaking, clearly struggling. "Well, I just don't think it's appropriate to even discuss it as a possibility. We need to trust in the Lord and keep our hearts filled with hope. Deborah is a strong young woman, and she has always had every reason to live." She glanced across at Julia. "Despite what you said downstairs, young lady."

"What Julia told you was true," Peter protested. "Debbie did feel desperate at KCA, Mom. I know she did. She used to give me poems she had written. They were filled with despair."

"All teenagers write moody poetry, Peter," his mom countered. "Feeling blue, thinking of running away — these are all common experiences during adolescence. And as for you and Julia thinking KCA was such a horrible place, well, let me remind you that you got a very good education there. You made lifelong friends, and you had some wonderful experiences. We loved you children. We still do. We would never have done anything to hurt you."

"Your mother is exactly right," Dad said. "We sent you to KCA because we felt it was the best opportunity for you to get a good education and build some strong friendships. If you'd stayed out in the bush with us the whole time, you wouldn't have had any idea how to function in the real world."

"The *real world?*" Peter exploded. "KCA was so far from the real world it might as well have been on the moon!"

His father held up a hand. "I'll admit, KCA was far from being a typical American school. But you did study the same subjects as American children, and you were with peers of your own faith and culture. Your mother and I felt that was very important. We wanted you to have as normal an upbringing as possible to prepare you for life in the States — and you wouldn't have gotten that in Maasailand."

"You would have been wild little things," Mom added. "Peter, you were practically an African anyway, running around with your spear and your toga and your sandals made out of old rubber tires. You don't have any idea the fear I lived with when you went off with your Maasai friends."

"The point I think we're trying to make here is that we did the best we could for you." Dad took off his glasses and blew on the lenses. "We followed our call to Africa to serve the Lord, and of course, we wanted children as a part of our family. That meant you needed schooling. In the early days of missions — when China and India were the frontiers — missionaries had to send their children back to America or England when they reached school age. We certainly didn't want to do that. We wanted you with us as often as possible."

"You followed your call," Peter echoed. "I think I started hearing that the day you left us in the Happy Room. All my life, people have been using it as an excuse. Was there really any such thing as a call?"

"God speaks to his people, Peter," Dad said in a low voice. "When I was a boy out fishing with my grandpa one day on the Osage River, I heard the voice of the Lord. Now, it wasn't a real sound — at least I don't think it was. But it seemed very real to me. You see, a missionary had visited our church, and he'd been talking about his work, about the great need for the unreached people of the world to learn about the love and forgiveness of Jesus Christ. And right there, on the banks of the Osage River when I was eleven years old, I felt God's presence telling me to go to Africa. He needed me there as his servant. I knew it! I still hear that voice speaking to me, calling me. It's a powerful thing, one that cannot be denied."

"I'm sure we've told you children this before," Mom said. "I was thirteen. I had not been brought up in a Christian home as your father was, but my older sister started going to a little country church there in Kentucky, and she took me along.

The things I heard there were so amazing! I can still remember how it felt to sit in that one-room church and hear about the love of God. And then I'd go home and . . . well, things were just . . . my daddy used to drink a little, you know. He would take a hickory switch to us kids. Not that we didn't deserve it, of course. I'm sure we did. But he was very strict. And it was such a contrast to what I'd been hearing in church. I wanted my daddy to know the Lord so bad! But he never would go with us."

She folded her hands together and sighed. "Anyhow, I was spending the night with a friend, Betty June, and she and I were reading the Bible together in bed. And that's when I heard the voice of the Lord, right there in that little old Kentucky clapboard house. 'Go to Africa,' is what he said. Scared me half to death, if you want to know the truth. I told my friend, I said, 'Betty June, God just called me to be a missionary in Africa.' So, we got down on our knees right there by the bed, and Betty June prayed for a good husband for me, and healthy children, and a long life serving the Lord in Africa. From that moment, I have not wavered. I know I was called out. I was chosen. I have been obedient, and the Lord has honored Betty June's prayer for my life."

Peter stared at his parents; then he looked at Julia to see if she was buying it. She swallowed. "Peter, God does speak to believers. He promised he would send his Holy Spirit to live in us, and sometimes the presence of the Lord does move in our hearts. There's a sense in which he really does speak. And if you're listening, you can hear him."

"Well, I've never heard him, and I hope I never do." Peter folded his arms across his chest and looked out the window. That was a lie, of course. He wished he could hear God. He wished he could understand his parents and Julia. But what could they possibly mean? It was ridiculous!

"You know, you've got the most fool-proof argument in the world," he told his mother. "How can any kid disagree with that? It's completely perfect for you. Anything you want to do, you just say, 'God told us to do this.' And if I don't like it, well, that's just too bad. It shifts the responsibility from you to God, and it puts me up against him."

"You shouldn't feel you have to be *against* anyone, Peter," Dad said. "What do you mean by that?"

"I mean there were plenty of things I didn't like about my childhood. I didn't like being carted all over creation for four-hour church services. I didn't like being forced to eat goat stew and drink warm Cokes because the pastor and the whole congregation was standing around the table watching me."

"They had walked miles to the nearest shop to get those Cokes for us!" Mom reminded him.

"I know. And I felt guilty for not wanting to drink them. Guilty, guilty, guilty. Julia, Debbie, and I always had to do everything you asked. Why? Because you said it was *God's will*. What chance did we have to express any real feelings? Did you know they took attendance at church at KCA? You couldn't skip or you'd be sent to detention. Everything I hated about my life was forced down my throat because *God* supposedly wanted it that way. And there wasn't a thing I could do about it."

"Well, the way I remember it, you certainly did express your feelings, Peter Mossman." Mom pursed her lips. "In fact, I had to wash your mouth out with soap several times for the awful things you said. We did all we could for you children, bringing you up with a comfortable home, a strong faith life, two loving parents, plenty to eat and drink, and clothes to wear. And what did we get for it? Especially from you, Peter? Ungratefulness."

"I'm sorry, Mom," Julia said, dabbing her cheek with the tissue, "but I felt some of those things, too. The feelings Peter was talking about. I just never said anything."

"Oh?"

"You had a kind of stranglehold on us with those two words: *God's will.* I realize God has a plan and a will for each of us. But when parents constantly put that on their children, they can't breathe. They can't feel anything negative, for fear they'll be disappointing God. Do you get what we're saying?"

"No, I do not." Mom checked for her purse again, making sure it was still there. "All I know is that your father and I went to Africa because we were called by the Lord. And I will never apologize for that."

Julia grabbed another tissue from the box beside Debbie's bed. She wished she could stop crying. Her tears had always been close to the surface, but it seemed that since she'd been pregnant, all she could do was weep. Why wouldn't her mother try to understand? Why couldn't her father see what she and Peter were trying to say?

"You know what this reminds me of, Don?" Mom asked. "It reminds me of that Christmas when Peter wanted the BB gun. Do you remember that?"

"Yes, Olive, but I'm not sure this is a good time to bring it up."

"I remember that Christmas," Peter said. "What does it have to do with this discussion?"

"It was the perfect example of your lack of understanding. You had no idea how much we loved you. All you could think about was that BB gun you wanted for Christmas . . ."

olive • africa • 1975

I would never admit this to the children, but I always dread Christmas. Here I am, out in the middle of Africa, trying to bake something that will taste like a pumpkin pie. It's nearly a hundred degrees inside the house, the candles on the mantel are melting, and it's Christmas Eve. But I will do my best.

Earlier in the afternoon, I sifted the flour

to clean out stones and weevils, combed through the sugar for ants, and measured out the very last grains of the ground nutmeg I carried here in my suitcase from furlough so many years ago. The pie isn't going to taste anything like pumpkin, because I'm actually using the pulp of some kind of a gourd that grows out here in the bush. Don found it at a roadside market on one of his preaching trips, and it was sort of orange in color. So he brought it home to me, in the hope that I could turn it into pumpkin pie.

The girls love to help me with the pie-crust. I'm so happy to have them home from boarding school for the holidays. I give each of them a little ball of dough, and they sit at our dining-room table shaping it into something special for me to bake. Julia is eleven and Deborah is eight, and they truly do look like little angels with their long gold curls and dimpled cheeks. They are so excited about opening their presents in the morning.

I've been working very hard on their Christmas gifts this year. Each July we try to order a few things from the Sears catalog, but no matter how early we place our order, we rarely get our box in time for the holiday. It's too expensive to airmail, so it has to come by boat across the Atlantic, across the Mediterranean Sea, through the Suez Canal, and down the east coast of Africa to Kenya. And when it finally does arrive at the post office in Nairobi, it has usually been opened by the customs officials who help themselves to almost everything. It's hardly worth mailing the order.

So, this year we didn't. I wrote to the children at school, as I faithfully do once a week, and I asked them what they wanted for Christmas. Julia wants clothes for Baby, the plastic doll someone gave her on the boat to Africa on our very first trip. Every time I can talk Don into turning on the generator, I start up my sewing machine. I've made a little nightgown, a party dress, and a pretty skirt for the doll. I think Julia's going to be so pleased. She's such a dear child, so gentle and loving. We rarely have a moment's trouble out of her.

Deborah asked for a rocking chair. She said she'd like to be able to sit with me and rock in it each evening. I think that's just the sweetest thing, though unfortunately it's not a very practical idea. Our house is too small for even one extra tiny piece of furniture, let alone a rocking chair that two people could sit in. Besides, Deborah is away at school so much, she'd hardly get to use it. So, I've made her a beautiful new dress. It's a pale blue cotton with a full skirt that will really stand out when she puts on her net petticoat. The sleeves are puffy, too, and I stitched white lace around the neck. I made a very deep hem, so I can let the skirt down as Deborah grows. She'll be able to wear it for years, and she's going to look adorable in it. Deborah is a lovely child, and I'm confident she'll eventually lose her baby fat and turn into a stunning young woman.

As I stir nutmeg into the squash, I study my little girls. They are growing up well in spite of this unusual life we've handed them. They're intelligent and kind and loving. I want them to adjust to life in America when they're older, so I'm doing all I can to give them a normal upbringing.

It's true we live in a house built of corrugated tin. The wood floor has been eaten through by termites so many times that we might as well live on dirt the way the Africans do. But I won't hear of it. Each time someone falls through the floor, I ask Don to go get some more wood and rebuild it. Then I lay my pretty area rugs right back down as though nothing ever happened. I've painted our walls a very nice white, which is about the only color we can get, and I keep them spotless. This is hard, because there are usually various lizards tracking across them day and night. They live behind our picture frames or up in the ceiling, along with the bats.

The bats plague me, I won't deny it. They hide in the rafters, crunch on beetles, and drop their shells on the floor at night when we're trying to sleep. Also, they leave piles of guano, which I have to clean up every morning. Don says it's a blessing from the Lord, because we can use the guano as fertilizer for our little garden, but I'm not sure I agree with him.

I insisted we have iron bars installed on the windows and a sturdy metal roof. This means if there's ever a fire inside, we're doomed. But it also means no one is likely to break in while we're at home, and I take comfort in that. I've hung lace curtains on the windows, and I made lovely pillows for our small sofa. We have a clean cloth on our dining table at every meal, and even though the termites have gnawed down the legs of the table, it's still quite a good piece of furniture.

Here comes Peter in from the kraal, where he's been playing with his friends. He is getting to be such a wild boy. I really worry about him. Years ago, he made friends with some of the youngsters from the kraal, and we were very happy about that. But as he gets older, he wants to spend all his time with them, and you know, the Maasai are not exactly the best role models for a young man. The warriors are downright promiscuous, and we won't be having our son behave that way. So, Don and I spend a lot of time talking about what we'll do as Peter grows. He's such a handful already.

Peter asked for a BB gun for Christmas. He had seen one in the Sears catalog, and he thought it was just the greatest thing. We tried to explain that gun ownership is severely restricted here in Kenya, but he won't listen. All he can talk about is that BB gun. He even prays about it during family devotions at night, as though God is somehow going to drop it right out of the sky.

When we were in Nairobi to shop for groceries a couple of months ago, Don tried to find a BB gun for sale, but there was nothing like that available. He also spoke to the police chief, who told him it was out of the question for a ten-year-old boy to own a weapon of any sort. Then Don remembered his favorite pastime as a child.

His grandfather had carved a plank of hard old pine into the shape of a pistol and attached a sturdy clothespin to the top of it. With a big supply of rubber bands, Don and his friends used to play along the banks of the Osage River, hiding behind trees and pretending to be cowboys and Indians. He recalls those times as some of the most enjoyable hours of his childhood.

So, he has carved a rubber-band gun for Peter. It's shaped like a rifle, so our son will feel like a real hunter. In Nairobi, we bought a whole packet of rubber bands. I've wrapped the gun and the rubber bands in a long box and put it under the little aluminum tree we brought from America years ago. Every time Peter looks at the box, he gets so excited. I can hardly wait to watch his face when he sees that fine gun his father has carved for him.

We eat a light supper of peanut butter sandwiches, because I'm preparing a big Christmas lunch for tomorrow. Don killed one of our chickens, and our houseboy plucked it. To tell the truth, it's a scrawny old thing. Safari ants got into the batch of chicks we bought in Nairobi and killed every one of them, so all we have left are a few ancient hens. Still, I'm going to bake that chicken as though it were the plumpest turkey ever. I've disinfected the salad greens and made up some dressing, so we're all set.

As I tuck the children into their beds, I praise the Lord for his many gracious gifts. These precious little ones are such a joy to me! I delight in them when they're home, and I miss them when they're away at school. When they do get to come home, I try to make everything peaceful and perfect for them. We all do our best not to argue or have any unpleasant moments. I think Don and I are bringing them up very well, with God's grace.

Once I fall asleep, I'm able to rest peacefully. I've been quite concerned because a missionary family not too far from here recently was attacked one night. They were all able to scramble down into a crawl space under their floor, and the attackers couldn't find them. The house was ransacked, but the missionaries escaped with their lives. Families in our mission have been shot, drugged, held up, mugged, and all sorts of things. I try my best not to think about it, and Don and I never discuss such troubles in front of the children. The Lord is watching over us.

Christmas Day dawns with the crowing of our rooster. It is barely daylight when the children jump out of bed and race into the living room. Don gathers us all around the tree and thanks God for the miracle of Christmas and the blessed gift of his Son. We light the candles on our mantel, read the Christmas story from the book of Luke, and sing a few carols. By this time, Peter is beside himself with anticipation, so we start to open presents.

Julia squeals with delight over the new doll clothes. Deborah gasps at the pretty blue dress. She never mentions a thing about the rocking chair, so I'm sure she must have forgotten it. She holds the dress up to her shoulders and dances around the room. Then everyone leans in close as Peter begins to unwrap his box. I glance at Don, and he gives me a wink.

"What's this?" Peter cries out, grabbing the gun from the box and thrusting it toward us. "This isn't a BB gun! Where's my BB gun?"

"We weren't able to get a BB gun, Peter," Don tries to explain.

"Your father made that for you," I say. "He worked very hard to carve it and —"

"These are rubber bands!" Peter shouts, jumping to his feet. "These won't kill anything! This gun is fake!"

I can hardly believe my eyes. My son

has turned bright red, tears are streaming down his cheeks, and he's jumping up and down in rage. "It's to play with, Peter," I say. "Daddy made that —"

"I don't want it! I want a real gun. I need a real gun."

"You do not need a real gun," I say.

"Yes, I do! I do!"

He runs out of the house in his bare feet. Julia bursts into tears. Deborah crawls into a corner of the couch and rocks back and forth.

"Don," I say, reaching out to my husband, "he doesn't really mean it."

Don stares at me. "I don't know my own children," he says in a low voice. "I don't know who they are."

This is nonsense, of course, and I find I am very upset with everyone, though I would never want to show it. How can Christmas have turned out as badly as this? I wish Peter weren't such a disrupting factor in our family. Why is he this way? What's wrong with him? The only thing I can think to do is get on with the day. I tell Don to start up the generator so we can play some Christmas music. Then I hurry into the kitchen, light the oven, and set to work making breakfast. We're having cinnamon rolls.

As I'm cutting the dough, I look out the kitchen window. That's when I notice a thin spiral of smoke near the incinerator, where we burn our trash. Peter has built a fire. Oh no. My heart sinks as I watch him snap the rubber-band gun in half with his knee. Then he feeds both pieces of it to the fire.

When he comes in for Christmas brunch, no one mentions the BB gun. I can tell Don is deeply hurt, but I decide it's best if we just try to put the whole thing out of our minds. The pumpkin pie tastes very good, if I do say so myself, and by the end of the day, the kids are swinging on the tire swing near the stream — playing with their old toys the way children always do.

A week later, Peter shows up at our house with a Maasai spear. I nearly have a heart attack. He says his friends in the kraal had it made for him, and they're teaching him to throw it. He won't hear of leaving it outside. That spear goes with him everywhere. He lays it on the floor by his bed at night.

It's not long before the children are ready to return to school. Don and I insist that Peter leave his spear at home. As they load the Land Rover with their trunks, I walk into their room to make sure they haven't left anything they might need. Julia has dressed Baby in one of her own old nighties and placed her on the pillow. Peter's spear is propped up in a corner of the room. That's when I notice that Deborah has forgotten to pack her blue dress! I grab it out of the closet and race outside with it, just in time to stuff it into her trunk.

Oh, these children, I think to myself as we drive away from the house. *We do all we can for them. But sometimes I wonder if they even notice.*

chapter twelve

"You say you needed us, and we weren't there for you?" Mom's eyes searched the faces in the small hospital room. "The only choices we had were to teach you ourselves by correspondence course, send you to boarding school, or leave Africa."

"Considering how isolated we were out in Maasailand," Dad added softly, "we felt home-schooling would be detrimental to your social growth."

"And as far as your father and I were concerned," Mom said, "leaving Africa was never really an option."

"Why not?" Julia asked. She'd always wondered why her parents hadn't considered returning to the States so they wouldn't have to send their kids away to boarding school.

Her mother stared at her. "Julia? You know we were called by God to work with the Maasai. You said so yourself."

"But other missionary families left Kenya when their kids got old enough to go to school."

"Yes, and we always felt it was such a shame. Every time a missionary couple resigned because their children couldn't handle boarding school, it was a setback to the kingdom's work."

Dad nodded slowly. "We were proud of you children for the way you seemed to take it all in stride."

Mom chimed in again. "We did all we could to give you a wonderful upbringing. We provided for your physical needs, and we worked very hard to make sure you had some of the luxuries children in America would have. You know we never had much money, but we rationed and saved to see that you had toys, special vacations to the beach, and good clothes. Most important, we tried very hard to bring you up with a love for the Lord. Now it seems that all we did was received with ingratitude, just like the rubber-band gun."

Julia studied Peter. She expected to find his anger boiling. Instead, he was sitting in silence, staring out the window and watching the rain puddle on the sidewalk. Had he known how much his act of rage had hurt his parents? Could he see the sting his rebellion and defiance had inflicted? She wondered if her brother realized how his rejection of Christianity still wounded his parents to the very core. They had given their lives to win souls for Christ, and they'd lost their own son in the process.

"I wanted the BB gun," Peter said in a low voice, his eyes now trained on his mother, "because of the time I heard you crying."

"Crying?"

"One night you were talking to Dad, and I could hear you through the wall. You said you felt like you never had enough meat to feed the family. Safari ants had gotten the baby chicks, and the gas freezer was too small to hold two weeks' worth of beef. You told Dad you didn't trust the pork or the fish in Nairobi to be fresh, and you were so tired of goat you could scream. Those chicks had been your only hope, and now all you had were a few tough old hens to feed us. And that's when you started to cry."

"I don't remember crying."

"I remember it. I had never heard you cry before. But that night I heard you, and I made up my mind that I was going to help you. I knew my friends in the kraal were training to become warriors, and I'd gone out into the bush to watch them practice their skills. There were so many animals roaming around — Thomson's gazelles, impalas, and game birds by the hundreds. I figured if I had a gun, I could bring you fresh meat every day, and you'd feel better."

"Peter, I had no idea."

"I searched through the Sears catalog and found that BB gun. I imagined myself as the hero of our family, coming in from the bush with a string of guinea fowl or a gazelle over my shoulder. But on Christmas morning when I opened the box and saw that rubber-band gun, I felt like my dream had been punctured."

Julia could hardly believe her brother was being so open with their parents. And even more amazing, the elder Mossmans seemed to be truly listening to their son — maybe for the first time.

Peter bent his head. "I told my friends at the kraal what had happened, and they somehow finagled with the elders to get me a spear. It wasn't a very big one, but it was just the right size for what I needed. I had a bow and a few arrows, too. I always left those with Saitoti in the kraal, because I was afraid you'd take them away from me. And after that, I started to do what I'd planned. I brought you fresh meat."

"And I did appreciate your efforts," Mom said.

"But you were always upset with me for having the spear."

"Well, it was a dangerous weapon! A Maasai spear, for heaven's sake, and you took it everywhere."

"I wanted to protect our family." Peter glanced at his father. "I knew about the attacks, the robberies, the muggings. You and Mom tried not to say much, but we could hear right through those thin walls. We knew everything — all the bloody details. And I knew our house wasn't secure. Someone broke into it every time we went on vacation. I figured if anyone tried to hurt our family, they'd have to deal with my spear. And that's why I never objected to leaving it at home when I went to school. I thought if there was any danger you could use it to defend yourselves."

"And we did, too. Don, remember the time that snake got into the house? It was a python, and you killed it with Peter's spear."

"Worse than a python, Olive. It was a puff adder."

"Oh, that's right." She gave a little

shudder. "The snakes were a drawback of that little house of ours. There was the time that boomslang came up through the drain and just lay there in the bathtub like he owned it."

"What about the time the bat-eared fox got into the henhouse?" Julia remembered. "Didn't Dad use Peter's spear?"

"I sure did." Don leaned back in his chair. "Threw it at him. Missed him by a mile, but it did scare him off."

"See?" Peter said. "I needed a weapon so I could give you fresh meat. But I wanted to protect our family, too."

"Well," Olive said. She fiddled with her purse for a moment, checking on the strap. "Well, Peter, I had no idea you wanted that BB gun so you could provide us with fresh meat. Did you, Don?"

"No. And I never realized you were so worried about our safety." He looked across at Julia. "Did you children have a lot of fears during our years in Africa?"

She shrugged. "It felt like things were always on the verge of coming apart. Like one little misstep could unravel our whole lives."

"How melodramatic," Mom said. "Really, Julia. Things weren't anywhere near that bad."

"Still," Peter insisted, "I was sure glad I

had that spear. I think everybody was glad I had it the time the Land Rover fell into the antbear hole."

Oh my. What a frightening day that had been! Julia was sure her parents would remember that. How could anyone have forgotten?

We're on our way to church. I hate church. Julia and Debbie don't seem to mind, but I can't stand it. We have to leave at the crack of dawn, and then we drive a million miles out into the middle of nowhere. Usually Dad maneuvers the Land Rover down a dry streambed, and so we run into plenty of rocks and holes and dust. The streambeds are the only roads out to some of the kraals where he's been setting up preaching posts, and since it rarely rains in Maasailand, at least we don't have to worry about getting stuck in the mud.

I'm sandwiched between my two sisters, who have decided to play with their dolls on my lap, which makes me mad. Why can't one of them take the middle seat? But no, they won't hear of it. It's my turn to be in the middle, so they're using me as their playground. Their game is all about brides and grooms, stupid junk like that.

My thoughts are on the hunt I know is taking place without me. My Maasai friends are all practicing for *emorata,* circumcision. They can't believe I got circumcised as a baby, and I'm not going to have a ceremony or get cows to start my herd, or anything. Sometimes I wish I had been born a Maasai.

It seems like my friends and I spend most of our time practicing. We pretend to be warriors, and we throw our spears again and again until we can hit our targets nearly every time. We pretend to be elders sitting around making important decisions for the clan. We play out all the rites of life that lie ahead. But for me, nothing lies ahead except more boarding school and then college. As near as I can figure, there aren't any ceremonies for Americans but marriages and funerals. In Maasai life, every little thing is done by ritual and ceremony. Each person knows who he is, and how he fits into the tribe, and what his future is going to be. I envy my friends.

Preparation for *emorata* is going to take a lot of work. The circumcision won't actually happen for a few years yet — not until they're about eighteen and have proven their worth as young men ready to become warriors. First of all, my friends will have to collect honey to be made into beer for their special guests at the ceremony. We practice this ahead of time by learning how to follow the little honey-guide birds, who lead us to fresh hives. We climb cliffs, carrying smoldering torches to smoke away the bees and toting bags to put the honey in. The wax from the honeycombs will be applied to the tips of brand-new arrows, which my friends get to carry with them everywhere. They'll put wax on the tips so they can shoot the girls they like. If they hit a girl with one of the blunt arrows, she'll give them a beaded finger ring. It's going to be a lot of fun, even for the girls.

Once the honey has been gathered, the boys will have to collect ostrich feathers. After circumcision, the feathers will be used to create their headdresses. So today while I'm sitting in church for too many hours to count, my friends are going to be out on the plains looking for ostriches. They want to get in some practice, because killing an ostrich is a tough business. Ostriches are hard to spear in spite of their size, because they're covered with layers of stiff feathers. And ostriches are mean, especially when they're mating or nesting.

I'd give just about anything to be out there tracking those birds. Later, when they're warriors, my friends will try to kill a lion to prove their manhood. They have great things to look forward to. But me? I'm stuffed into a Land Rover with my dumb sisters and their dolls on our way to church. None of my friends would submit to the humiliation I have to go through. But what choice do I have? I'm not a warrior in training. I wish I was.

We finally get to the church. It's a tin roof propped up on four posts. There aren't any walls, so we can see that the benches are already lined with people. One of the pastors is up front, standing by the pulpit. Dad built a whole bunch of pulpits out of the packing crates that held our refrigerator and beds and stuff we shipped from America. Those pulpits are scattered all over Maasailand.

Sometimes I think about the churches we used to visit on furlough in the States. They have lobbies like hotels. The maintenance crew changes the lobby flower arrangements to match the season. They have lights you can dim when the preacher is praying so everyone will feel more holy. They have carpets and stained-glass windows and recreation halls where people play basketball or Ping-Pong. Frankly, it's enough to make me sick. Why don't they send some of that money over here? The cost of a few of those bouquets on the altar could pay for a couple of church walls in Maasailand.

The Maasai pastor is leading the singing, and most of the congregation is joining in. They're all wearing their Sunday best — cotton togas printed in red-and-white checks. I have been in barbecue restaurants in America and thought how my Maasai friends would give their eyeteeth to get their hands on those tablecloths.

Small children roam around between the benches. When they need to go to the bathroom, it's no big deal. They just squat down right where they are. Dogs wander through the church, too. People pat them even though they're mangy old curs, and I'm glad. Babies hang on to their mothers, who sometimes remember to fan away the flies that cluster around the mouths and eyes of every living thing out here.

The smell of these people is familiar to me — woodsmoke and sweat and cow dung. I start to feel kind of comfortable after a while, because this is a smell and a language and a people I know well. Dad stands up and preaches a little in Swahili. The pastor translates. I don't usually listen to my dad preaching. He always says the same boring stuff. So I kind of drift off, thinking about the ostrich hunt that's going on without me.

Then Julia, Debbie, and I are invited to get up and say a few words of greeting. I speak in the Maa language, which just about knocks the congregation dead with delight. Then Mom stands up and tells everyone about the women's meetings she's going to be having in a few weeks. She will be teaching basic first aid, and this causes a lot of excitement. Sickness is a big problem out here. We sing some more hymns. The pastor preaches for a while. Dad gets up and says some more stuff.

Now it's time for the offering. People get up one by one and put a shilling or two in the basket by the pulpit. One lady brings an egg. Another lady brings three eggs. Then an old guy walks forward carrying a scrawny old chicken. This is a very big deal. Everybody claps. I have a bad feeling I am looking at our lunch.

About one in the afternoon, when we're all about to starve to death, they decide it's time to end the service. There's lots of praying, more singing, and then everyone files past us. My sisters and I bow our heads to receive the customary Maasai blessing from the elders, and we place our hands on the children's foreheads to bless them.

Then, while we wait in an agony of hunger, someone kills the chicken. Mom sneaks us some crackers. They're stale, but I eat them anyway. We all sit around under a thorn tree while they roast the chicken. Somebody shows up from the kraal carrying bottles of warm Coke, Fanta, and Sprite. Wow, they've gone all out for us today.

Dad's busy talking to the pastor and the other men. Mom visits with the ladies. She admires their babies while secretly checking for eye diseases or skin infections. I know my parents will be back here in a few weeks with a missionary doctor who can take care of some of those problems.

Well, it's halfway through the afternoon. My friends have probably killed an ostrich by now, drunk some of the cow's-blood-and-milk mixture they carry around in their calabashes, and wandered on home. Here I sit gnawing on a tough old chicken leg.

All the members of the church are squatting on the ground and staring at us like we're the luckiest dogs on the planet, and I know that to them, we are. Maasai rarely eat meat — only on very special occasions like us showing up at their church.

Debbie looks like she's about to cry, she's so miserable. Julia's starting to turn green. But I know neither of them will say a word. They'll just chew the meat the best they can and swallow it down with their warm soda.

Dad and Mom do some more praying with the pastor and the remaining members of the congregation. It's clear these people love my parents, who have brought them the good news about Jesus and his great sacrifice for their sins. A lady gives my mom a beaded necklace for a gift. A man presses a shilling into my dad's hands. It's the best they can do.

Finally we all pile back into the Land Rover and head off down the dry streambed. We barely get out of sight of the church when Julia, Debbie, and I start pleading for more food. Mom has packed sandwiches and potato chips and sugar cookies. We're about to stop by the side of the road to eat when Dad notices something.

"Hey, look at those vultures, Olive," he

says. "You don't suppose there's a kill over by that baobab tree, do you?"

Before we can get a word out, he swings the Land Rover off the track, and we barrel out into the bush. Scrub thorns screech along the metal undercarriage, dust billows up inside, the car bounces and jolts as we go faster and faster.

"There they are!" Dad shouts. "Lions!"

This is the most excited my father ever gets, except sometimes when he's preaching. It turns out a couple of lionesses have killed a big zebra, and the whole pride is having a feast. The males take the main places at the belly, the females hang out around the haunches, and the cubs scamper back and forth trying to sneak a strip of meat without getting cuffed in the head.

Huge vultures and marabou storks form a ring around the dead zebra, waiting for their turn. And I know that even though we can't see them, jackals and hyenas are lurking in the brush. By tomorrow morning, that zebra will be nothing but a pile of bones bleaching in the sun.

Watching a kill is big entertainment for our family, so Dad pulls the Land Rover to a stop. Mom gets out the peanut butter and jelly sandwiches and passes them around.

And then we join with the lions in scarfing down every scrap we can get our hands on.

By now the sun is hanging really low in the sky, and we never like to drive at night. It's time to head for home, so Dad cranks up the Land Rover. He releases the emergency brake, and the car rolls forward about six inches — and the right front wheel drops straight into an antbear hole.

The hole is so deep, the fender is sitting on the ground. Mom bangs her head on the windshield. Julia screams. Dad says a word I never realized he knew. It's not the worst word I've ever heard, but it's something we're sure not allowed to say.

"Goodness gracious, Don, what happened?" Mom's voice is shaking.

"I think we're in a hole of some sort. We must have been parked right in front of it."

The lions stare at us, panting, their mouths and tongues covered with blood. The vultures do a little sideways dance, like yippee, yippee, more dinner is on the way!

"How are we going to get out?" Julia asks. "Daddy, I'm scared!"

"Me, too!" Debbie whimpers.

I realize we're in a major pickle now. The only thing in our favor is that these lions have already been eating for a while. Maybe they won't have a hankering to sample a few missionaries for dessert. On the other hand, this is a big pride, and some of the females don't look like they've had enough dinner to satisfy them.

Dad reaches for the door handle. Mom grabs his arm. "Don't you open that door, Donald Mossman!" she orders. "Don't even think about it!"

"I have to see what's happened to the Land Rover, Olive," he tells her.

"It fell in an antbear hole; that's what happened," I inform them.

Antbears are digging animals that no one ever really sees. They're kind of like aardvarks or anteaters or badgers, but nobody knows for sure. They make huge holes, and after they've lived there awhile, they move on. Other animals take refuge in the antbear holes — snakes, civet cats, bat-eared foxes, warthogs, stuff like that.

"We can't sit out here all night, Olive," Don says. "The newsletter to our supporting churches needs to go out tomorrow morning, and that means I've got to head to town bright and early if I'm going to make it to the post office in time."

"Well, what do you think you're going to

do — lift the front end of the Land Rover out of that hole?"

"I think that's our only option."

"You'll get eaten by a lion, Daddy!" Julia cries. "Don't go outside!"

By now dusk is settling in. I'm remembering how fast we ate those sandwiches and how hungry I already feel.

"I need to go to the bathroom," Debbie whispers in my ear. "Don't tell!"

I look at her. She's so weird sometimes. "Debbie needs to go to the bathroom," I announce.

"Well, she'll just have to hold it," Mom says. Her mouth is so tight it looks like she just ate a lemon. She's mad, but she'll never admit it. "Maybe another car will come along, Don. What do you think?"

This is a good joke. The chances of another car coming along at this hour in the middle of nowhere without even a road nearby are about a jillion to one. That's when I have an idea.

"Here's what we'll do," I say. "I'll get my spear and stand in front of the Land Rover. If the lions make any move in our direction, I'll threaten them. Then you guys all jump outside, lift the wheel out of the antbear hole, and roll the car back a few feet."

My idea causes a mighty hullabaloo.

Mom says absolutely not. Dad says it might be the best idea we have. Julia says we'll all get killed, our throats ripped open by hungry lions, and our intestines spread all over Africa for the vultures to eat. Debbie says she really, really needs to go to the bathroom. We all argue and fight about this for a while, but finally everyone admits that we don't have any better options.

Actually, I'm pretty excited about the whole thing. I get my spear from the back of the Land Rover. The minute I open the door, every lion in the pride stops eating, looks up, and stares at me. One of the females gets to her feet.

"She's getting up!" Mom warns. "Don't get out of the car, Peter!"

But I step outside, leaving the door ajar. The lioness cocks her ears forward, her yellow eyes focused on mine. I walk toward the front of the Land Rover. It's bad news up there. One wheel is deep in the antbear hole, and it's going to take some doing to get it out.

Keeping my eyes on the pride, especially that lioness, I beckon everyone out of the Land Rover.

Dad starts counting. "One, two, three."

Everyone else in the Mossman family

305

bolts out of the car, races to the front, and grabs the fender.

"Lift," Dad says in a hoarse whisper.

The Land Rover doesn't budge. The lioness takes a single step toward us, the way cats do when they're stalking prey. Another lioness gets to her feet. They're not happy about having their meal interrupted.

"Again!" Dad says. "Everybody lift!"

This time, the fender comes up a few inches. I can see right away that my plan is not going to work. Girls are just too weak for this kind of thing. I study my spear for a moment. It has three parts — the sharpened steel blade, a central shaft of wood, and the steel butt. The butt is actually pointed, so I jam it into the ground right in front of me.

Without turning around, I back up to the Land Rover, grab the fender, and tell everybody to lift again. I have to say, I am pretty strong these days. Also, I can see the two lionesses padding slowly toward us, their heads held low and their eyes trained on me. I feel power coursing through me as I bend my knees and strain upward.

With all five of us lifting, the Land Rover rises out of the hole. We push backward, and it rolls to safety. As my family races back to the car, I jerk my spear from the ground. The lionesses pause. That's when a huge male leaps up and runs straight at me.

I see his bloody teeth bared, his wet black mane glistening. His paws eat up the ground between us. All the females in the car start screaming. Dad hits the horn. The lion keeps coming. There's no time for me to run to safety. I clench my spear, drop to one knee, and tense up just the way my friends and I have practiced over and over. The lion leaps at me, and I jam the butt of the spear into the ground again, its tip aimed at his heart. As his huge head and body plunge toward me, the spear pierces his chest, straight through the heart. Blood sprays across his tawny skin, and the lion drops to the ground, dead in his tracks.

The other lions jump to their feet. A few of them roar, a deafening sound that rumbles the ground under my shoes. A moment of confusion reigns, and then the whole pride pads away into the darkness, leaving the dead zebra to the hyenas and vultures.

Finally, I begin to distinguish the noise coming from the Land Rover. "Get in this car, Peter Mossman!" my mother is screaming.

Dad is leaning on the horn. "Peter, Peter!" he yells.

I turn around and look at them. What are they so afraid of? The danger is over now. I saunter toward the dead lion.

Dad backs the Land Rover away from the antbear hole and pulls along beside me. "Peter, get in the car," he commands.

"I killed a lion," I say.

I look into his eyes, and I see that he understands. For once in my life, my father understands me. This is more than playing with a toy spear. This is more than saving my family.

Today I have killed a lion.

Today I am a man.

"Stop screaming, Olive," my dad says. "Peter's all right."

"Make him get in the car!"

"He's going to get his spear," Dad tells her. "And then we'll put the lion on the roof of the Land Rover and take it home."

"Are you crazy, Donald Mossman?" she says. "That lion could have killed our son! And you expect us to get out of the car again?"

"Yes, I do."

"Why? What do we need an old tick-infested lion for, anyway? Please, Don. Don't do this."

For once, my dad isn't having anything to do with Mom or her opinions. He pulls the Land Rover between the dead lion and the pride lurking just beyond it in the dark grass. I take out my spear and wipe the blood on my jeans. Then Dad and I try to lift the big cat onto the car. It weighs too much, but before I know it, here come Julia and Debbie. And then to my surprise, even Mom gets out of the Land Rover and helps us lug that lion up onto the roof. Dad and I tie it down, and then we all pile back into the car and set off.

For some reason, I feel full of emotion. Like I want to cry or laugh or something. No one says a word for a long time.

Finally, Dad speaks up. "You did a fine thing out there, young man."

"Yes, Peter," Mom says. "Thank you. We're proud of you."

Julia and Debbie start playing with their dolls on my lap again, but this time it doesn't bother me.

Now I know who I am.

---

chapter thirteen

"Well, my goodness." Olive shook her head. "I suppose there are several things we never truly understood about you children. Maybe even things we never knew at all — like that incident with Deborah at the train tracks — though I certainly believe we were doing all we could to give you a happy childhood. Anyway, we're all tired right now. I know your father and I are exhausted from our trip, and then everyone's worried about Deborah."

Peter sighed. He guessed it was too much to hope that his mom would ever admit to having done anything that might have hurt her children.

"I think I'll go check at the nurses' station," Julia said. "I want to know if she's out of the operating room yet."

"I'll go with you, honey." Mom collected her purse and followed her daughter out into the hall.

The rain seemed to have stopped, Peter noticed as he studied the parking lot outside. Though it was dark, the puddles on the sidewalk were still and glassy, reflecting the yellow lights overhead. How long had it been since he'd known exactly who he was? Peter wondered. Once upon a time, years ago when he was a boy, the world had made sense. Things fit. Everyone belonged. But Julia was right. There had been a constant tension, an ongoing sense of impending disaster. As Peter thought back over his life, he realized that for him it finally *had* fallen apart. All of it unraveled and ground into dust. Everything important had vanished. Including hope.

"Peter," his dad said gently. "I feel I need to talk with you, Son. It seems that over the years, we've grown apart. I'd like to understand how you're feeling about your life. I want to know if there's anything I can do."

"Grown apart?" Peter studied his father. "Were we ever close, Dad?"

"I thought we were. I certainly loved you and your sisters very —"

"She's out of surgery!" Mom announced, marching back into the room and flipping on the light, filling the space with a glaring brightness. "Gracious, it's dark in here. I had no idea how late it had gotten. We talked to the nurse for a moment. The doctor's on his way."

As Olive spoke, Dr. Bryant followed Julia into the room. He gave the family a nod of greeting and seated himself on the edge of Debbie's bed. "We have inserted a jugular central line, what you might call a heavy-duty IV line. We were having trouble keeping Debbie's veins open for the antibiotics and pain medication she needs. She does have an infection, but I'm not sure of the source. I changed her antibiotic, and this one may be more effective. I also had her hip and pelvis x-rayed again. We're seeing some healing there, but you need to understand that the bone is very weak and fragile because of the osteoporosis. Only time will tell if she's going to be strong enough to battle what lies ahead of her."

"What do you mean?" Mom asked. "What does lie ahead of her?"

"First, she's going to have to come to an acceptance of her condition. As long as she keeps denying the anorexia, we're not going to see much improvement. Once we get over that hurdle, she'll need to work with a physical therapist and a psychiatrist. The main concern is that we've got to get her eating again. I'm going to continue feeding her through the nasogastric feeding tube, but she'll need to begin eating solid foods again before we can say she's on the road to real healing."

He glanced at each of them. "Do you have any questions?" When no one spoke, he stood. "She'll be in recovery for a while. I'll tell the nurses to let you know when she's able to have visitors."

Turning in the doorway, he gave them a perfunctory smile. "Keep up those prayers. They'll help more than anything I can do for her right now."

As the door shut behind him, Mom let out a shuddering breath. "Well, this is just unbelievable. How can she have gotten so sick so quickly? I just can't understand it."

"Mom, it hasn't been quick," Julia said. "Deborah's been sick a long time."

Olive stared at Julia for a moment, then shook her head. "I think it's that boyfriend of hers. That Dave Hornburg fellow. Do you realize how long they've been dating? And he won't even broach the subject of marriage. What do you suppose is wrong with him? Can't he see what a wonderful wife and mother Deborah would make?"

"Maybe he's gay," Peter said.

"He is a Sunday school director, Peter Mossman!" Mom's cheeks flushed a bright pink. "Honestly, I never know what's going to come out of your mouth. Where do you get such ideas?"

"Peter," Dad said, laying his hand on his son's arm, "would you come with me a moment?"

"Where?"

"I thought we could take a walk outside. The rain seems to have stopped."

Peter glanced across at Julia. This was it. His dad was probably going to give him a big sermon on proper Christian behavior. There would be a few admonitions on using gentlemanly language, several references to Scriptures about honoring your parents, and a couple of anecdotes about when Dad was a boy in Missouri. How many times had Peter heard his father's sermons — both in church and out? Sometimes it seemed like they never had a normal conversation. When his dad did speak to Peter privately, he always launched into monologues about his speaking engagements, his plans for the churches he had started, or some other topic that didn't really interest Peter. Had the two of them ever understood anything about each other?

"Sure," Peter said, standing. "Maybe when we get back, Debbie will be out of the recovery room."

As they walked down the hall, Dad took off his glasses and cleaned them. Always a bad sign. Peter could just imagine his father rehearsing the pearls of sage wisdom he was about to cast before his son, that thankless swine. As always, Peter would listen, nod a few times, maybe even make an appropriate comment or two. Then he'd go off and do whatever he wanted. He'd learned that if he tried to disagree with his dad, the conversation came to an abrupt end. For some reason, Don Mossman couldn't bear conflict of any kind, and so he always sort of shrank into himself, falling into an unhappy silence until the moment he could walk away and escape.

"Looks like the storm has passed on by," Don said as they stepped out onto the sidewalk. "I always liked a good ol' Missouri thunderstorm. When I was a boy, I'd sit on the front porch with my grandpa, and we'd watch the lightning just fire up the sky. What a sight."

"Dad, how come you always talk about your grandpa? Didn't you ever spend time with your own dad?"

"Well, he was a farmer, you know. I helped him out a lot. But he was usually busy from dawn till dusk. Grandpa had lost his leg in a tractor accident, and my dad pretty much had to take over the farm when he was still just a teenager. I never saw my dad that he wasn't working. Even in the evenings, he'd sit by the fire making diagrams of what he was going to plant."

"Sounds like you. Planting your churches."

Don looked across at his son. "I never thought of it that way."

"Remember all your charts and maps? You had every church marked with a little pin and a flag. It seemed like there were hundreds of them."

"A hundred and twenty-seven by the time we left Kenya."

Peter recalled the way his father had carefully shown him each pin, described the church it represented, explained his plans for evangelizing that area. Because the Maasai were a nomadic people, sometimes the pins had to move, too. Dad always placed each pin in the exact spot where the church was located. With his many multicolored highlighting pens, he would line out the dry riverbeds and dirt roads he needed to follow, the tiny towns where he might find a soda to drink, and of course, the kraals where hundreds of unsaved souls lived in sin.

One time, Peter had slipped into his father's study and switched all the pins around. He'd even thrown a few into the trash can just to be ornery. Olive had given her son the spanking to end all spankings. But Don had quietly shut the door and gone back to work returning each pin to its proper place.

"You miss your churches, don't you, Dad?" Peter asked, feeling a knot of guilt in his stomach.

"I miss the people. The relationships." He led his son across the parking lot. "I miss the work, too. It hasn't been easy knowing there are still so many who do not know Christ as Savior. If the mission board would let me, I'd be back there in a heartbeat. The people are so hungry for God. And who's there to feed them? No one but their pastors — men I felt I had barely started training. I had so much more to teach them. Now I sit around in my La-Z-Boy recliner watching my big-screen TV and eating Fritos. And that's supposed to make me content." He paused. "But I guess you know a little bit of what I'm talking about, Peter. I don't think I'd realized how much you miss Africa."

"It was my whole world. It was who I was." Peter noticed they had approached his parents' car. "You, too, huh?"

317

"Yes." Don's voice was just above a whisper. "Peter, I have something to give you. Something I think you'll want."

He fumbled with his keys for a moment, and then he opened the large trunk. Peter recognized the boxes of items his parents dragged around with them while they were speaking at churches in the States — carved African animals, woven baskets, samples of Maasai beadwork, lengths of pretty African fabrics.

Don leaned into the trunk and pushed a few of the boxes around. Then he lifted out a long, shiny object. "Here's your spear, Peter."

He laid the weapon across his son's extended arms. Peter stared down at his spear, disbelief and amazement coursing through him. In the lights of the parking lot, he could see the tiny marks he'd carved for each animal he had killed. He ran his finger over the cold steel blade, caressing the familiar edge he had sharpened to a razor thinness. The butt end, also steel, had come a little loose, and he wiggled it back and forth, instantly worrying about how he was going to repair it — before he remembered who he had become.

Tears filled his eyes as he looked across at his father. "Thanks," he managed.

"After you left for college, it stayed in your bedroom for years, propped right next to your bed the way you always kept it. We never moved it. But when I was packing to come back to the States for our retirement, I slipped your spear down the side of one of the crates. We've been taking it around to the churches when we speak. Showing it to the congregations, you know. I want you to have it back. It's yours."

Peter found he couldn't speak. Fighting to keep tears from sliding down his cheeks, he swallowed again and again. A thousand memories rushed through him — practicing on the plains with his friends, animals he had taken, the grand moment when he'd killed his lion. The spear had gone with him everywhere, always in his hand, so comfortable it had felt as though it were a part of his body.

He turned it over, studying the glint of light off the leaf-shaped blade. He felt as though that painful thorn had just slipped right out of his heart.

"Peter," his father said slowly, "I'm sorry about the BB gun."

"No, Dad —"

"There were a lot of things about you I didn't understand. Maybe I didn't try hard enough to listen to you. I wanted to give you everything, but when I see you now, I think all I gave you was loss . . . things you wanted and needed . . . and never got."

Amazed at the words his father spoke, words he had been sure he would never hear, Peter felt the terrible wound inside him begin to heal. As his father's words penetrated the angry, red place where so much hurt had been, Peter wanted to reach out to his father as well.

"Dad, I'm the one who should apologize about the BB gun. I didn't know how much work you'd put into making that rubber-band gun, how it was something from your own childhood that you were trying to give me. I didn't think beyond my disappointment. And my anger." He gripped his spear. "I'm sorry I broke the gun you made me. I'm sorry I burned it."

Don took off his glasses, but this time it was his eyes he wiped. "Well, you keep your spear now. This was the better thing for you to have, anyway. God always knows to give us what we really need, even if the process sometimes hurts."

Peter looked into his father's face, sensing the wound beginning to fester again. "What do you mean, Dad? Sometimes I feel like you're talking a language I never learned."

Don nodded. "Funny thing, isn't it? You understood your Maasai friends, and you took years of lessons in Kiswahili. But when God spoke, it seemed to be a mystery to you."

"Not always," Peter said, remembering his experience under the palm tree on the beach. That childhood faith had been real — he was sure of it. But he'd buried it along with all the other things that had been too painful and confusing to understand. Now for the first time, he wanted to risk letting his father see what had been hiding inside him for such a long time. "I know what you and Mom and the others think. You don't believe I'm a Christian. You think I'm some kind of heathen. But I'm not. I do believe in Jesus. It's just that a lot of pain rises up inside me when I think about religion. I have too many questions, too much anger."

"You've been reluctant to surrender your heart. And that's what holds you back from the fullness of salvation."

"This is what I'm trying to tell you." Peter fought the urge to shout. "*Surrender your heart* — what does that mean? *Fullness of salvation* — it's like some kind of religious code that makes a guy feel like an outcast. Talk like real people, Dad!"

"Real people?" Don thought for a minute. Then he sat down on a wet bench and beckoned his son to join him. *"Oyiote?"* he asked.

Peter recognized the familiar question as the start to every Maasai riddle. *Oyiote* meant "Are you ready?" He shrugged and squatted beside his father in the fashion of a warrior, his spear poised at his side.

"E-euo," Peter said, stating the common response that meant "It has come."

Don sat in silence for a while, and Peter was mentally transported back to countless nights when he had sat inside the home of the old woman, Ko-ko-o, who had been like a grandmother to him and his sisters. Adults and children gathered around the fire and listened to the rain on the roof of the dung-plastered hut. Then slowly one or another of the Maasai would begin to speak, telling stories, jokes, riddles, until Peter and the other children were so sleepy they had to be carried to their homes. Of all the rich experiences of his childhood, those had been the most precious. A wave of homesickness swept over him.

"Kilikuai oshe kop," his dad said.

Peter glanced up, surprised his father could remember this riddle. He hadn't realized that his father had been as immersed in the Maasai culture as he had been. His father's revelation that he, too, missed Africa built a bridge between them. "There is a message that stretches across the world," the words meant.

And Peter knew the answer. *"Enkoitoi,"* he said in a low voice. "A path."

Dad smiled and nodded. He continued, speaking slowly in Maa. "You are on a path, my son. Your path has stretched across the world, across many seas. Is this not true?"

"Ee, neijia," Peter answered — "yes, it is like that."

"Your path took you to *Maasaini,* the land of the Maasai. There you stayed many years. I also stayed many years, and now I am an elder. Is this not true?"

"Ee, neijia," Peter said again in a low voice. He knew his father had aged, but somehow Peter had failed to accord him the honor due an elder of the tribe. Hearing his father speak in Maa, Peter suddenly saw his father differently and felt a newfound respect for the older man's years of experience and his greater wisdom. Just as he had done around the fire in the kraal, Peter found himself listening — and listening carefully.

"The elder must know and understand

all the rules of the clan so he can sit in judgment over his people. He must use the art of the tongue and the wisdom of the mind in place of the spear." Dad gestured at the weapon that Peter held. "And this is what my tongue wishes to say to you, my son. You know it is the way of the Maasai that every wrong done must be repaid. If someone steals a goat or a sheep, he must pay with a two-year-old calf. Is this not true?"

"*Ee, neijia,*" Peter said.

"But if the thief confesses before he is caught, he may ask forgiveness, saying, *Muro,* 'mercy.' He will still have to pay, but perhaps it will be only a small ewe. Now, if someone steals a cow, the fine will be much greater. He must pay seven cows for this crime. And if the stolen cow is pregnant, it will be even more, because the unborn calf is taken into account. What if someone breaks the bone or the tooth of another man? Then he must pay a ewe. But if he kills another man, he must first hide so that the dead man's relatives will not kill him in revenge. Later, when he comes out of hiding, he must pay forty-nine cattle, for this is the fine for murder. And so, my son, you can see that for each wrong committed on this earth a payment must be made. If payment is not made, the wrongdoer is cursed. Is this not so?"

"*Ee, neijia.*"

"Every man commits wrongdoings with his hand, and this is a well-known truth. But there is another truth. Wrong also lives inside man. These wrongs are many. They include lying, pride, bad temper, the telling of rumors, disrespect for elders, the desire to violate sexual rules, and many other things. For example, the Maasai say, *Moti nayier esayiet enkutuk* — 'An angry mouth is a pot that cooks poison.' My son, poison fills each person in a way that no fine of ewes or cattle can repay. It is a poison that separates each man from his Creator, from the God who made him, and therefore, man is cursed. There is no sacrifice great enough to cover all the wrongdoings of man. Is this not true?"

Peter bowed his head in respect. He knew the answer. "*Papaai,*" he said, "my father." "You are wrong. There was already a sacrifice great enough to cover all the wrongdoings of man."

"*E-sipa,*" Dad said — "It is truly spoken." "And that sacrifice was not a cow or a goat or a ewe. That sacrifice was *Kristu,* the very Son of God. God, the one who was wronged, paid the fine for those of us who cannot pay it. He sent his Son to earth to become the greatest sacrifice. You have said you believe in this Kristu, my son. And yet, I must tell you that believing is not enough."

"What do you mean, *Paapai?*" Peter felt that he had bared the wound in his heart, willing it to begin to heal, wanting to hear his father's words, trying to understand. Like an impala lying in grass with its soft underbelly exposed, he felt vulnerable and even fearful. Yet he didn't want to hide any longer. He wanted to understand the answer to these riddles that had mystified him all his life. Why wasn't belief enough? What more was there?

"A man must do more than believe that forty-nine cows are the fine for murder. He must take those cows into his own kraal. They must become part of his own herd, living with him and his family and providing the nourishment he needs through their milk and blood and meat. In this same way, each man must take Kristu into his life, surrendering completely to him, acknowledging that without Kristu he cannot live. He must follow Kristu's guidance, drawing nourishment from himself, and worshiping him because he is God. Do you understand these words, my son?"

Peter stared at the damp pavement beneath his feet. This was not the dusty, beaten ground of a Maasai kraal. And yet, for the first time in his life, he truly understood who Jesus was and what he had done. He understood the sacrifice, the payment for the wrongs mankind had committed. The wrongs Peter himself had done. Not murder and thievery and physical violence. But those wrongs his father had spoken of, the evil that lived inside him and separated him from God. Just as important, he also knew now that believing wasn't enough. More than simply finding healing for the wound in his heart or opening the door to his childhood faith, he needed to invite Christ into his life, turn the controls of his life over to God.

"I understand," Peter said, speaking in English. "You told it in a way that I understand."

"King'as Olemaayi nikintoki oleng'eno," Dad said. "We begin by being foolish, but we later become knowledgeable."

Peter smiled at the familiar proverb. "I've been pretty foolish."

"Now that you understand my words, your wisdom can begin. Are you willing to accept Christ's sacrifice, take him into your life, and give him control?"

A strange swelling of elation filled Peter's chest. Accepting the sacrifice . . . taking Christ into his life . . . surrendering control . . . it was about time. *"Ee, papaai,"* he said. "Yes, my father." He closed his eyes, gripping his spear. "God, I am full of wrongdoings," he whispered in the Maa language. "I cannot pay the fine for all of my sins. They are too many and too great. I thank you for sending your Son, Kristu, to give his life as the fine I could not pay. I accept this sacrifice as the payment for my wrongdoings, and I ask you to come into me, to live in my life now and forever. I submit my will to you, God."

"Naai," his father said — "Let it be."

"I worship you."

"Naai."

"I serve you."

"Naai."

"I draw nourishment from you."

"Naai."

"I follow your guidance down the path that is my life. *Eesai,* 'amen.' " Peter opened his eyes and saw that his father was weeping. There was still one more thing Peter needed to do. Still crouching on the sidewalk next to his father, he tugged a clump of green grass from the lawn. In the Maasai gesture of asking for forgiveness, he held out the grass to his father.

"Oh, Peter," Dad said, taking the grass and clutching it tightly. "You don't need my forgiveness."

"I've not only wronged God," Peter said. "I've wronged you. For years now, I haven't respected you and Mom. I haven't tried to understand you. And I've held a lot of anger in my heart."

"We certainly haven't been perfect parents, Peter."

"Yeah, well, I know I caused you a lot of trouble when I was young."

"You know that old saying, *Aimenye marmali anaa menye maata?* Which would you rather be, the father of the mischievous one, or the father of no one?" Dad slipped his arm around his son. "*Menya marmali.* I'd rather be your dad than anything else on earth."

They sat in silence, watching the clouds drift across the moon and listening to the patter of raindrops as they slid from the leaves to the ground when the wind blew. Peter turned his spear over and pondered it. The smooth feel of the African olivewood in his palm showed him that just as his father was an elder, he too had a place in the tribe — the body of Christ. He was a warrior. The elder's role was to judge and keep order. The warrior's work was to use his spear, not for destruction but for good. To stand up for the truth. To defend the weak. To fight for what was right. As a warrior, Peter could take the anger inside him and use it for good, God-given purposes.

Peter knew that giving Christ control of his life wouldn't erase the beat of Africa that still pounded in his breast and made him ache inside. But things seemed clearer than they had in years.

Not only did the past make sense, the present moment was clear and real. And that meant the future could not be ignored. If Christ was living in him, then he knew change was possible. He didn't know how it would come, and he didn't know how he would be different. He hardly even knew where to begin.

But that was the point, wasn't it? He wasn't in charge anymore. What did God want him to do? In an almost blinding vision, a face came into his mind. Maria. His wife.

"I need to call Maria," he said. "I have to talk to her. I can't let my son grow up without me."

"You do that. And I'll go find out how Deborah's getting along."

They stood and embraced. As his father started back to the hospital, Peter hurried to a pay phone he remembered seeing outside. He quickly punched in the numbers to Maria's family home.

As the phone rang far away in New Mexico, Peter closed his eyes and addressed the Spirit of God he had accepted into his life. "Please, Lord," he murmured, "let Maria answer." He didn't know what he would do if his mother-in-law refused to let him speak to his wife.

"*Hola?*"

It wasn't Maria. "Hello, this is Peter Mossman — please don't hang up!"

"Pedro?" The voice sounded familiar.

"Abuela?" Maria's grandmother. Even better! "Is that you?"

"Yes, Pedro, it is I."

"Abuelita, please let me talk to Maria. I have important things to say to her."

"You may speak, Pedrito. But Maria is not here. She's at her cousin's house making tamales. Tell me what you want to say to my little Maria."

"Abuelita, please tell Maria I'm sorry for all the hurt I've caused her. I know I've done many things wrong. Will you tell her that for me? Please, Abuelita, will you speak to Maria on my behalf? Will you tell

331

her I love her, and I beg her to give me another chance?"

The phone in his hand was silent for a moment. Finally, the old woman spoke. "I will tell Maria what you have said."

Before he could respond, the line went dead. He turned away from the pay phone and spotted his sister coming through the door of the hospital. "Hey, Peter!" she called, waving at him. "Debbie's out of the recovery room. She looks better!"

Ever the optimist, he thought. He walked toward her.

"Peter, what have you got there? Is that your spear?" She stopped on the sidewalk. "It is! Where'd you get it? Oh, this is so weird."

"Dad had it in his trunk. They've been carrying it around with all their other curios."

"Are you serious?" She took the spear and passed it from hand to hand. Then she gave it back to him. "You look like you did when you were a kid. Just the same."

"But I'm different," he said.

She cocked her head, staring at him. "Maybe so." Then she shrugged. "Listen, Mom and Dad are going to stay here with Debbie for a few minutes until she's asleep. Then they're driving back to Lebanon.

Would you mind taking me back to Deb's house? I'm exhausted."

"Come on, big sister," he said, slipping his arm around her shoulders. "Here's a song for you."

He slowly hummed the tune of a Maasai blessing song. But when he began to sing, his sister joined in, and the words blessed him, too.

"*Miliyau sii iyie Enkai*
　　May God bring you back
Taa oipotori
　　May you be the one that people talk about
Oipotoo Maasai
　　One that the Maasai talk of
Oipotoo Ashumba
　　One that other people talk of
Meiruko Enkai olekukuya
　　May God hear this prayer
Meiruko emagilani
　　Make us bear for each other
Entoiki olari
　　Make us produce in time of plenty
Entoiki olmeynaai
　　Make us produce in time of famine
Naai!
　　Oh, God, hear our prayer!"

chapter fourteen

Peter had his spear. Mom and Dad had promised to be back at the hospital by ten the next morning, right after their church's early worship service. And Debbie was on a new antibiotic and resting again. Julia jammed a couch pillow under her back, wondering why she didn't feel any better. Something inside her felt restless and awake, and it wasn't the babies. She ran her hand over the hump in her middle and let out a sigh.

They'd been back at Debbie's house for a while now, but neither she nor Peter had been able to sleep. She had emerged from the bedroom to find him sitting in a chair reading the Bible. Pete reading the Bible? If that wasn't enough to unsettle her, she didn't know what was.

She had stretched out on the couch and wondered whether to flip on the television or read a magazine. Instead, she stared at the paintings on the wall and felt miserable.

She'd talked to Mike an hour earlier. He and the girls were missing her, they said. But the truth was, all seemed just fine without her. They'd fallen into a comfortable pattern, eating out a lot and taking turns with the laundry. No one had remembered to clean the cat box for a few days, but the smell finally alerted them, and Heather actually volunteered to do it. Jessica had even baked a cake and made lasagna the other night.

Julia pushed at the couch pillows. Why couldn't she get comfortable? And why was Peter reading the Bible, anyway?

"What are you doing?" she asked, twisting her shoulders around to look at him.

"Drawing."

"I thought you were reading."

"Nope."

"Well, what are you drawing?"

"You."

"Me?" She pushed herself into a sitting position. "Peter, don't draw me. I look like a whale."

"No you don't. You look like a Maasai woman."

"What?" Getting to her feet, she padded across to his chair and peered down at his sketchbook. The rough beginnings of a young Maasai woman emerged from the paper. She sat against the wall of her mud-plastered house, her feet stretched out in front of her, and her pregnancy evident under the checkered cloths wrapped around her body.

"Peter, that's really good."

He gave her a little push. "Sit down, Jules. You know I hate it when anyone watches me draw. Sit on the couch and put your feet up on the coffee table. And don't move."

"I thought you said you weren't drawing much these days."

"And don't talk."

Frowning, she did as instructed. Peter was a good artist, she thought as she sat there trying to look like a Maasai woman. What was he doing working as a mailman? He ought to be using his art in some way. Maybe he could go back to college and get his degree. Then he could teach.

Oh, who was she to tell anyone else what to do with his life? She'd wanted to be a nurse for as long as she could remember. And now, just when it had seemed possible — surprise! She ran her fingertips over her stomach.

Well, babies, she thought, *you're going to be stuck with a fuddy-duddy old mom you won't really need. Or miss when she's gone. And you'll probably grow up in some backwater town in Wyoming, because your dad got tired of being a youth minister.*

She stared at her toenails. "Why were you reading the Bible, Peter?"

"Don't talk. I'm trying to concentrate."

"Just tell me that one thing."

"I need to know what the Bible says."

"You've heard it all a million times."

"Yeah, but I didn't pay attention. I just believed what I wanted to believe and ignored the rest. It doesn't work that way. God gave us the whole thing, so we can't just pick and choose. I need to find out what the Bible really says — not just what I've wanted to believe."

Julia stared at him. Was this her brother talking?

Peter looked up at her. "You know those little metal thingies that hang from the ends of their necklaces? How are they shaped?"

"Triangles. Like arrow tips." She paused a moment. "Peter?"

He frowned at her. "Julia, would you be quiet? I haven't been able to draw for a long time, and I'm really getting into this. So, please, hush."

She folded her hands across her middle and resumed her examination of her toenails. How many years had it been since she'd painted them? Come to think of it, had she ever painted them? She was such a boring, traditional nobody. She'd worn the same hairstyle since high school. Most of her clothes went back fifteen years. She never played around with any of her recipes, and she rarely tried to cook anything new. Even her garden looked the same year after year. Why did she always do the right thing? Why did she always do what people expected? She was so goody-goody and predictable, it just about made her sick.

"You know something I just realized?" Peter said. "You're pretty."

"Ha."

"Seriously, Jules, you've got a classic face. Really nice lines. You ought to wear your hair up on top of your head. Or cut it off short. You have a good chin."

"Yeah, and I ought to paint my toenails purple, too."

"Sure."

"Sure." She stared at her feet. "And be a nurse."

"Why not? You could go back to college."

"Have you forgotten this?" She pointed at her stomach. "I'm not foisting my babies off on day care or a nanny or something. Boarding school taught me that, at least. Whether it's good for these kids or not, they're stuck with me."

"So? College doesn't take twenty-four hours a day. You could go to night classes and leave the babies with Mike."

"Mike does most of his ministry at night."

"Then take day classes. What's your problem tonight, Julia? You're being a total grouch."

"You'd be grouchy, too, if you were me. Don't you get it? I'm stuck. I'm stuck, stuck, stuck! I made my choices, and now I'm stuck with them. I'm stuck with Mike and his midlife crisis. I'm stuck with my two teenage monster daughters. I'm stuck with these babies. And I'm stuck with my stupid unpainted toenails!"

She hauled herself off the couch. "I'm going to bed. You can finish your drawing without me."

As she stomped toward the bedroom, she could hear Peter behind her. "You're only stuck because you're such a doormat!" he called.

"I'm not a doormat!" she shouted, slamming the door between them.

"You are, too!" he said. She could tell from the sound of his voice that he was walking toward the closed door. "You said so yourself the other day. And it's true.

339

You're a doormat. You let everybody walk all over you, and you always have. And you know why you do that? Huh?"

"Shut up, Peter!" She flopped down on the bed and reached for the Kleenex box. "Just shut up!"

"You're a doormat because you think that's how Christians are supposed to act!"

"I do not!"

"Yes, you do. You think you're supposed to be nice and kind and agreeable and submissive all the time, because that's real Christlike. That's what you think."

"Well, what would you know about how Christians are supposed to act, Peter? Huh? Tell me that!"

There was a silence from the other side of the door. Julia tugged a tissue from the box and blotted her damp cheeks. She shouldn't have said that. She shouldn't have said anything tonight. Sucking down a ragged breath, she prayed that God would forgive her for resenting her new babies and her husband and her lot in life. She had been given so much. So very much!

"Jesus wasn't a doormat! He was a warrior!" Peter bellowed, throwing open the door and bursting into her bedroom. He held his spear high in his hand like Moses with his holy staff. "He whipped the money changers out of the temple. He stood up for the woman who was getting stoned for adultery. When people asked him tricky questions, he gave them tricky answers. He did all kinds of brave stuff. Jesus was not a wimp, and you — Julia Mossman Chappell — you don't have to be a wimp either!"

"I was raised to be a wimp," Julia said. "I've been a wimp all my life, and I'll always be a wimp. And don't talk to me about Jesus, because you don't know anything about him."

"Yes, I do! Dad explained it to me tonight, and it finally made sense. So, I'm a Christian just as much as you are — and Christians don't have to be wimps!"

"Well, Christians can't be fighting and yelling all the time!" She could hardly believe that she was shouting at the top of her lungs. For the first time in her life, Julia was yelling at someone besides the glue lady. And the more she yelled, the more she felt the long-buried sparks of anger beginning to flare up within her. "What about *love one another?*" she challenged. "What about *be kind to one another?* What about *honor thy father and thy —*"

"Yeah, what about it? You can love people and be kind to them without turning yourself into a total worm."

"Well, maybe I *like* being a worm! Did you ever think about *that?* I'm really *good* at it! I've had years of practice."

"Fine, be a worm. Just don't write it off as acting like a Christian. Because I'm a Christian, and I'm not a worm."

"Okay, hotshot, what are you then?"

"I'm a warrior." He began to pound his spear on the floor for emphasis. "Warriors fight. Warriors stand up for right and truth. Warriors defend the weak."

Standing beside the bed, he lifted his voice in the high-pitched notes of the warrior's song:

"*Abuaaki emutiy o endaruna*
   I call out at twilight as well as
      in the morn
Olmurrani lai lenkila enkopiro
   I the warrior with the black cloak
Pee mejo Enkai memjo enkop
   So that neither the heavens nor the
      earth can say
Kalo ting'idai ele lemebuak ebuaki
   I am arrogant, for not calling out
      loud enough like the others."

"You're calling out loud enough, Peter!" Julia said, cutting into his song. "Stop it.

The neighbors are going to send the police over here."

"I'm a warrior!" Peter cried, pounding his spear on the floor again.

"Okay, you're a warrior. You're a Christian warrior! Now be quiet!"

"I fight for truth and justice. I will fight for my wife's love, and I will win her back! I'll fight for my son! I know who I am — I'm a warrior!"

"Stop it, Peter!" He was beginning to scare her now. "You're shaking the whole house."

"I'm a warrior!"

"You're a mailman!"

He glanced at her, took a deep breath, and collapsed laughing onto the bed. "You're right! I'm a mailman. I'm a warrior mailman. Oh, Jules, don't you get it? It makes sense now. Christians walk down God's path. They do what he tells them to do. They listen to his voice, and they follow him."

"I thought you said you'd never heard God's voice, and you hoped you never would."

"I hear him now. He's telling me I'm a warrior."

"You're freaking me out, Peter."

"Be a warrior, too, Julia."

"I'm a woman. I don't want to be a warrior."

"Well, the song sure doesn't say, 'Onward Christian *Doormats.*' Maybe you're not supposed to be a warrior, but you're supposed to be something! Get up on your feet and be who you're supposed to be."

She looked across at him. Never in her life had she seen her brother look so happy, so filled with joy. What she had longed for, for so many years, seemed to be happening to Peter. She should be happy. But all she felt was misery.

Peter stood from the bed and carried his spear to the door. "I love you, Julia," he said. "I'm glad you're my sister. And you're a good Christian. Even if you are a total wimp."

As he shut the door behind him, she reached for another tissue.

"Where are they?" Julia paced beside Debbie's bed. "They said they'd be here at ten o'clock. They promised!"

"Maybe they got stopped after church." Debbie picked at her covers. "I bet they had people to talk to or something."

"Don't make excuses for them, Debs. They said they'd be here, and they should be here."

Debbie looked over at her brother, who was studying the second day of rain pouring down outside the hospital window.

He shrugged. "Don't worry about Jules," he told Debbie. "I think it's hormones." After Julia blew up at him last night, he had heard her alternately crying and thumping things around in her room. While a part of him was glad to see his big sister finally expressing some honest emotions, he couldn't help worrying about her and her unborn babies. He really wished Julia would calm down.

"It's not hormones," Julia objected. "Debs, don't listen to him. Pete doesn't know anything. He says I'm a doormat."

"You *are* a doormat," Debbie said. "But I've always liked having you around."

"Yeah, we like wiping our feet on you, Jules," Peter added, hoping he could joke her out of her bad mood. "Mom and Dad, too. It's your role in our family to be the doormat."

"Peter, I've just about had it with you!"

He laughed. Julia looked like a steam locomotive chugging around the room and getting nowhere. He didn't know why she was so upset about their parents' being late. Their parents had never been on time for anything, and it never seemed to bother

Julia before. At the end of every school term, all the buses would leave with kids heading away to their parents' homes in Zaire or Tanzania or somewhere at the end of the world. But the Mossmans, who could actually drive from their mission post to pick up their children, never seemed to arrive until a good hour or two after the campus was deserted.

Peter remembered how angry he used to get, standing forlornly on the porch of the administration building waiting for the tell-tale puff of dust that meant the old Land Rover was on its way. But sweet, compliant Julia had never let it bother her. She just found something to amuse herself with, and eventually, Peter would join her. But Debbie never left her post, watching and waiting, until at last she would shout, "They're here! They came for us! They came!"

He studied his little sister this morning. She looked awful. Really, really bad. Her skin was translucent and her face skeletal. The fake blonde hairpiece Ralph had found for her in the cancer ward was lying on the table beside the bed. She kept picking and picking at the sheets, as though their weight was too heavy for her fragile body to bear.

A knock on the door drew his attention

as Dr. Bryant walked into the room. "Good morning, Deborah. How are you feeling today?"

The grin she gave him was almost frightening. "I'm fine," she said. "How are you, Dr. Bryant?"

"Well, I'm all right, but I'm concerned about you, young lady. The nurses tell me you had a rough night and your temperature is still elevated. Is that right?"

"I feel okay."

"Deborah, I have something to tell you. You know I've been consulting with Dr. Baines, an eating disorders specialist who works at Cox Medical Center down in Springfield. I spoke with him again this morning, and both of us agree it would be to your benefit if we transferred you over there today. Dr. Baines has been very successful in treating your kinds of problems. He's a fine doctor, and I think he can help you get better."

Debbie lowered her eyes. "I'm fine, Dr. Bryant. I really don't want to go to Springfield."

"I know you don't want to go, but that's my recommendation. We're concerned about some of your lab results. Frankly, we don't have the facility or the specialists to provide the kind of care you need,

Deborah. I want to transfer you to Cox. May I have your permission to do that?"

Peter could feel his heart slamming against his chest. This was not a minor setback. The doctor was telling them that Debbie wasn't getting better. That she needed more help. He sat forward.

"Debs," he said. "I think you ought to go."

"Oh, Peter."

"You'd better do what the doctor says," Julia added.

"Please, Debbie." Peter stood and took her hand. "Come on. It'll be nice to have a change of scenery. Jules and I will go with you." He focused on the doctor. "Will she be taken in an ambulance?"

"No!" Debbie protested. "I'm not going anywhere. I'm not riding in an ambulance again. Please don't make me! I won't go if I have to ride in an ambulance. I hate that!"

"She would certainly be safer in an ambulance," Dr. Bryant said, looking at Peter. "But if it's the only way to get her to agree, I believe I could let you drive your sister to Springfield instead. We can have the nurse flush her IV line and cap it off for the time it will take you to get there. Debbie could lie in the backseat. As long as you'll take her straight to Cox, I think she can manage the ride."

"There," Julia said. "Peter and I will drive you. It'll be fun. An adventure."

Peter frowned at her. Did Julia have to try to put a happy face on every situation? This was not an adventure. This was a ride to the hospital with a very sick patient. But he could see the fear in Julia's eyes, and he knew her gut reaction had been to search for something comforting to say.

"Yeah, an adventure," he confirmed. "Like a safari. Come on, Debs. Let's do it."

She plucked at the sheet. "Oh, all right. I guess so."

The doctor looked relieved. "I'll let the nurses' station know and get them started on the transfer papers. Hopefully, we can get you on your way within the hour."

"Great." Julia marched to the closet to begin gathering up her sister's possessions. "Now if we could just get hold of Mom and Dad, we could tell them not to bother coming to Bolivar. But, of course, they don't have a cell phone. That would be too showy, and you know good missionaries are supposed to be humble and poverty-stricken."

Peter gave the doctor a shrug and tapped his stomach to indicate the source of his sister's moodiness. Dr. Bryant smiled and spoke a few words of farewell to Debbie as Julia began filling a tote bag.

"If you're a missionary," Julia was saying, imitating her mother's voice, "you can only buy your clothes off sale racks or get them at the secondhand store. On furlough, you wear other people's hand-me-down winter coats. You live in a borrowed house." She paused and looked across the room. "Hey, Pete, remember that place we stayed that one time? We were washing the dog in the bathtub, and you sat on the sink. The whole sink fell right off the wall."

"I remember," Peter said. "Hot water sprayed everywhere."

"Wonderful houses they give missionaries. But, of course, you have to be grateful and smile and be nicey-nice all the time. Remember what Mom used to tell us? 'Don't do anything to make us ashamed of you.' That was it — the main message of our childhood. Be good and sweet and perfect all the time. Be the perfect children, the perfect family. And whatever you do, don't look like you have any money."

"What is Julia ranting about?" Debbie whispered to her brother. "Is this some kind of a joke, or what?"

"It's a mood, I think. She's mad."

"Mad? Julia?"

"She got mad last night, and she's still upset this morning."

"What did you do to her?"

"Me? Why do I get blamed for everything in this family?" Peter crossed his arms. "I didn't do a thing."

"We had hand-me-down Christmas trees, of course," Julia continued as she stuffed Debbie's clothes into a tote bag. "People's leftover, broken ornaments. Their half-melted candles. But, of course, we were just grateful, grateful, grateful. Oh, and then they'd send boxes of their used clothing all the way to Africa. Stained blouses. Ripped hems. Jeans with torn knees. Remember how we'd get those boxes sent by one missions-minded church or another, and we'd just go crazy with excitement? Yay, I get to wear somebody's sweat-stained bra. Whoopee."

"Do you need some help there, Jules?" Peter asked.

"Well, what are you waiting for, Pete?" she snapped back at him. "You'd better pull the car around to the front of the hospital so we can load Debbie from the wheelchair."

"All right, I'm going." Although the

doctor had indicated that it would be half an hour or more before the necessary paperwork was completed, Peter was glad to get out of there. It was like somebody had flipped a switch inside Julia. Instead of the pliant, kind, and loving sister they had always known, they suddenly had the Wicked Witch of the West on their hands.

Was her pregnancy bothering her? Physical discomfort? Or maybe she was struggling with the emotional impact of raising two new children when her other two were nearly grown. She had mentioned a desire to go back to college and become a nurse. Maybe that's what was getting to her. Whatever it was, Peter didn't like it. Julia was the nice one of the family, and seeing her in this sarcastic, angry mood didn't sit well with him. He also wondered if he had brought it on by telling her she didn't have to be a doormat. Oh, well.

He found the car, pulled it around to the front of the building, and got out to wait on a bench. Maybe Julia was worried about Debbie. And no wonder. Despite his best intentions, Peter found himself projecting all kinds of terrible endings to this situation. And where was this so-called boyfriend who had been with Debbie for years? Where were her friends? Her

Sunday school class? Her coworkers at the boutique? Yeah, she'd had a few bouquets and a couple of visitors. But it seemed like in the past couple of days, Debbie had dropped off everyone's radar.

"Ralph!" The sight of the small man with his odd gray mustache lifted Peter's heart.

The nurse gave a cheery wave. "Mornin' to ya, Peter!" It was drizzling, but nothing seemed to dampen the man's spirits.

"I thought you were off duty."

"Aw, I called over to check on Miss Deborah this morning, and I got the news about the transfer. So, I hoofed it over here. I don't live too far away — just across the street really. She'll be all right," he said. "I'm sure of it."

"How can you be sure? Debbie just seems to be getting weaker and weaker." Peter looked into the man's warm brown eyes. "It's like she doesn't even realize what's happening to her."

"Your sister talked to me a lot about her faith," Ralph said. "She told me the only one who had been with her throughout her whole life was Jesus. She said she's traveled here and there all around the world, and sometimes she felt lost or confused. Sometimes she didn't know who loved her — or if anybody did. But she always remembered that Jesus Christ lives in her heart, and he is with her, no matter what happens to her. She knows he loves her. So, I know she's going to be all right."

"But God doesn't promise to heal every sickness, Ralph," Peter said. "You can't count on that."

"Oh, I don't mean she's going to get well. I don't know the answer to that. Miss Deborah's body is pretty near all used up. But she'll be all right anyway. When my wife was sick, she told me it didn't matter if her body never healed because her soul was as healthy as a horse."

Peter tried to smile. He knew Ralph's wife had died, and the man had endured a great deal of suffering. But how could he stand there and dismiss Debbie's condition as being "all right" just because she was a Christian? It sounded trite.

"The verse I put on my wife's headstone really kind of sums it up," Ralph continued. "It's from Revelation 2:10. It says, 'Remain faithful even when facing death, and I will give you the crown of life.' She's in great shape now, my wife. She's wearing her crown and dancing in heaven. It's me who's doing the suffering these days. I miss her, and you'll miss your sister, too, if she goes on to heaven. But she'll be with the Lord, don't you see? She'll be all right."

Peter looked up and saw Julia wheeling Debbie through the big double doors of the hospital. Julia spotted the two of them and headed in their direction.

"Hey, why don't you come to Springfield with us, Ralph?" Peter asked. "You could ride in the back with Debs. Keep an eye on her."

"Oh, that would be wonderful," Debbie said, as the wheelchair rolled to a stop near the car.

"Well, I've got a pot of soup on the stove, and I wouldn't want it to burn down my house. Tell you what, Miss Deborah, I'll call over to Cox this afternoon and check up on you."

"Okay." Debbie looked down at her lap. "Thank you."

Peter focused on Ralph's kind face and warm brown eyes. Last night Peter had declared himself a Christian warrior, and that meant fighting for what was right. But how? He'd always used his mouth, his angry and accusing words. How would Christ have handled this?

"I wish you'd come with us, Ralph," he said. "We need you."

"Oh, Peter," Julia said. "Didn't you hear

him say he's making soup?"

"Look, I think Ralph really cares what happens to Debbie, and right now, she could use his help." He turned on the nurse. "Isn't that right, Ralph?"

Ralph took a step back. "Well, sure I care about Miss Deborah —" he gave her a shy grin — "but —"

"Peter, don't try to *guilt* people into doing what you want," Julia said.

"I'm not 'guilting' Ralph."

"Yes you are. You're doing just what Mom and Dad always did. If you're a Christian, you'll do this and this and this. Well, Christians don't have to be doormats, remember?"

Peter gazed at her for a moment, letting her words sink in. She was right. As a warrior, he would be strong enough to admit that without anger. "You know, Ralph," he said, "I really do hope you call Debs later. And maybe you'll have time to visit another day."

Julia splashed through the puddles to the trunk and tossed Debbie's tote bag in. She couldn't figure out what had gotten into her brother. Here they were — in a terrible crisis with their little sister — and Peter kept coming off like this major Christian. It was almost like he was making fun of her.

And where were their parents? At church — like always. Ralph was more faithful to Debbie than her own parents were! The more Julia had thought about it last night, the more she came to realize how selfish Don and Olive Mossman had always been. Had it bothered them to drag their children halfway around the world? Had they cared in the least when they sent three tiny children off to boarding school one by one? Did anything matter but their precious mission work? Even now?

Julia slung Debbie's bag into the trunk and assisted Peter in helping their sister into the backseat of the rental car. By now, Julia was damp to the skin. Come to think of it, did anyone ever consider how *she* might feel about anything? Did Mike care that she might not want to move to Wyoming and be a pastor's wife? It was one thing to entertain groups of teenagers in their home once in a while. But a pastor's wife would have a lot more responsibilities — especially in a small church. What if they expected her to play the piano on Sunday mornings? She was terrible at playing the piano!

Slumping down into the seat, Julia jerked her shoulder belt across her stomach. The bulge seemed to stick out from here to eternity. Did her daughters ever consider that their mother was a real human being? Hardly! She was just the convenient cook, laundress, chauffeur, nurse, handyman, and psychologist all rolled into one. Did anyone even care that she was pregnant? Did it matter to anyone how she felt? Peter had been right. She was a worm. A pregnant worm.

"I don't feel very good," Debbie said from the backseat. "My hip hurts."

"Just hang tight," Peter said. "It won't take long to get there. Why don't you take a little nap?"

Julia glared out the window, searching for her parents' car. They would probably drive up just after Peter pulled away from the hospital. It was nearly eleven o'clock. An hour late. This was cute. This was just too cute.

Peter switched on the radio and found an instrumental station. The wipers swished back and forth. This ride might actually be kind of nice, he realized. It had been years since he'd been in a car with his sisters.

In spite of her bad mood, Julia was looking kind of stylish in her maternity dress. He noticed she'd pulled her hair up into a topknot. It suited her. And Debbie was on her way to get the help of a specialist. Ralph was a good guy. Peter liked him. Maybe he and Debbie would hit it off. Maybe they'd get married and have kids, and this whole ugly thing would just turn into a dim memory.

After a while, Debbie fell asleep. Julia sat staring out the window at the rain. She still seemed to be seething over something. It was weird to know that his sister was angry. Oh, Julia had been mad before — little snits, an occasional angry glare. But he'd never seen it go on for more than a few minutes.

He wondered if he'd hurt her by calling her a worm. He doubted that Christ would have done such name-calling. On the other hand, wasn't there some place in the Bible where he'd called the Pharisees a brood of vipers? Or maybe that had been John the Baptist. Peter wished he'd listened better during all those years of mandatory church.

Debbie suddenly let out a gasp from the backseat. "Where am I?" she cried out. Her voice was shrill, panic-stricken. "What's happening? Who's —"

"It's okay, Debs," Peter said. "You just dozed off for a few minutes. We're on our way to Springfield, to the hospital."

"Oh."

"Why don't you rest now?"

"I didn't know where I was."

"You're right here with us."

"I thought I was lost." Her voice drifted. "I thought I was lost at Fort Jesus. That's a place in Africa where I got lost."

"You got lost lots of places," Peter reminded her.

"But I thought I was back in Africa. I thought it was the time I got lost at Fort Jesus."

debbie • africa • 1976

When we're on our family vacation to the beach, we always visit Fort Jesus. Of all the places I have been to in the world, it is my favorite. A long, long time ago, in 1593, somebody built the fort out of big coral blocks. In the sunset, it glows pink, just like heaven.

I wish I lived inside Fort Jesus. I don't think I could ever get kidnapped or killed there, because it is very big and very strong. The walls are so thick, people can walk across the top of them. Not even a cannonball can knock down those walls. The gates — nestled up high on the walls

— are made out of iron, and they have sharp spikes on the bottom. If an enemy tried to get me, I could just cut the rope and drop the gate right down on them. They would be stabbed to death. That would teach them.

At Fort Jesus, our family is always happy. Mom and Dad hold hands and walk along the walls, just like they're in love. Peter pretends he's a Portuguese soldier fighting to suppress the Arab rebellion. Julia takes my hand, walks with me into the museum, and reads the inscriptions on all the displays. She doesn't want to miss a single plaque. Someone went to all the work to write up this information, she tells me. So we ought to read it. Julia is thoughtful like that.

The thing I like best in the museum is the broken plates. These plates are blue-and-white china, and somebody found them at the bottom of the ocean in the shipwreck of a Portuguese frigate. I stand beside Julia and stare at those plates. We don't have china plates at our house. We have melamine plates, which won't break. A sprig of purple violets sits right in the middle of each of our plates, and when it's my turn to set the table, I turn the sprigs so they face the right direction. Peter doesn't care at all about violet sprigs. He sets the plates any old way, and the same with the silverware — which isn't really silver, but that's a different subject. The violets on our plates are scratched up from all the knives cutting them day after day. But the blue-and-white china plates in the museum at Fort Jesus just gleam, even though they sat at the bottom of the ocean for no telling how long.

At boarding school, we don't have plates at all. We have metal trays. The trays are divided into sections, and we're supposed to have a different food in each section. Sometimes I get a tray with dried-up food stuck on it. But everyone's in such a hurry to get through the line and eat, that I can't do anything but let the cooks put new food on the old food. Eating at KCA is not my favorite thing.

At Fort Jesus, I keep looking at those blue china plates and thinking about how much I love them. Julia is moving on down the aisle, reading all the signs in the displays. I don't think she would understand why I love those plates. For one thing, Julia is very practical. She thinks we should be happy with what God has given us and stop wishing for more.

I've tried to think this way, but I'm not

very good at it. I always want more. Last year at school, the cooks decided to give us an afternoon snack. They spread strawberry jelly between two slices of bread, cut the sandwich in half, and set it on a little metal cart. After they had made a bunch of these jelly sandwiches, they would roll the cart out onto the porch in front of the student center.

This was very exciting for us kids, and we would wait like vultures, hopping on one foot and then the other, hoping the cooks would hurry up and bring out the jelly sandwiches. The minute the cart came into view, we swooped down on it, grabbing sandwiches and stuffing them in our mouths and pockets.

The first time I came for the afternoon snack, I didn't make it to the cart in time. I was standing at the back of the crowd, and by the time everyone cleared away, there was nothing but a few crumbs left. The next day, I elbowed and fought my way through to the cart just like everybody else. I snatched as many sandwiches as I could get. I didn't care about the people at the back of the crowd because I was hungry, and those were good jelly sandwiches.

But the cooks decided this whole idea of afternoon snacks was too much trouble.

We were too rowdy. We made too much of a mess. So, it only lasted a couple of weeks, and that was the end of the jelly sandwiches.

When I look at the blue-and-white china plates in the museum at Fort Jesus, I don't feel like a hungry vulture. I don't even care that the cooks stopped serving jelly sandwiches. I'm a fine lady who lives at Fort Jesus and eats every meal on fine china plates. I have three servants to wait on me, and I have a cook who makes lobster and prawns and roast beef. I don't ever wear a uniform. My clothes are all made out of silk, and I swish when I walk.

My husband is very handsome and brave and strong. He loves me, and he hugs me all the time. He tells me I'm beautiful. We have seven children, four girls and three boys. They all eat on blue-and-white china plates, and they sleep in the same bed with us at night, so nobody ever gets afraid. We never worry if our plates get broken, because we have more than enough.

As I stroll down the hallway of the museum, I can almost feel my long flowing green dress. My tiny silk slippers go pitter-pat on the stone floor. I smile, nodding from side to side as my servants bow to me. They all love me, because I'm very kind and I keep them safe and healthy.

I float out the museum door and search around for my sister, Princess Julia. Wait a minute. Did she leave without me? Feeling a little flutter of anxiety, I turn and head back into the museum. I'm not a fine lady in a green silk dress anymore. I'm very worried that I've lost my big sister, so I run up and down the aisles looking for her.

"Julia!" I call out in a loud whisper. No one says anything.

I race back out into the courtyard. Where is Julia? I can't see any people at all. I look up on the walls, but my mom and dad aren't up there strolling hand in hand. I search the line of black cannons, but Peter isn't there pretending to be a soldier. Where did they go? Did they forget about me?

I hurry over to the fort's church. This is a broken-down building, but we all like to sit on the stone benches in there and pray. Well, not Peter. The rest of us do. I look for everyone, but the church is empty. I start to feel really scared. Where is my family? Why did they forget about me? Leaving the church, I cross over to the cistern. This is a big deep hole where the soldiers used to store water in case of an attack. As I peer down into the murky water, I suddenly re-member where I am.

Fort Jesus!

I don't have to be scared here. These walls are too thick for any robbers to break in. No one is going to hurt me at Fort Jesus. Feeling a little better, I set out across the courtyard again. This time I come to a house. It's an old Arab house, and I wander around in it, thinking that if I just had a bed, this would make a nice place to sleep. Even if my parents have forgotten all about me, I will be safe in Fort Jesus. I can just curl up and rest, safe and sound.

Walking alongside the wall, I run my hand over the rough coral blocks. The sun is going down — my favorite time. As I watch, the walls slowly turn from gray to pink. Bright orange pink. They glow and glow.

I come to a corner of the fort, so I sit down on the grass and snuggle my shoulders into the warm, sunbaked walls. It feels just like a big hug. Like Jesus is hugging me while I'm sitting in heaven and watching the glory of God all around me. This is the best I have felt in a hundred years.

"Debbie!"

Someone is calling me. It sounds like

Julia. Her voice is far away, and I realize I am hidden here in the corner of the fort. I'm safe and quiet and warm, and suddenly I know I don't want to be found. I close my eyes.

"Deborah Mossman, where are you?"

That's my mother. She didn't leave me! She didn't forget about me. Well, maybe she forgot me for a while. But not forever. I wonder if I should get up and go look for my family. I can hear them calling, but I don't want to move away from this perfect place.

If I stay here, I won't have to go back to boarding school and eat off a dirty tray. I won't have to go to America for furlough and stand in front of all those churches and pretend to love my relatives who I don't even know. I won't have to go home and worry about finishing all the food Mom has managed to cook for us or accidentally running out of all the water Dad has been able to collect in his big metal drum.

If I stay right here, I can melt into this warm wall, just like the bosom of Abraham. And I won't have to fight for jelly sandwiches or covet blue-and-white china plates or any of the other sinful things I do in my life. Like forgetting to read my Bible every night. Like eating the last cookie on the plate. Like telling my mom I don't mind that I didn't get a rocking chair for Christmas, when really I feel mad, mad, mad about that! I wanted that rocking chair, and I wanted to sit on my mother's lap and rock back and forth. I wanted to smell her neck and hear the sound of her humming down deep in her chest. But I tell her it's okay about the rocking chair. Lying is a terrible sin.

I will fade into this wall, and I will become part of Fort Jesus, and no one will ever find me. All the hurts and all the sins and all the ugly things that fill me up inside will disappear. I'll just be a piece of pink coral, glowing like the walls of heaven.

"Debbie, come back! We love you. Debbie!"

Glory be to God.

"Debbie, what's wrong? Why don't you answer?"

Glory in the highest.

"Deb-bie!"

"Debbie!" Julia reached back between the car seats and shook her sister's shoulder. "Debbie, wake up. Peter, something's the matter with her. She's so gray! Why won't she open her eyes?"

chapter fifteen

Julia was thankful for the comfort of Peter's arms around her. They sat side by side in the emergency room waiting to hear from the doctors who had wheeled Debbie away. Why had this terrible thing happened to Debbie? She had looked awful — completely still, blue gray, and barely breathing. "I don't want Debbie to die," she said out loud. She felt almost desperate, as though she needed to physically hold on to her sister.

"Neither do I," Peter said. "But Ralph told me something we need to remember. Before you and Debs came out, he reminded me that Debbie will be all right even . . . even if we lose her. This faith thing has always been real to her. You know God won't let her down."

"I don't want her to be 'all right' in heaven! I want her to be all right here on earth with us. I want us to have the chance

369

to be a better family to her. I want her to know how much we love her. She can't die!"

"Debbie knows we love her, Jules," Peter said. "I'm sure she does."

"Oh, right. Where were we when she was going downhill? We were off in New Mexico living our own lives, hardly even checking in on her. I was a lousy sister. I let Debbie go, just like I've let everyone I've loved slip away from me."

"What do you mean by that?"

"I said so many good-byes in my life — and each time it hurt so much that I forced myself to stop caring when people left me. I shut off the part of me that grieved every time I had to lose someone I loved. I closed myself away from Debbie — and from you, too, Peter."

"But I've always known you loved me, Jules."

"How can you say that? Until we got back together this week, I hardly knew anything about you. I didn't even realize you and Maria were having trouble!" She faced him. How had she failed so miserably to maintain the bond she'd had with her brother? "What a great sister I've been."

"You are a great sister."

"No! No, I'm not."

"Well, look at what we were taught about family loyalty, Jules. The message our parents gave us was pretty pathetic: We love you so much, and now we're abandoning you to fend for yourself."

"Good-bye, good-bye," Julia murmured, feeling once again the desolation that had threatened to envelop her as a child, first in the Happy Room, then every time she was forced to leave someone or something she loved. "Say good-bye to your grandparents and aunts and uncles and friends. Say good-bye to your teachers and your classmates. Say good-bye to your house and your pets and your city and your country and your continent! And now, say good-bye to your parents — and be sure not to care about any of it. Do it over and over and over again. Be big and accept all this, because it's God's will for your life."

She blew her nose into a tissue. "What kind of a lesson was that, Peter? *Don't care too much.* And we learned it really well, didn't we? So well that we let our own sister drift away from us without even realizing it."

"Calm down, Julia." He picked up a strand of hair that had fallen from her topknot. "You're exaggerating this."

"I'm not exaggerating. You called me a

worm — and I am. I admit that. I am a squashed-flat, stepped-on bug of a human being. And you know why? Because I learned the best way to keep from feeling the pain that was with me my whole childhood was to shut down. Don't feel anything. Don't be mad or sad or lonely or frustrated. Make peace with everybody, avoid all conflict, and do everything perfectly. And then I might not feel the pain."

"Julia," Peter said. He tried tucking the loose strand of hair back into her topknot, but she waved his hand away. "Julia, don't blame yourself."

"What lets me off the hook, Peter? Did I stop being Debbie's sister just because I became an adult and had a family of my own? I should have been there for her. I should have seen what was —" She paused and looked down the hall. "There they are!"

She pushed herself from her chair and ran toward her parents, arms outstretched. Her father reached to embrace her, but she grabbed his shoulders and began to shake him violently.

"Where were you?" she shouted, unable to contain her anger. "You promised to be at the hospital in Bolivar at ten! It was nearly eleven when we left, and you weren't there!"

"We were on our way," Mom said. "Julia, what's happened to Debbie? Why are you so upset?"

"On your way? You made a promise! What kept you?"

"The pastor needed to talk to us after the service." Her father tried to pry her hands from his damp raincoat. "There's a committee meeting this afternoon, and he had some questions about the neighborhood evangelization project I'm spearheading. And then as we were walking out the door, your mother was stopped by one of the ladies in the Sunday school class she teaches."

"Louella is such a talker, and —"

"Church? You didn't come because you had to do church work?" Julia was sobbing now. Would her parents never learn? "Debbie is more important than church work!" she cried. "We're your children! We're more important than your church responsibilities. Don't you get that? Don't you see?"

She couldn't stand to even be in their presence anymore. She tore away from her father and began running down the hall. She heard Peter following her, calling her name. Ramming her shoulder into the ER doors, she pushed through and headed into the lobby. She heard sobs echoing through the cavernous rooms and only dimly realized they were her own.

"Julia, wait!" Peter cried.

The electronic door barely opened in time to let her through. She burst out into the rain and started down the stairs. On the second step, her foot hit a puddle and her heel skidded off the marble. Surprise surged through her, followed immediately by horror. She reached for a handhold but couldn't find one. A sense of unreality swept over her. Time seemed to slow. Unbalanced by the weight of her pregnancy, she was unable to regain her footing. She fell to her knees. The sharp edges of the stairway tore at her palms and ripped her shins. When the world stopped spinning, she realized she was lying flat on her stomach on the wet, cold sidewalk.

"Julia!" Peter's voice penetrated. "Julia, are you all right?"

Instinctively trying to undo the damage, she rolled over and tried to sit. A jagged, slashing pain tore through her, and she curled into a fetal position, grasping her bloody knees, crying soundlessly.

"Julia, are you hurt?" Peter was kneeling

beside her. "Stay here. Don't move! I'm going to get some help."

At the sound of Peter's voice, rage displaced her shock. "I hate them, Peter," she sobbed, feeling it all over again. "I hate them so much. I hate what they did to Debbie. I hate what they did to me . . . and you, too."

"Don't try to stand up, Julia," Peter commanded. He cupped her face in his hands and forced her to look at him. "Stay here! I have to get you some help!"

She clutched him, leaning her forehead on his arm. "No, Peter, don't leave me! I'm so mad. I'm so full of . . . anger and rage and every horrible thing that's pushed down inside me. I hated boarding school, and I hated saying good-bye, and I hated my whole horrible, wretched childhood."

"No, you didn't." He stripped off his T-shirt and dabbed it on her bloody knees. "We had fun. We loved Africa. Most of the time, things were all right."

"But I was lonely. I was so lonely! Where were our parents when we needed them? We needed them, Peter. I needed them. Oh, I don't want anything to happen to Debbie . . . and my stomach hurts, Peter. Everything hurts. My babies hurt. Oh . . . my babies . . ."

"Sir?" Someone stood on the step above Peter. "Is she all right?" He looked up to find a security guard peering at him. "Someone said they thought they saw a woman fall down the steps."

"Yeah, get help. She's pregnant, and her stomach is hurting, and there's some blood —"

"Oh, good golly. I'll be right back."

Julia vaguely recognized that Peter was trying to protect her head from the rain as he crouched against her. "Julia, it's okay to be angry."

"I hate God," she said, unable to repress a shudder. "And I hate myself. I hate who I am. And I hate God for letting me turn into this ugly, stinking nothing."

"Julia, you don't hate God."

"Yes, I do! I hate him."

"No, you don't."

"And you know what else I hate? I hate church. I hate the stupid building programs and the pretentious services and the Ph.D. preachers with their sermon points that all start with the same letter of the alphabet." She groaned. She knew she was babbling, sounding hysterical, but she had to get it all out. "Oh, but Peter, I don't hate you. You're a good little brother. I love you. I love Debbie . . . and I don't want her to . . . to die."

"Calm down, Jules. You have to try to calm down."

"I love Mike, too, even though he's driving me crazy. I really do love my husband. And I love Jessica and Heather! I miss my girls! I wish I was home."

"We'll call them. You can talk to them."

She caught his arm and squeezed it. "Don't let Debbie die, Peter."

"I'll go check on her, okay? The paramedics are here. They're going to take care of you, and I'll see you in a few minutes. Remember what Ralph told us. Debbie's going to be all right."

As desperation threatened to overtake her again, she reached for her brother. But he was already gone.

"She's pretty far along," someone said as she was lifted onto a stretcher. "We'd better get on this right away. She's losing a lot of blood."

"I want to see Debbie." Julia was startled by the rattle of a sizeable piece of equipment being pushed into the room, but it didn't deter her. Through the hissing oxygen mask that had been placed over her mouth and nose, she repeated her request. "I need to see my sister. I can't do this right now. I have to be with my sister."

"Mrs. Chappell, we need to do an ultrasound here. I'm Dr. Carson, a perinatologist, which means I deal with complicated or high-risk pregnancies. The fetal monitor is showing us that your babies are having some difficulty, and the nurse tells me you're bleeding significantly." The doctor peered at her, his face serious. A deep-pitched hum filled the room as the nurse turned on the ultrasound machine. In tones of gray and black, the screen slowly came to life. "I know you're upset about your sister, but you need to concentrate on yourself. I see you're also having frequent contractions."

"But what's happened to Debbie?"

"We'll find out about that later, honey," the nurse said as she removed the fetal monitor pieces from Julia's abdomen, then reached up and switched off the overhead lights. "No, no. Don't try to turn onto your back. Remember? You need to stay tilted to your left side so your babies get all the oxygen they can. Can you rate your contractions on a one-to-ten scale?"

"I don't know . . . eight or nine." Julia squeezed her eyes shut. Her tears had mingled with the rain, and her hair lay damp on the pillow beneath her head. What had happened? The contractions were so strong now, so intense, she could hardly remember the sequence of events that had led to this moment. She and Peter had driven Debbie to the hospital. And then their little sister had almost quit breathing. And then Mom and Dad showed up. . . . A gasping sob contracted her chest. She had practically beaten her own father in rage . . . and then she had slipped and tumbled down the steps.

Dear God, please! Julia opened her eyes again and stared at the light. She had told Peter she hated God. Was that true? Blinking, she tried to keep the tears from spilling down her face into her wet hair.

God, are you here? Are you here with me?

"Julia Mossman," the missionary woman announces. It is my turn in the program to recite a verse of Scripture.

I step forward, open my mouth, and speak as loudly as I can. "Joshua 1:9. 'Yes, be bold and strong! Banish fear and doubt! For remember, the Lord your God is with you wherever you go.' "

My friends and I are standing up at Mission Meeting in front of all the missionaries. I am so happy I can hardly keep my feet still on the stage, and these are the reasons why: First of all, ten minutes ago, when I was walking into chapel for the Bible memorization awards ceremony, Paul Davis started chasing me. "I'm gonna get Julia," he yelled. I shrieked and ran away as fast as I could, but not fast enough for Paul. He caught up to me and yanked on my braid! He said, "Gotcha, Pigtails." It was so wonderful that I will never forget it as long as I live.

Oops, time for me to say another verse. It's a long one, but I know every word. "Isaiah 41:10," I announce in my clearest voice. " 'Fear not, for I am with you. Do not be dismayed. I am your God. I will strengthen you; I will help you; I will uphold you with my victorious right hand.' "

The weight of the ultrasound device on Julia's abdomen caused her belly to draw tight. Dr. Carson continued his examination as gently as he could, scanning and measuring, while a lengthening strip of pictures emerged from the machine. "Right here," he said to the nurse, pointing to the screen. "A good-sized clot behind the placenta. Mrs. Chappell," he went on, speaking to Julia, "your fall most likely caused what is known as placental abruption, which is causing internal bleeding as well as the bleeding that's visible. I've measured your babies at about twenty-four weeks' gestation. Does that correspond to the dates of your pregnancy?"

"I don't know," Julia said. "I don't know how many weeks I am. I'm about six months along. I've only known about the pregnancy for a couple of months."

"Let me tell you what is happening," he said, his voice grave. "A portion of your placenta has come away from the uterine wall. In addition to the bleeding caused by that, your babies are not getting the oxygen they need. Baby B, on top, is showing us he's in real trouble. My recommendation is for an immediate cesarean section."

"What's happened to Debbie?"

"Do you have family members waiting outside?" Turning to the nurse, he said, "Find the family, notify anesthesia, and tell the charge nurse to get the OR ready for an emergency section."

"What's happening?" Julia cried, closing her eyes as another contraction curled through her abdomen. *Dear Lord, you promised to be with me! Keep my babies safe. Take care of Debbie.*

The second reason I'm so happy is because I have on the cutest pants of anybody at the awards ceremony. They are pink. A few months ago, I was trying to climb a baobab tree near our house, and I tore holes right through both knees. I was so sad. But then my mom found an old dress of hers with blue, green, yellow, pink, and red stripes on it. She cut two shapes — a star and a heart — out of that dress, and she sewed them on the knees of my pink pants. They are so pretty I'm just about to burst!

Oh, it's my turn again. I take a step out onto the stage and hold my head high. "James 4:8," I say loudly. " 'When you draw close to God, God will draw close to you.' "

"Get NICU over here, stat," spoke Dr. Carson to yet another nurse who had appeared in the doorway with a clipboard.

"Twenty-four week twins. Abruption." Julia was aware of more people in the room now, one with IV paraphernalia, another with laboratory tubes with brightly colored tops.

"NICU? What's that?" Peter's voice drew Julia out of the wave of agony racking through her. "Is my sister having her babies? Are they going to be okay?"

"Peter!" Julia grabbed his hand. "What happened to Debbie?"

He bent over and kissed her forehead. "She's all right," he said, laying his damp cheek against her skin.

"Ralph's kind of 'all right'?"

Peter let out a groaning sob and closed his eyes. "She's dancing in heaven, Jules. She's wearing the crown of life."

"No."

"Her heart. The doctor said she had heart failure caused by an electrolyte imbalance. Her heart gave up."

"No, Peter."

"She's gone, Julia."

"No."

"Okay, we're moving into the operating room now," the doctor announced. "Sir, you'll have to step back from the bed. Mrs. Chappell, I want you to focus on staying with me, doing exactly what I say, and we're going to see what we can do to make this happen the best way possible."

"Peter!" Julia cried out as the bed began to move away from him. "Oh, Peter, call Mike. I need Mike."

"I will, Jules. I'll call him right away." His voice faded. "You take care of yourself!"

"I can't lose my babies. I love my babies."

"Hang on, Julia!" Peter said somewhere far away. "Hang on for those babies . . . and for us."

The third reason I'm so happy is because I can see my mom and dad right there on the third row of chairs in the chapel. They're looking up at me with the proudest light shining in their eyes. They're proud because I won second place in the Scripture-memorizing contest, and now I'm getting to say my verses in front of all the missionaries. Debbie earned a ribbon for effort, but Peter didn't even try. The other kids in the contest are reciting some verses, too, but I'm saying the second most.

I love my mom and dad, and I want them to be proud of me. There just isn't anything I like better than knowing I've made them happy.

"Psalm 50:15," I say in a loud voice. " 'Trust me in your times of trouble, so I can rescue you and you can give me glory.' "

In the rain that had continued all afternoon and evening, Peter and his dad drove toward the Springfield airport. Neither spoke. Peter kept seeing Debbie as he had looked at her for the last time, lying on that gurney, her beautiful blue eyes shut and her body perfectly at rest.

Cardiac arrest. How could that have happened to a thirty-four-year-old? It seemed like once Debbie broke her pelvis, everything else started breaking down. She couldn't fight the infection, and she wouldn't eat, and then her heart gave out.

How could that be? It didn't seem real.

He turned the car into the well-lit airport parking lot and took a ticket from the device. And now Julia was facing the possibility of losing her twins. They had been born only minutes before Peter and his father left for the airport to pick up Mike and the girls. Mom insisted on staying with

Julia. She wanted to pray, she said.

Pray? Would prayer keep the two tiny boys alive — boys who couldn't breathe on their own, who weighed barely a pound each, who looked as scrawny and skeletal as Debbie had on her deathbed? Prayer hadn't kept his sister alive, Peter thought. So, what was the point?

He pulled the car to a stop and set the parking brake. As he reached for the door, his father laid a hand on Peter's arm. "After last night, when you asked Christ to live in your heart," Dad said, "I haven't stopped praying for you. I couldn't sleep last night because I was praying so hard. And I'm fearing that now . . . now that Deborah and Julia . . ."

He broke into tears, and Peter covered his father's hand with his. "You're afraid I'm doubting God. Doubting his power. You're scared I'll turn away from him again."

Dad took off his glasses and laid them on his knee. He rubbed his damp eyes for a moment. "I know it hasn't always looked that way to you, Son, but your mother and I love you children very much. I can't bear to think we've lost our Deborah. Our precious baby. But, Peter . . . to me, it would be even worse . . . much worse! . . . to have you turn away from God . . . to have you reject him."

Peter sucked down a breath at the significance behind those words. He thought about the hours that had passed since his acceptance of Christ. In between one crisis or another, he had spent those hours praying and reading the Bible he'd found in Debbie's house. Then his sister had died and the twins had been born. But for some reason — something he was sure he could never explain — he felt an undeniable sense of peace in his heart. Peace and hope and comfort. And he knew it was the presence of God inside him. God and the power of the countless prayers he had been lifting up. He and his father.

"Dad, you might remember that I'm a pretty stubborn little cuss," he said. "Once I make up my mind about something, I rarely change it. I made up my mind last night. For the first time in my adult life, I know who I am. I'm a warrior for Christ. Life is a battle, and today I've been fighting with every ounce of my strength. This time, Dad, I'm not going anywhere without my spear."

Dad nodded as he wept. Peter reached across and gave his father a hug. "There's the plane taxiing in. Let's go tell Mike he's the father of twin boys. That ought to be an interesting moment."

Trying to force a smile onto his face, Peter climbed out of the car and walked beside his father into the terminal building. They stood near the bank of large glass windows and watched the passengers slowly make their way out of the small jet standing on the runway. And then they spotted Mike Chappell, followed by Jessica and Heather on the stairs. Peter hurried to greet them as they made their way across the tarmac and into the terminal.

"Peter!" Mike gave him a crushing hug. "What's happened? How's Julia?"

"Uncle Peter! Grandpa!" The girls surrounded the two men, hugging and kissing them, shedding tears and clamoring for information.

"Boys," Peter managed. "Julia had twin boys!"

"They're all right," Dad said. "They're in the neonatal ICU and they're struggling, but they're alive."

"Boys?" Mike stared at Peter. *"Boys?"*

"Brothers!" Heather cried out. "Oh, wow. This is just too cool!"

"It's weird, is what it is," Jessica said. "I feel so happy and sad at the same time." Peter knew exactly how she felt.

"Uncle Peter," Heather said, "turn around. Look who came with us!"

She clamped her hands on his shoulders and pivoted him right into the path of Maria and Angelo.

Peter caught his breath. "Maria? How . . . ? What . . . ?"

His wife studied him with her dark eyes. The baby held out his hands. "Pa-pa-pa-pa!" he babbled.

"My angel," Peter cried, taking the boy in his arms. "Aw, Angelo, how's my big boy? Maria . . ."

He looked at his wife's beautiful, anxious face, and his eyes flooded with tears. Her black hair hung around her shoulders like a silky cape, and her pretty lips trembled. He didn't know how she had known to come, but right now she was the most beautiful sight he could imagine. He caught her in his arms and held her tightly so she could never slip away. "Maria, I love you. I love you so much!"

"I'm sorry about your sister, Peter," she whispered. Her breath smelled sweet, as it always did, and the fragrance of her favorite perfume clung to her hair. "I had no idea she was so sick."

"Neither did we," he said. "It's been terrible . . . but you're here. You came.

How did you know?"

"My *abuela* told me about your phone call yesterday. She said you had begged her to talk with me and tell me you've changed. I decided right then to come and see you. I didn't know about Debbie until I got to Albuquerque and called Mike to say hello. They were just about to leave for the airport, and we got on the same flight."

"I *have* changed, Maria. I love you, and I want to start over with you. I want to be the husband you deserve. The father Angelo needs."

She stood on tiptoe and pressed her sweet lips to his cheek. "We'll talk," she said softly. "But first, let's go see Angelo's new little cousins."

chapter sixteen

Julia gazed at her sons through the transparent hoods of their Isolettes. Twin boys, still nameless, laced with wires and tubes, and connected to monitors. They were impossibly small. Too small for her to hold. Too small to breathe on their own or to nurse at her breast or even to wear diapers. They hardly looked alive, but they were, and she thanked God with every breath that filled their tiny lungs. The doctor had explained that her fall had caused the placenta to tear away from the wall of her uterus. That was what caused all the bleeding. And it meant they'd had to perform an emergency C-section to try to save the boys' lives.

Three days had passed since Debbie's death and the birth of the twins. Mike and their daughters had arrived from New Mexico, filling the hospital room with their noisy concern. Somehow, Peter's wife and son miraculously appeared, too. Lots of news and questions and expressions of sympathy poured over Julia, and she tried to soak everything into her heart.

But Debbie was dead.

And two tiny boys lay fighting for life.

Julia ached to the very core of her being — and not just from the pain of her incision. She felt as though she had been rolled through a bed of hot coals — her body burned, her mind tortured, her very soul battered. And who could she talk to about all this? Who would understand the impossible combination of nothingness and fullness inside her?

The whole family had gone to Bolivar to attend Debbie's funeral that afternoon, but Julia had refused to leave the side of her babies. How could she? She loved them so much!

Guilt tore through her in huge crashing waves. It was her fault that her sons lay so precariously close to death. Her fault that they might not have a chance at a normal life — might battle cerebral palsy, blindness, lung problems, and any number of other complications associated with premature birth. If she hadn't gotten so angry at her parents, run like a madwoman through the hospital, and fallen down the steps, her babies would still be safely incubating in her womb, maturing until the day they were ready to be born.

And what had she ranted about during that headlong, maniacal dash through the hospital? She'd said she hated her parents, hated God, hated church. She had verbally violated every value she held sacred. Never in her life had she felt so angry. And look what had come of her rage. Nothing but tragedy.

Those things she'd said weren't even true.

Were they?

Shutting her eyes, Julia bowed her head and tried not to cry. In the past days, she had wept more than she thought possible. Did she hate her mom and dad? Everything within her commanded the proper response: *No, you love your parents. They were wonderful parents. You had a fantastic childhood in Africa — experiences you wouldn't trade for anything.*

But something deep down inside Julia whispered another truth: *Your parents abandoned you. They hurt you and neglected you when you needed them most. You will never look at them in the same way again, because now you see reality. Your mother and father put their church work above their family. They always did. They always will.*

Oh, it was too awful, the way she felt now. She wanted to go back to her blind acceptance of the pretty image she had painted of her childhood. She wished she could pray.

But she'd said she hated God. No, she didn't hate God. She loved and worshiped him. She was placing her tiny sons in his loving hands each moment of their lives. God had been with her and in her through everything she had endured. She did not hate him.

And then that little voice began to whisper again: *Everything that hurt you was done in God's name. Every painful loss came because of God's will. God sent your parents to Africa. God allowed your parents to send you to boarding school. God allowed Debbie to die and your babies to be born too early. What kind of a God do you worship, Julia? Who is God, and why do you confess him as Savior and Lord?*

"I'm sorry, God!" Julia whispered through her tears. "I'm sorry I'm mad at you. I don't want to be angry. But everything inside me hurts. You're supposed to be loving and nurturing. Are you? Why is it that every time I think of you, I feel hurt? I feel pain. Are you the God of pain or the God of healing?

"And what about your church? Each time the doors are open, Lord, there I am working away for you. Or singing. Or listening to some preacher. In Africa, out in the bush, I knew you. At least I thought I did. Are you in America — in these fancy churches with their gymnasiums and committees and building programs? Why doesn't the pastor ever come see me? I know I'm the youth minister's wife. But I need feeding, too! I need help. Does my pastor even know I exist?"

"Julia?" A nurse laid a hand on her back. "We have to ask you to leave now. I'm sorry. We'll call you from the waiting room when it's time to come back in."

Wordless, Julia nodded. She ran her gaze over her little boys, memorizing them, as if somehow this could keep them alive until the next time she saw them. She walked out into the waiting room, curled up on a couch, and shut her eyes. She was so weary. So worn. And so very lost.

As she lay half asleep, drowsy but in too much pain to rest, she thought of her sister. Why had Debbie let herself get into such terrible shape? It was her own fault she had died! She had killed herself. Suicide by starvation.

But why had Debbie wanted to die?

What had been so awful in her life that she hadn't wanted to go on living? Julia shuddered and turned over on the sofa. She didn't want to be angry anymore. But now that the emotion had been released, it curled through her, refusing to be tamed into submission.

She was angry with her parents. Angry with God. And angry with Debbie. *You shouldn't have done it, Debbie! You shouldn't have gone and died!* The rage tearing through her reminded her of the countless incidents in which she'd been furious with her little sister . . . like the time Debbie had beaten her at Old Maid seven games in a row . . . or the time Debbie had opened her private dresser drawer and played with her paper dolls without asking . . . or the time Debbie had cut Julia's Skipper doll's hair . . .

julia • africa • 1974

Debbie and I don't have very many Barbies, but we play with them all the time. We have two Barbies who used to have ponytails, but we took out the rubber bands and found out they have bald spots on the backs of their heads. Their eyelashes are black and solid, one long lump that would probably blind them if they ever had to blink. My Barbie has brown hair, and Debbie's is blonde. They don't bend or anything fancy like that. We saw some bendy, twisty Barbies in the Sears catalog, but our mom didn't have enough money to get them. That's okay.

We have two Kens. They used to have crew cuts, but now they have bald, pointy foreheads where the hair is starting to wear away. Our Kens are blond and brunet, too, but we don't always make them marry the Barbie with the same color hair. We mix and match.

Mom made most of the clothes for our Barbies. We have a wedding dress and some skirts and coats and regular dresses. We don't have any shoes or purses at all. Our Kens only have one pair of pants each, but that doesn't matter to us. Sometimes Ken has to be Barbie's mother, so he wears a dress. Sometimes he's her best girlfriend. But he's kind of ugly for a girl.

Over the years, we've bought a few other dolls in Nairobi to go with our Barbie collection. They aren't genuine Barbies, of course. They have *China* printed on their behinds, and they look kind of pale and sickly. Still, they join in all the games that Debbie and I play with the real Barbies. Sometimes we pull their heads off and switch them around, and it's a lot of fun.

The most exciting thing that happened to us lately was this past Christmas. What should appear under our little aluminum tree but a pair of Skippers who came in a box all the way from America! Barbie's little sister was more than we had ever hoped for. But we have two of them with straight, silky hair that goes all the way to their waists. My Skipper has red hair, and Debbie's is a brunette. They are so cute. Mom has made them several little dresses, and we're so glad to have them join all our other dolls. We play big games, and we make houses for them on the card table. The tissue box is a perfect-sized bed, and washcloths make great carpets.

Our Barbies have been to the moon. They've been pioneers. They've been mermaids under the ocean. There is nothing they can't do. Today we're playing "beauty parlor." The Barbies are hairdressers, and all the other dolls are coming into the salon for new styles. Debbie and I braid their hair, make ponytails and buns, and use our colored markers to give Ken something better looking than that dumb crew cut.

"Julia, I'm going to do something special just for you," Debbie tells me. Her blue eyes are shining, and I can't wait to see what she's thinking of.

"Okay!" I tell her as she takes my red-haired Skipper and crawls behind the bed. I'm busy putting tiny little cornrows in one of the fake Barbie's hair. It's hard to get them to stay. I have to really concentrate hard.

"Ta-dah!" Debbie cries out suddenly. She whisks Skipper from behind the bed and holds her in the air like a trophy.

I stare. Then I blink and stare some more. Most of Skipper's beautiful red hair is gone. What's left sticks straight out all the way around. She looks like she jammed her finger in an electric socket.

"Isn't she pretty?" Debbie asks. "I gave her a bob."

Our grandma got a bob when she was eighteen. There's a picture of her hanging on the living-room wall. Mom told us all about the roaring twenties and flappers and bobs. Bobs are smooth. They have little waves in them which you make with bobby pins. They curl up under your chin and look very darling.

"That's not a bob," I say.

"Yes, it is." Debbie studies Skipper. "It's a bob."

"No, it's not."

"Is too."

"Is not!"

"Is too!"

"Gimme that!" I grab Skipper and touch her flyaway hair. That's when I start to cry. I can't help it. She had the prettiest red hair, all the way to her waist. Now it's so ugly. None of the boys will like her at all. They won't ask her out on dates. She isn't fit to be anything but a laughingstock.

"It's a bob!" Debbie shouts and jerks Skipper from me. She mashes down the hair to show me how it comes down to her chin, just like Grandma's hair in the living-room picture. "See, it's pretty!"

"It sticks out. You ruined my Skipper!"

"I did not."

"Did too!"

"Shut up!"

This is something we're never allowed to say, and I can't believe those words just came out of my sister's mouth. I'm sobbing, and I reach out and smack her across the cheek.

"How dare you tell me that!" I wail. "You shut up!"

"Shut up, shut up, shut up!" Debbie pounds me on the leg with her fist. Now she's crying, too, but I don't care at all. She ruined my Skipper, and she had no right. Nothing she can ever do will bring back my beautiful doll.

"You're stupid!" I tell her. We're not supposed to say this, either. I grab her arm and sink my fingernails into her skin.

"Stop," she shouts. "You're hurting me!"

"You deserve it." I rake my nails down her arm.

"Ow, ow! Your Skipper had dumb red hair to start with. She's ugly!"

"You're ugly!"

"You're stupid!"

"Shut up!"

By now, we are down on the rug slapping each other and yanking on each other's hair. I pound on her with my poor, half-bald Skipper. Debbie kicks me in the knee.

Finally, I scramble to my feet and head for the bedroom door. "I'm telling! I'm telling on you!"

"You can't tell!" she screams. Her arm is bleeding where I scratched it. "Mom is at a women's meeting at Sultan Hamud, so ha! ha! You can't even tell Dad, 'cause he's over at the kraal talking to the elders."

"Shut up!" I say one last time, because I know she's right, and there's nothing Mom or Dad can do about my poor Skipper anyway.

"Stupid!" she yells as I run out the door, sobbing. "Idiot, stupid, dumb, shut up!"

These are the worst words we know, and this has been the most awful fight Debbie and I have ever had. I hate her so much I think I would kill her if I could. I run out to the incinerator and climb up onto a rock and cry. I wish I could throw Debbie in the incinerator and burn her up. I wish I could knock her out and let the lions eat her. I wish I could tie her to an anthill and watch while the ants swarm over her, nibbling away at her stupid, ugly, dumb self.

For a long time I sit on that rock and cry. Then gradually I start to notice how warm I feel. I'm sweating. I lift my head and rub my eyes with my fists. Wow, I'm really hot. I stare at nothing for a long time. Then I start to look at the things in our incinerator.

Banana skins don't burn all the way up. I never knew that. I wonder if Debbie knows. There's a broken drinking glass. The other day at lunch, Peter banged it into his mouth and chipped his tooth on it — and that broke the glass. Now here it is in the incinerator. I notice a few scraps of paper that haven't burned. They look like Bible lessons Dad has been writing. He has to teach the Maasai pastors so much stuff because they can't read very well. They hardly know what the Bible says at all.

I spot a piece of aluminum foil. It must be really old to have wound up in the burn barrel. Mom almost never throws foil away. She smooths out each sheet and washes it. Then she props it up around the sink to dry. She does the same thing with plastic bags. She uses them over and over until they can't be used again. I think about how many possible leftovers that scrap of foil has covered in its lifetime. And now here it is, wadded up in the incinerator.

It's really hot out by the burn barrel. Two lizards watch me from a rock near the one I'm sitting on. I start to wonder if there might be a snake under my rock. I prop up my feet and hug my knees. I think about what Debbie's doing in the house. I really hate her. She's an awful sister.

I'm sweating a whole lot. And I'm thirsty, too. That snake under my rock might be thinking about coming out and looking for something to eat. What if it's a puff adder or a boomslang or a cobra? Snakes don't strike people just out of meanness, but what if he doesn't like me sitting on his rock?

I look at the lace curtains in our windows. Even though it's made out of corrugated tin, our house stays cooler than the outside air. I think it must have something to do with the shade from the acacia tree nearby. I am very hot.

Although I hate my little sister, we usually do have a lot of fun together. Every school holiday, we play all kinds of games. She knows everything about me, and I know everything about her. If one of us has an idea, the other one will know exactly what to do. We hardly even have to talk to each other.

One of our most favorite games is pretending to be shipwrecked on an island. The area rug is the island, and the couch is our lookout post. If we set one foot off the island, the sharks will get us. But there's always other stuff to worry about, too. Pirates invade the island a lot, and we have to make traps for them. Sometimes an elephant will go mad and storm around, trying to knock things over.

I stare at the window of the bedroom Debbie and I share. I suppose it wouldn't be such a terrible thing to have a Skipper with short hair. She could be the boy and invite the other Skipper out on dates. We could ask Mom to sew some jeans and a T-shirt for her.

I really wish I hadn't scratched Debbie. She was bleeding something awful. God is not happy with me about that — I'm sure of it. Why did I get so mad? Debbie was just trying to do a nice surprise for me. She thought she could give Skipper a bob, and even though it didn't turn out quite right, I shouldn't have hit her.

Is it possible to be mad, mad, mad — and love somebody at the same time?

I lean across the space between my rock and the burn barrel, hoping the snake won't strike suddenly. I tug out one of the scraps of paper from Dad's Bible lesson. It's half burned, but there's some white space on the other side. I break off a piece of a charred stick. I spread the paper on my knee, and I write a message in charcoal:

Dear Debbie,
I am sorry I scratched you. Want to play shipwreck?

Love, Julia

I toss the stick on the ground and fold the paper into a nice square. Then I haul myself onto my feet on top of the rock and tense up for the biggest jump of my life, because there's no way I'm going to let that snake come out and bite me. I have a lot of fun things to do.

I leap at least five feet away from the rock and tear across the patch of dry grass toward the house. We don't have screens on our windows, and we keep them open to let in fresh air. Standing outside the bedroom Debbie and I share, I pull aside the lace curtain and peer inside. Debbie has her back to me. She's sitting on the bed trying to glue Skipper's hair back on. She has made a terrible mess, and Mom's going to be mad about the glue all over the bedspread. I rear back and hurl the folded note across the room, hitting Debbie on the arm. As she swings around, I duck.

Pretty soon, I hear the front door open. "Julia?" she calls.

I creep around the side of the house and peep out. She's been crying. Her nose is red and her eyes are all swollen up. She sees me.

"You can be captain of the ship," she says.

This is a very big deal because we always argue over who gets to be captain. I walk toward her. "Where are our swords?"

"Mom hid them on top of the refrigerator."

"You get the swords, and I'll find a treasure chest." I pause. "Should we have a treasure chest this time?"

She smiles. "Yeah! And let's put my birdcage necklace in it!"

Wow, this is wonderful. Debbie loves that necklace, and she never lets me touch it. A church in America gave it to her for a going-away present when we left for Africa. The small golden cage is filled with tiny stones of every color — like emeralds and rubies and sapphires. Peter says they're all fake, but we don't care. Debbie and I both think that necklace is the most beautiful thing we've ever seen. I can't believe she's going to let us use it in our game.

"I'll get it for us," she says.

"Okay!" I head off into the kitchen to look for a box we can use as a treasure chest. This is going to be a lot of fun!

chapter seventeen

"Julia!" Peter sat down on the small couch beside his sister and put his hand on her arm. "Julia, let me take you to the hotel so you can get some rest."

She opened her eyes and looked at him without seeming to see anything. Peter gave her a little shake. "Come on, Jules. Let me take you to the hotel where Mike and the girls are staying. Mom and Dad went home hours ago."

"Are my babies okay?" she mumbled.

"They're fine. And the nurse told me you need to sleep in a real bed tonight. She'll call us if there's any trouble at all."

"No, I can't leave them."

"Julia, it's nearly two in the morning, and I've been sitting here with you until I can barely stay awake myself. Let's go home and get some sleep."

"I can't leave the hospital, Peter." She

pushed herself up and raked a hand through her hair. His sister looked about as bad as Peter had ever seen her. Dark circles shadowed her eyes, and she was as pale as the shaft of moonlight across the floor of the waiting room.

"Julia, you can't keep your babies alive just by sitting here day and night," he said as gently as he could. "You need to trust the nurses to take care of the boys. That's what they're trained to do. The best thing for you would be a good night's sleep."

She shook her head, and Peter knew it was a losing battle. Mike had been trying to pry his wife away from the hospital for several days now, but she refused to leave.

"Where's Maria?" she asked, stifling a yawn.

"She and Angelo are staying at the same hotel as your family."

"How are things going with the two of you, Pete?"

He shrugged. "All right, I think. We're talking a lot. Dad's been helping us some, trying to get us to look at the real problems in our marriage. We were fighting over lots of little things, but Dad thinks there might be something deeper."

"Do you agree?"

"Maybe. This afternoon, Maria told me

she feels like I've never really been committed to her. She says it's like I'm only halfway in the marriage. Like I'm keeping one foot out the door in case I need to run." He studied the floor for a moment. "I think she could be right. You know all that stuff you said the other day — about the good-byes that were such a part of our lives? I realized I'm afraid to let myself get too close to anyone because I might lose them."

"Oh, Peter."

"I'd rather cut the ties than be cut loose myself."

"Well, you can't keep Maria at arm's length. Not if you want your marriage to work."

"I'm trying to let her into my heart. She told me I killed the love inside her, and I know it's true. I've asked her to give me one more chance. I want to show her I've changed. I'm different now. I know I'm not perfect, and I know we'll still have problems, but I'm determined to be the husband Maria deserves."

"That's good," Julia said vaguely.

"Maria was right when she told me that in all the years she's known me, my thoughts have been on one person — myself. She's having trouble believing I can be different."

"Can you?" Julia's interest seemed to pick up a little.

"Yes I can, because of Jesus Christ. I used to be filled with myself. I had no room for Maria or Angelo or anyone but me. But when Dad spoke to me and explained the truth, I understood it. For the first time I understood it and accepted it. I'm not filled with myself anymore. I'm filled with the Spirit of God. As I learn who I am, I'm trying to let Maria see the changes, too."

"That's good," Julia said.

Peter was afraid he was losing her again. "I'm talking more about Africa, too, about what it meant to me and how it feels to have lost all that. And I'm trying to grow as a Christian. I've been reading the Bible."

Julia stared at him as though her mind had suddenly gone blank. Her eyes were expressionless, like a pair of television sets with the power turned off. He put his arm around her and gave a squeeze.

"Please let me take you home, Julia. You're about to collapse."

"No, it's just . . . I can't make sense of everything. You're reading the Bible?"

"Yeah. I want to know what it says. I think it's going to help me repair the mess

411

I've made with Maria."

"Is she planning to move back in with you?"

"She says she will. But she's scared." He paused. "So am I."

Julia laid her head on his shoulder. "I'm proud of you, Peter. You're a warrior, and you're going to win back your wife. Just like you said."

"I couldn't protect Debbie, though. I couldn't keep her alive."

"No." She trembled a little. "Is she really dead, Peter? It just doesn't seem possible."

"I'll take you to the cemetery tomorrow. You need to see where she's buried. That'll help you start to accept it."

"No, I can't leave my boys."

"Why not, Julia? They may be here in this NICU for weeks. Even months. You can't live at the hospital."

"Yes I can."

"Why?"

"Because I love them."

"Because you feel guilty. You're blaming yourself that they were born prematurely, isn't that right?"

"Partly."

"And you feel guilty because you didn't really want to be pregnant in the first place."

"Yes." She gulped down a sob. "And also because they're my children, and I'm not going to abandon them the way we were abandoned. I'm going to stay beside them every minute."

"You have other children, too, Julia. Your daughters are very worried about you. And so is Mike. He told me he doesn't know what to do. It's like you're hiding in some kind of a tunnel, and he can't get to you. Don't abandon the rest of your family because of the babies, Julia."

"I don't have enough energy for all of them. I can only take care of the boys right now."

"But you *can't* take care of them. You can't even hold them."

"They need me!"

"Yes, but you're too tired to do them or anybody else any good. You have to take care of yourself first."

"How can you say that?" she cried out, jerking away from him. "I have to do more. I have to do better . . . I can't . . . can't . . ."

"Julia, come here." He drew his sister into his arms. "I'm a warrior, but I'm not the head elder of the tribe. And even though you've spent your whole life trying to do everything perfectly, you're just a woman, just a human being. You've done a lot of things right, and you've made a few mistakes."

"I said I hated God."

"You were upset."

"But I said that!"

"Look, I've said hundreds of things I didn't really mean."

"I think I meant it, Peter." She covered her eyes with her hands. "Not really, but sort of. See, there are some things I've been thinking about. Some angry feelings I've been having. And I'm furious inside. God has let some horrible things happen to me. I hate that!"

Peter rubbed his sister's back, thinking of all the times his own thoughts had been exactly the same. And now here sat good, perfect little Julia — finally facing up to reality. Funny that she had landed here, when he had finally grown past this stage. He could remember the anger, the feelings of betrayal that had always been associated in his mind with God. He knew just how Julia was feeling. But now — finally, unbelievably — he could see beyond the hurt.

"Julia, here's what I want to tell you," he said. "You might not believe me now, but later on you will." He sighed. How could he put into words the truths he was only beginning to understand himself? "I'm starting to see that it's okay to feel angry about the things that hurt us in the past. And it's all right to admit that God was there when those painful things happened. We don't have to choose one or the other."

"What do you mean?"

"Pain and faith. I wouldn't have believed it myself a couple of months ago, but I'm starting to get it. Pain and faith can co-exist, Jules." He pushed her tangled hair back behind her shoulders, as if he could somehow straighten her into some kind of order and peace. "We can remember the pain of feeling abandoned by Mom and Dad, even feeling forsaken and betrayed by God — and we can also know that God was with us through it, loving us and shaping us into the kind of people he wanted us to be. The fact that awful, painful things happened to us doesn't mean God didn't love us."

"I don't know, Peter. All I know is how bad I feel."

"You feel angry, and you don't think God can be a part of that. You think in order to be a good Christian, you've somehow got to eliminate the hurt, pretend it isn't there. But it is."

"Yes, it is."

"You know what I was reading this morning? It was that passage in the Bible when Jesus was in the Garden of Gethsemane. He knew his death was coming, and he was in a lot of pain over it. He didn't want that pain, Julia. He sweated blood and begged God not to make him go through it. Jesus felt hurt and rejected and afraid at the same time he loved his Father. He suffered a lot — more than we ever did in Africa, that's for sure. But the thing was, Jesus never rejected God. He begged for the pain to stop, he even felt like God had forsaken him — abandoned him, Julia! But he just kept on talking to God and trusting God to be with him. And he was."

Julia nodded. "You know, I remembered some things about Debbie. About how I could be so angry with her . . . and still love her at the same time."

"Yeah. And after a while — after you have time to think about it clearly — you'll figure out that you don't have to pretend anymore. You don't have to pretend you had a perfect childhood to avoid damaging your rosy picture of God. God's not rosy. He's real. And you can be honest about the pain you've gone through without having to stay angry at God and everyone else who had a part in it. You'll get to where you can admit the pain — and love God, too."

"You're ahead of me," she said. "All this time, I thought you were so messed up because you lived in your anger. But now you're past the rage and into this stage where you're accepting both pain and faith."

"Uh-oh, I can feel my straight-A sister getting nervous here. I'm ahead of you, huh? I've got you beat?" He shook his head. "You're so far ahead of me in understanding faith — in knowing the Bible and understanding God — that I'll never catch up."

"I don't understand God."

"Who does?" He elbowed her. "Seriously, who does?"

"Billy Graham?"

He laughed. "I bet if he could, Billy Graham would tell you he never even got close."

"I wish I hadn't said I hated God. Or our parents. Or even church. I don't really hate any of that. I'm just feeling angry."

"Ask forgiveness. You know how."

"Yeah." She rubbed her eyes. "I do."

"Now, come on, Jules. Let's go over to the hotel and put you to bed."

"No," she said, shaking her head. "I'm

serious, Peter. I won't leave my babies. I need to be with them."

He let out a deep breath. "All right, but I'm going home. I can't do this night after night."

She leaned over and kissed him on the cheek. "Thanks, little brother."

As he left the waiting room, he turned to find her curled up on the couch again, and it looked like her lips were moving in prayer.

Mike sat beside Julia and held her hand as they gazed down at their sons. "Something that starts with a *D*," he said. "In memory of Debbie, and in honor of your dad. But not Donald. I can't handle having a son named Donald. I can't say it without adding 'Duck.' "

"David . . . Dustin . . . Darrell . . . Derek." She could hear the toneless quality to her voice, and she wished she could inject some spark into herself. "Or Daniel. I like Daniel."

"I like it, too. Daniel in the lions' den. That would be a fitting description of either one of these two little rascals."

Now that it seemed the babies might actually survive, Julia had agreed to name them. Her husband had found a collection of name-your-baby books in the waiting room, and they'd spent hours poring through them.

"What about David?" Mike suggested. "David in the Bible was a fighter. He slew Goliath."

"Don't say things like that."

"Like what?"

"Like *slew*. It's not a real word. It's a preacher word. A fake word."

Mike let out a breath of frustration. "Julia, honey, how long are you going to be in this bad mood?"

"Forever."

"Well, it's getting old."

"Too bad. I'm sick of being a doormat. I'm going to say what I feel."

He shifted in the chair. "Do you think it's your hormones? Or the baby blues, or something? Maybe we should get you to a therapist."

"Not right now. I want to stay with the babies."

"Julia, look, Peter told me how upset you were right before the babies came. He's tried to explain all of it to me — the things you guys were talking about. I think I sort of understand. At least I would if you'd talk to me without biting my head off."

"I'm sorry, Mike. I just can't handle

everything all at once."

"Well, if your frustration has anything to do with blaming yourself because you didn't really want to be pregnant — because you were thinking about going back to college for your degree —"

"How did you know about that?"

"I'm married to you, remember? You've talked about it off and on ever since you quit school. I know you want to be a nurse. And I support that. I really do." He took her hand. "Julia, I realize I've been pretty unstable lately. It seems like God has been dealing with me —"

"Don't say that, Mike. 'God has been dealing with me.' It's so preachy sounding."

He scratched the back of his head. "Okay. Good grief."

"Well, I'm just tired of hearing it. I've heard it all my life — that religious language everybody speaks. Don't do it anymore. I can't stand it."

"All right." He rubbed his thumb over her knuckles. "I haven't been comfortable as a youth minister because I thought I was getting too old to relate to teens. And I've been praying about it . . . is it okay if I say that? Praying about it?"

She glanced at him. "It's okay." She felt

kind of bad now, wishing she hadn't come down so hard on her husband. Mike was worn out, too. He had suffered greatly over the condition of their sons. He had wept many tears, and he could hardly tear himself away from the NICU each evening.

"Anyway, I feel like our boys . . . are we calling them Daniel and David?"

She nodded. "Daniel and David."

"I feel like Daniel and David are gifts. They're God's way of teaching me some important things. Like I'd better be in the business of relating to young people for a long time to come."

She smiled. "You're wonderful with youth, Mike."

"I really love kids. All ages of them. I just don't want to get boring."

"You're never boring."

"Neither are you. But, Julia, if you feel like a doormat being a stay-at-home mom, I'll support your going back to college. I'll work it out with the church so I can be with the boys while you take classes. We can do this. I know it."

"Thanks, Mike," she said. "That means a lot to me. But I'm beginning to see that God is telling me the same thing he told you. Daniel and David are our gifts. I want to care for people and develop my skills in the nursing area. If the boys have special needs — which the doctor says they may — then I'll have plenty of stay-at-home nursing to keep me busy. Why don't we give it a year or so and see how they're doing?"

"Are you sure, Julia?"

She nodded. "I just want to take our babies home and get back to living again."

"Well, that brings up another point." He squeezed her hand. "Julia, you know how I've been talking about moving to Wyoming?"

She felt her heart constrict. If he thought they could take two premature babies to the middle of the northern wilderness —

"Well, I've been doing some checking around," he said, running on breathlessly the way he did when he was nervous, "and there's a church here in Springfield that's looking for a youth minister. Yesterday afternoon I went ahead and talked to their pastor, and he seemed very interested." He studied her for a moment. "Now, please don't get upset. I know Peter said you're struggling with your feelings about your parents. But I figure there's no way we can live in some remote place if the boys have these special needs. So Wyoming is out. And I feel like I'm just ready to move away from Santa Fe. I'd like to get back here closer to where I grew up. My parents are very concerned about the babies, and they want to help out. Julia, your mom and dad have really encouraged us to move here, too. They said they would love to be near us and be a part of our lives."

"They said that?" Julia didn't know whether to be pleased or suspicious.

"I don't know why that's so hard for you to believe. Your mom's been going nuts organizing a baby shower for you and keeping all her prayer chains informed on the condition of the boys. Your dad has done everything he could to make Jessica and Heather feel comfortable while they're here. He even loaned them his car so they could go out for pizza. Your parents are pretty wonderful people, Julia. I know you had some hard times as a kid, but they love you a lot."

Julia felt a tendril of hope stirring in her heart. "I do have a lot of things to work through with my parents. I don't know if it's too late, but I'd really like to try. Living closer might help." She lifted her husband's hand and kissed it. "I love New Mexico," she whispered, "but it might be good to move here."

"Then you'd support me if I put my

name in with the search committee for that church?"

"Go for it, Mike."

He hugged her. "We'll make it, Julia. You'll see."

"I love you."

"I love you, too. And now I have one more request for you. See those people out there?" He pointed to the large window that looked out onto the waiting room. She could see her parents, her daughters, Peter and his family, and even Mike's parents, who had driven from the northern part of the state to visit the babies. She knew all of them had been coming to the NICU every day, spending hours there. She'd just been too wrapped up in her own pain to take much notice of anyone else.

"I see them."

"We all want to take you to the cemetery. We want you to leave the babies here for a few minutes and trust the nurses to take care of them. You need to do this, honey."

Julia let her eyes drift over her tiny sons. Then she stood. "I have a better plan," she said. As Mike followed her out of the room, she walked toward her parents.

"Hey, Mom and Dad," she said. They each embraced her, holding her tightly. "Listen, I need to go see about Debbie. It's another good-bye, you know."

"Yes, Julia," Mom said. "We know."

"I was wondering though . . . I really hate to leave the boys alone, without any family around. Would you stay with my sons? Would you watch them for me?"

"Oh, sweetheart, we're so sorry we were late to Bolivar the other day." Mom began to cry. "We didn't realize how much we were upsetting you. We didn't know Debbie was —"

"Mom, are you listening to me? I'm telling you I trust you. I'm giving you charge over our babies, to take my place while I'm gone. Will you do that?"

"Of course we will, Julia," Dad said. "We won't leave their side. We promise."

Julia nodded. Jessica and Heather slipped their arms around her, one on each side. "We're here for you, Mom," Jessica whispered. "We're all together now."

"Dad just told us you're going to call our brothers Daniel and David," Heather said. "Can we choose their middle names? Me and Jessica?"

"I think that would be a great idea."

"Cool!"

Julia stretched out on the grass and unfolded her legs. Peter tucked his jacket under her head and took his place beside her. Debbie lay not far away, in the shade of an oak tree. It would be months before the grass grew over the scar in the earth that marked her resting place. Peter and the others had ordered a headstone. Julia planned to decorate it with flowers.

"I'm glad everybody else went for a walk," she told her brother. "It's nice to be here, just the three of us."

"Well, Debbie's in heaven, but I kind of feel her spirit. Do you?"

"A lot. I think Ralph knew what he was talking about when he said she was going to be all right."

"She *is* all right. . . . But I miss her."

"Me, too." She studied the canopy of oak leaves overhead. "I hope Ralph is okay."

"He didn't do too great at the funeral. Cried a lot." Peter twirled a fallen leaf between his thumb and forefinger. "I'm kind of glad in a way. The rest of the people who showed up hardly made it to the hospital to visit her. But Ralph . . . I think he loved Debs."

"I think so, too. I can't help wondering what might have happened between them if . . ." She faltered. "I'm going to write to him. Thank him, you know. Tell him how much we appreciate him. Keep him in touch with our family."

"That's a good idea." He fell silent. "Speaking of keeping in touch, I want to do a better job of that myself. I don't want us to drift apart again like we did."

"Oh, Peter, I don't want that either. That's going to be one of the hard things about leaving New Mexico — being so far away from you and Maria."

"Yeah, but it will be good for you to be closer to Mom and Dad."

"I hope so," Julia said. "I know it didn't really help Debbie to have them living nearby, but maybe I can take some steps to building a better relationship with them. I'm sure going to try."

A comfortable silence grew between them. How many changes had occurred in such a short time, Julia thought. And yet there was still so much more to be done. She felt like there was a forest ahead, and she'd just found the road.

"You know what this reminds me of? The trees and the green grass and all?" Peter's voice broke into her thoughts.

"The graves?" she asked.

"Not that part. Mostly the trees and the blue sky." He paused. "It makes me think of the arboretum in Nairobi."

She remembered. "Oh, I loved going there when we were little. We used to have wonderful picnics — remember how you and Debbie and I would ride the Saturday bus down from KCA, and Mom and Dad would meet us? And then we'd all go to the arboretum and walk through the trees together."

"Remember the time Debbie got lost in the hedge maze?"

"She was always getting lost." Julia reflected on her statement, wondering if Debbie finally felt at home, secure and safe at last.

"And remember the time we walked around the bend in the path and ran into that whole gang of grass cutters with their *pangas?*"

"That scared me to death. I was sure they were going to come after us. But they just waved and went back to cutting the grass."

"Do you remember the most exciting thing that ever happened to us at the arboretum?" Peter asked.

"Of course. How could I forget? We were lying out under a tree just like this. Mom had stretched out with her purse under her head for a pillow."

"Dad and I had gone for a walk. He was

chewing me out about my grades at school — as usual . . ."

We have to get on the KCA bus at six o'clock on a Saturday morning. I like to sneak out of the dorm late on Friday nights and hunt with my friends, so it's not my favorite thing to get up early on Saturdays. But Julia and Debbie are excited because Mom and Dad wrote that they'll be in Nairobi for a grocery-shopping trip, and they want us to come see them for a few hours. The last thing I want to do is walk around in boring old Nairobi. But I don't like to disappoint my sisters, so here we are bouncing along on the bus.

Outside the sun is just coming up, and the whole Rift Valley is coated with a pink glow. I can see Mt. Longonot, a volcano that's full of caves and bats. Sometimes a group of us boys talks one of our teachers into taking us there to explore. It's fun.

Several lakes glimmer gold on the floor of the valley. I know the zebras, giraffes, and gazelles are cautiously making their way toward the water to get a drink. They'll

429

bend down to take a sip, then jerk up and scout around for any scent of lion or cheetah. But the cats are probably sprawled under trees somewhere, too lazy to bother hunting for breakfast.

After what seems like hours, the bus finally comes to the edge of the city. We pass the slums where thousands of people live in cardboard boxes covered with plastic or sheets of corrugated tin. They make their living through prostitution or the black market or other illegal things. Even at this early hour, we see naked children wandering around in the open sewers and picking through the piles of trash, scrounging for something to eat. When I get to feeling bad about stuff in my life, I remember the slums of Nairobi. I've got it good compared to them.

The bus heads into the city, and now we can see skyscrapers with the morning sun glinting off their rows of windows. People bustle up and down the sidewalks, opening their shops or hurrying to buy food at the market. The smells of fresh bread and spices and diesel fumes fill the air.

"There they are!" Debbie squeals, poking me in the back. I don't know why she's always so excited to see our parents. To her, it's like a miracle every time they appear. "They came! They're right here to see us!"

"Cool your jets, Debs," I tell her. "It's just Mom and Dad."

To tell the truth, I'd rather make the long drive out to our house than do this Nairobi get-together. It's not that I don't want to see our parents, but I like to go over to the kraal and visit my friends. Sometimes Mom and Dad just feel like strangers to me.

Both of them give me a hug as Debbie and Julia dance around on their tiptoes, telling about one thing and another. KCA gossip — as though Mom and Dad even know who their daughters' friends are. Dad rumples my hair and asks about school. I figure he really wants to find out if my grades are okay. I tell him I'm having a great time. He smiles, but he's pretty nervous. Each year, it's kind of touch and go whether I'm going to pass on to the next grade, and Dad worries about this a lot.

"We have a surprise for you!" Mom says. She always does things like this. When we're together as a family, she tries to make everything special and perfect. If anyone gets mad or upset or frustrated, she just about can't stand it. We have to be happy and cheerful all the time, especially if anyone outside the family is around to see us.

"We're going to the arboretum for a picnic breakfast!" Mom announces.

"Wow!" Julia gives Debbie a hug of excitement, as if there's going to be a pot of gold waiting for them there. "The arboretum!"

"Can we explore the hedge maze?" Debbie asks. "I promise not to get lost this time. I'll hold on to Peter's hand real tight."

"We'll see," Dad says in his cheerful voice. "Hop in the Land Rover everyone. Off we go!"

Mom and Dad review their grocery list as we ride down the streets of Nairobi toward the arboretum. After we get back on the bus, they'll do their twice-monthly shopping. They have to make sure they don't leave anything off their list, or they'll be stuck out in the bush without it. They discuss how they're going to arrange the small cooler and debate whether there's room for all the perishables they need to buy. Mom moans a little, wishing she could have fresh milk instead of the stuff they buy. It's specially treated so it won't go bad in the heat. You can leave your milk out on the table for days and it won't go sour, but it tastes funky no matter what.

I have heard this conversation two thousand times, so I close my eyes and drift off until the Land Rover comes to a stop at the arboretum. It's a big park — kind of like a zoo for trees. Every imaginable species of tree is planted in the arboretum, and each tree has a sign telling what it is. Julia reads every sign she sees, as though it's her obligation and the trees will be disappointed if she skips one of them.

We all wander into the arboretum carrying blankets or baskets of food or jugs of drinking water. The grass is soft and thick under our feet. I don't think any place in Africa has better grass than the arboretum. Dad chooses a big shady tree, and we spread out the picnic.

"This is a red flowering gum," Julia informs us. "*Eucalyptus ficifolia* of the family *Myrtaceae*. It originated in Australia."

She and Debbie skip around, hand in hand, reading the plaques on the nearby trees. "Here's a camel's foot," Debbie sings out. "This is a cape chestnut! And this is a floss-silk tree!"

If they would bother asking me, I'd tell them the last one is really a kapok tree, and before long those big fruits are going to pop open to reveal the cotton-type stuff that cushions the seeds. If you gather enough kapok, you can make it into a pillow and take a nap. I know stuff like that, but nobody cares.

Mom has brought Vitabix cereal for us. She also brought that nasty heat-treated milk. She made a big fruit salad with mangoes and bananas and tangerines. And she fried hunks of ham, which are cold but very tasty. We eat and talk, mostly the girls blabbering about what they've been doing and how great their grades are. Mom tells about her women's work, and Dad drones on and on explaining his latest plan to teach the Bible to the pastors. Julia, of course, listens to Dad as if this is the most exciting thing she's ever heard. She's such a goody-goody. Debbie picks pieces of grass and makes a pattern on the blanket. I daydream about my friends at the kraal and wonder what they're doing right now. Probably taking the goats out to pasture. I wish I was home.

"Well, I am going to stretch out right here on this blanket and shut my eyes," Mom says after she puts away the picnic. "You girls want to rest with me?"

Julia and Debbie plop down beside her, just like two little puppets. Dad looks at me. "Peter, shall we take a walk?"

Uh-oh. I have a bad feeling about this. Dad never spends much time with me unless he's got a sermon to preach. I shrug and get to my feet. We stroll away from the blanket and he starts in on me.

"Peter, we've had a letter from the school," he says. "Your teachers are quite concerned about your grades. Particularly in math."

"I don't like math."

"Math is a very important skill, Son. You need to know your math so you can have a good job as an adult."

"When I'm an adult, I'm not going to do a job with math in it."

"But, Peter, it's important to know math."

"Why?"

"Because it is." Dad walks along, his hands behind his back and his head hunched forward like a marabou stork. I know he's frustrated with me, but I can't help him. Math just doesn't make sense to me. I'd rather hunt. Or draw.

"Peter, your mother and I expect you to pull up your grades," Dad says. He's using his preacher voice now. I figure he's about to say something about hell and damnation and come to the Lord before it's too late.

"I'll try," I tell him.

"Do you want to have to repeat this whole year?"

"No."

"Well, you're in danger of doing just that. You're barely passing social studies and English, and your science grade is just above average. Your Bible teacher tells us you never listen to a word she says, and your grades show it. Now, Peter, why would you not listen in Bible class?"

"I'm sorry, Dad." I really do feel bad that he's so upset. But I think Bible class is boring. Who cares about the Amalekites and Amorites, anyway? Not me, that's for sure.

Dad goes on talking about the importance of good grades and how the Bible says to study to show yourself approved unto God — whatever that means. I look at all the trees, and I wonder if there are any wild animals living in the arboretum. It's right in the city, but it would sure make a nice place for an impala herd.

"Do you see what I'm saying, Son?" Dad asks.

"Yes," I tell him, but I haven't really been listening too well. "I'll try harder."

"Now, God has called our family here to Kenya to do a very special work, and you need to do your part by —"

"Daddy! Peter!" Debbie is screaming her head off, running through the trees toward us, waving her hands around in the air, all hysterical. "Daddy, Daddy! A man stole Mommy's purse!"

"What?" Dad stiffens up. "Is your mother all right?"

"He jerked the purse out from under her head, and she and Julia went running after him, and I'm scared they're going to catch him! Oh, Daddy!"

Dad and I both take off running back toward the picnic spot. We leave Debbie behind, going around in circles because she's too scared to follow us. She's crying and jumping up and down. I think about running back to get her, but there's a thief out here, and we have to catch him!

The minute we arrive at the blanket, we see Mom standing at the edge of a bunch of trees in the distance, yelling at Julia to come back. Mom is barefooted, and her hair is a mess. I've never seen my mom like this. She's always in control of everything, but right now it looks like the world is coming to an end.

"Oh, Don!" she hollers when she spots us. "Julia's chasing that thief! What if he has a knife or a gun? Oh, Don, you've got to find her!"

I'm more interested in catching the thief than in saving my sister. Dad and I race down the path in the direction Mom pointed. It's not long before we hear Julia screaming, *"Mwivi, mwivi!"* which means "thief" in Swahili.

We catch up to her, and she points out a clump of bushes with hundreds of flowers all over them. "He's in there," she says. She glances at the plaque. "In the lantana!"

Leave it to Julia to get the exact name of the dumb bush.

"I'll go in after him," Dad tells me. "You stand down there, and if he comes out, grab him!"

I've never seen my father like this. He's always got his nose in a Bible commentary or something. This is amazing. We're like warriors together, Dad and me. I wish I had my spear.

"I'm going in," he yells.

"I've got this side covered!" I crouch down, waiting for the thief. Sure enough, an African man comes charging out of the lantana bushes straight into my path. I throw myself onto him, the best rugby tackle I've ever made. We both fall to the ground.

"I've got him!" I grunt. "I've got him!"

"Hold on!" Julia barrels around the bush and grabs at the thief's leg. The next minute, Dad is pushing through the undergrowth. I do my best to keep my grip on the guy, but he's scared and sweating, and he smells like African honey beer, even at this hour of the morning.

And before Dad and Julia can pin him down, he smacks me in the jaw with his fist and takes off. For a moment I'm stunned. I just lie there looking up at the sky. Then I see my sister's face, spinning around and around overhead.

"Get up, Peter!" she shouts at me. "You let him go. He got away!"

I've never seen my sister this way. She looks like a queen, all powerful and commanding. I roll onto my knees and get up and follow Dad down the path after the thief. Behind me, Mom and Julia are diving into the lantana, because they've noticed something.

The thief didn't have the purse when he came out.

"I've got it!" Mom yells. "I've found my purse! Don, let him go! I have my purse."

Dad and I don't care a bit about her old purse. We want to catch this guy. We run up behind the thief just as he squeezes through a tall cedar hedge and bursts out

439

into the parking lot.

"He's getting away!" I roar.

"No, he won't!" Dad beckons me. "Come on, Son. Let's get the car!"

We tear through the hedge and, lo and behold, Debbie has rounded up a couple of policemen! All her screaming and crying must have alerted them, and here they come, jogging into the parking lot with my little sister running along between them. She looks so proud of herself, and I give her a big slap on the back for being so awesome.

Then everybody piles into the Land Rover. Dad and one of the policemen jump into the front seats. Debbie and Julia and I throw ourselves into the backseats. As Dad roars out of the parking lot, he spots Mom jumping up and down in her bare feet. The Land Rover squeals to a stop, I open the back door, and Mom climbs in on top of all us kids.

"There he goes!" Dad yells.

We see the thief bicycling down the street toward the middle of Nairobi. If we don't catch him right now, he'll get away. Where did he come up with that bike? How will we catch him?

"Drive along beside him, bwana!" the African policeman orders my dad.

"He's going to turn the corner."

"No, just go with him now."

We roar up alongside the thief on his bicycle, and the policeman throws open his door. It knocks the man right off his bike and into a ditch. The policeman, Dad, and the rest of us Mossmans pile out of the car onto the thief, all of us wrestling around in the long grass. And before we know it, the policeman snaps a pair of handcuffs on the guy's wrists.

"Well done!" the policeman says. He's beaming as a crowd of people gathers around us.

Mom holds up her purse. "I got it back," she says. "But my money's gone."

"How much money was stolen from you, *memsahib?*"

She looks embarrassed, and I know why. She and Dad were going to do their grocery shopping, so she had a lot of money in her purse. All these poor Africans will hear her say how much money she had, and they'll think we're rich Americans. This is the last thing my mom wants. She has spent her whole life trying to look humble and meek. I just know she's going to tell the policeman to forget about the money.

"Five hundred shillings," she boldly announces.

I can hardly believe it! My mom actually spoke up for herself!

"It was to buy food, because we live in Maasailand far away," she explains. "We are missionaries."

The policeman digs around in the thief's pockets, and sure enough, he fishes out a wad of paper money. With everyone in the crowd watching, the policeman counts the money.

"Five hundred shillings," he says, handing the money to my mother. She nods in gratitude and puts the money back into her purse.

"And now you must come to the police station to make a report on this thief," the policeman tells my dad.

We all pile back into the Land Rover, including the thief, and we drive over to the station. It takes an hour or so before all the testimony is given and the thief has been searched and beaten a little bit and questioned. As it turns out, he has already been in prison for robbery and rape. So, we're feeling kind of nervous about the fact that we chased him down. What if he'd had a knife? What if he'd tried to kill one of us?

After the police let us go, we all walk back out to the car. Dad says he wants to pray. So, we hold hands in a circle and he prays a long prayer, asking God to open the doors to the thief's heart. Then he thanks God that none of us got hurt. And finally he tells God how proud he is to have such a fine family.

Before it's time to catch the bus back to boarding school, Dad drives us all over to the Dari-Frost. We each buy a huge vanilla cone dipped in chocolate. As we're sitting there licking our ice cream, I look down and notice that my mother is still barefoot.

Suddenly it all comes back to me, and I feel warm and happy inside. I study each person in my family, one at a time. Mom and Julia ran after the thief. Debbie found the policemen. I tackled the thief. Okay, I let him get away, too, but I did knock him down for a minute or two. And Dad tore into those lantana bushes and drove the Land Rover around Nairobi chasing after that guy. Wow!

Even though it's time to go back to boarding school . . . even though we have to say good-bye and feel a little lonely . . . even though things aren't perfect, I have a feeling we're going to be all right. We're a pretty amazing family. Us Mossmans.

"You know, as scary as it was, that's one

of my favorite memories," Julia said.

"The time the thief stole Mom's purse?"

"Yeah. I wonder why."

Peter was silent, considering. Reminiscing with his sisters these past couple of weeks had reminded him of some important truths. In their memories, Africa was alive; childhood was alive; the world that had made them who they were continued to shape them even now. Their family was no closer to being perfect than it had been when Peter was a kid, but once again, he had the feeling they were going to be all right. Just as he'd realized the day the thief stole Mom's purse, the Mossmans were a pretty amazing family.

Answering Julia's question, he said, "It's probably because we each did our part. The time the thief stole Mom's purse, we were a team — the Mossman family — and there was nothing we couldn't do."

"We couldn't keep Debbie from dying."

"No, there are some things that will always be beyond our control. But Debs will always be a part of our family — who we were, and to some extent, who we will become."

Julia was quiet for a long moment. Then she gave Peter the first genuine smile he'd seen from her in a long time. "You're right.

She will. And we *are* an amazing family."

"Those boys of yours don't know what they're in for," Peter said, grinning as he came to his feet and held out his hand to his sister. "C'mon. Let's go find the rest of the Amazing Mossmans and see what's happening for dinner."

acknowledgments

I was not going to write this book. Not ever, never, no way. But Francine Rivers kept telling me I had to write it. In fact, she pushed me right into that corner where I gave God my brilliant ultimatum. "Lord," I informed him, "I'm not going to write this book. First of all, I don't really have a plot, you know. Second, nobody wants to publish a book about things like this. And third, I'm afraid it would upset my family."

God heard me, of course. He waited a couple of weeks and then dropped the plot right into my head. A day later, Ron Beers of Tyndale House insisted he wanted to publish the "book of my heart." And within a short time, my loving, understanding parents had given me their permission to write about pain, joy, healing — all the things that have made up my life and the lives of so many others I have known.

So, thank you Frani, Ron, and Mom and Dad for letting God work through you. And thank you, Lord, for leading me down the right paths even when I didn't want to go. I love you, my heavenly Father.

My gratitude also extends to many others who have helped shape this book. Ken Petersen and Jan Stob listened patiently to the earliest, fumbling plot, and their enthusiasm urged me on. Ken followed through later as the story took shape. Thanks for reading all those multicolored notes! Rebekah Nesbitt, as always, provided a strong undergirding of support for my writing. And the staff at Tyndale turned pages into print, created a cover, promoted the book, sold it to bookstores, packaged thousands of copies, and shipped them out. Without these dear people my ministry would not exist.

An enormous debt of gratitude also goes to Kathy Olson, my outstanding editor. She believed in this story from the very start. Her support, encouragement, and enthusiasm carried me through many dark days. Her careful editing and sensitive hand is felt throughout this and each of my books. Bless you, Kathy.

I am also very grateful to those who read this story in its early stages and passed along their heartfelt response. Dan and Heidi Elliott, your words still echo in my heart. Dan, thanks also for sending me the excellent book *The Third Culture Kid Experience: Growing Up Among Worlds* by David C. Pollock and Ruth E. Van Reken. It helped to make sense of the confusion. Diane Eble, your tears taught me that my work was not in vain.

I also want to express my love and gratitude to those who lived this story with me. Elizabeth Bennett is the one soul with whom I most fully shared my childhood. Thank you for being my sister, Libby. I love you. The missionary kids of East Pakistan and Kenya were my family: Janice, Sheri, Gayle, Mary, Bev, Marilyn, Rollin, Joel, Milton, Rick, Mike, Donna, Bethel, Terrie, Margaret, Cindy, Linda . . . to all of you, too many to name, and especially to the Rift Valley Academy class of 1974, thank you for who you were . . . and who you have become.

Most of all, I thank my husband, Timothy Charles Palmer, who has been my anchor in the stormy seas of anger and sorrow, and who has walked beside me toward a place of healing. I love you, Tim.